P9-CQA-800

LUCK, LOVE & LEMON PIE

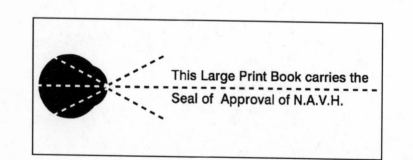

This Large Print Book carries the
Seal of Approval of N.A.V.H.

Luck, Love & Lemon Pie

Amy E. Reichert

THORNDIKE PRESS
A part of Gale, Cengage Learning

Dwight Foster Public Library
209 Merchants Avenue
Fort Atkinson, WI. 53538

GALE
CENGAGE Learning·

Farmington Hills, Mich • San Francisco • New York • Waterville, Maine
Meriden, Conn • Mason, Ohio • Chicago

GALE
CENGAGE Learning®

LIBRARY OF CONGRESS CATALOGING-IN-PUBLICATION DATA

Names: Reichert, Amy E., 1974– author.
Title: Luck, love & lemon pie / Amy E. Reichert.
Other titles: Luck, love and lemon pie
Description: Large print edition. | Waterville, Maine : Thorndike Press, 2017. | Series: Thorndike Press large print women's fiction
Identifiers: LCCN 2016054123| ISBN 9781410498359 (hardback) | ISBN 1410498352 (hardcover)
Subjects: LCSH: Large type books. | BISAC: FICTION / Contemporary Women. | GSAFD: Love stories.
Classification: LCC PS3618.E52385 L83 2017 | DDC 813/.6—dc23
LC record available at https://lccn.loc.gov/2016054123

Published in 2017 by arrangement with Gallery Books, an imprint of Simon & Schuster, Inc.

Printed in the United States of America
1 2 3 4 5 6 7 21 20 19 18 17

"Deliciously entertaining! Reichert's voice is warm and funny in this delightful ode to second chances and the healing power of a meal cooked with love."
— Meg Donohue, *USA Today* bestselling author of *Dog Crazy* and *All the Summer Girls*

"Reichert takes the cake with this charming tale of food, friendship, and fate."
— Beth Harbison, *New York Times* bestselling author of *If I Could Turn Back Time*

"*The Coincidence of Coconut Cake* is a delicious story of food and love, and a wink at what people will do to have their cake and eat it, too."
— Ann Garvin, author of *The Dog Year* and *On Maggie's Watch*

"*The Coincidence of Coconut Cake* is a read as satisfying as the last bite of dessert after a lovingly prepared meal. The novel is as much a celebration of the Midwest and regional food as it is a love story between chef Lou and food critic Al. I adored Lou and her quirky makeshift family of restaurant customers and coworkers. Their missteps and milestones kept me racing through the chapters."

— Susan Gloss, author of *Vintage*

"What a wonderful treat! Delicious descriptions of food and love and Milwaukee (I know! Who knew?). A sweet, endearing read."

— Megan Mulry, *USA Today* bestselling author of *A Royal Pain*

"Reichert whips up the perfect recipe for a deliciously fun read. Combine humor and romance with a dash of drama, then let it simmer. The sprinkle of Wisconsin pride is icing on an already irresistible cake. Warning: Do not read this book hungry!"

— Elizabeth Eulberg, author of *The Lonely Hearts Club* and *Better Off Friends*

"Reichert brings sweetness and substance to her scrumptious debut. Sign me up for second helpings!"

— Lisa Patton, bestselling author of *Whistlin' Dixie in a Nor'Easter*

To Mom,
for being the strongest woman I know.

To John,
for always giving me new reasons
to fall in love with you.

"A successful marriage involves falling in love many times, always with the same person."
— Mignon McLaughlin

CHAPTER ONE

It took MJ one hour forty-seven minutes and three old-fashioneds to eat the entire anniversary pie herself. All that remained in the empty tin were a few smudges of lemon cream sprinkled with flakes of crust, but her stomach didn't seem to mind the alarming influx of calories. She waved to the nearby waiter to order another cocktail and have the pie tin removed. In minutes, the gluttonous evidence had vanished and she sipped her next drink, letting the brandy burn as it went down — and appreciating that it was more booze than soda. Somehow, bartenders always knew when to give a generous pour.

Fellow patrons had arrived, dined, and left, all while she had waited for Chris. She sat alone on the small patio behind their favorite local restaurant. The late-summer sun found the first changing leaves in the nearby trees that lined the meandering stream below the deck, speckling the few afternoon diners who shared the patio, finishing their bowls of handmade pasta. A waiter peeked around the corner, clearly checking to see if she was ready to pay her bill. She knew he wanted her to leave soon so he could collect his tip, but now she was too tipsy to drive herself home. Time to hydrate.

MJ reached for her phone on the edge of the small table but missed on the first attempt. With a shaky swipe across the screen, she saw the time. Three thirty. She sent him a quick, fairly passive-aggressive text.

Still at restaurant. Sorry you couldn't make it.

Chris was supposed to have met her three hours ago for lunch, but he had never appeared, so she'd eaten without him.

Again.

It wasn't until the server had appeared with the pie that MJ had remembered special-ordering it for today's lunch. She'd called the chef weeks ago to arrange for her to make this particular pie and serve it at lunch, when Chris wouldn't be expecting it. For anniversaries past, Chris had always baked it, but last year he had said he didn't have time. So after twenty years, she decided it was her turn to bake. She'd attempted

14

and failed to make it three times before accepting her culinary limits, and gave his recipe to the chef. It was meant to be a surprise, a romantic gesture on their twentieth anniversary — a celebration. Instead, alone, she had grabbed the pie and a fork and settled into her dining chair, mollifying her disappointment one flaky bite at a time, ignoring the judgey looks of the other restaurant guests.

She set her half-empty old-fashioned on the cleared table and rested in her chair, embracing the rare afternoon solitude and booze-induced tipsiness. With her right thumb, she rubbed the inside of her left wrist where a tiny faded tree marred the thin skin. Covering an area no bigger than a dime, the scraggly ink branches were dotted with tiny purple-pink flowers as familiar to her as the sound of her children thumping through the house. Her head rested on the deck railing behind her chair, and her eyes drooped closed behind her large sunglasses as she relished the sun soaking into her skin.

Nineteen years ago, she had come home to an apartment glowing with enough candles to trigger a flash of worry about their cost. Scents of lemon and recently extinguished matches mingled to set her at ease as MJ kicked off her shoes with a sigh and yanked off her too-tight control-top panty hose, her skin prickling with relief. Leaving the offending items by the door with her purse and keys, she scampered to the kitchen with a quick adjustment to her lace underwear, noticing the freshly vacuumed carpet.

Still wearing his suit, Chris stood at the kitchen counter spreading the last swirl of whipped cream onto the top of a pie. She hugged him from behind, wrapping her arms around his taut torso, her nose buried in the back of his shirt, inhaling the smell of Chris. It wasn't just his deodorant or shampoo or the dryer sheets she used, but a little bit of everything combined with him to create a scent that was indescribable and uniquely Chris. She could pick him out in a pitch-black room by that scent alone. When he was gone on overnights for work, she'd wear a dirty shirt from the hamper just to smell him near her.

"Happy anniversary," MJ whispered in his ear.

Chris turned in her arms, still holding the spatula covered in whipped cream.

"You're just in time, Moon," he said, tapping the spatula on her lips. But before she could lick them clean, he leaned down for a kiss, the whipped cream sweetening the moment.

MJ pulled back, sucking the remaining cream off her mouth.

"So what did you make?" she asked. Chris was the cook in their marriage, conjuring up delicious creations for the two of them.

Chris tilted his head and smiled.

"Lemon custard pie."

MJ leaned to look around him at the dessert.

"*The* lemon custard pie?"

"It seemed like the right way to celebrate our first anniversary."

MJ put her hands on each side of Chris's face. Every fiber of her wanted to flip with giddiness that she had found the very best man to marry. His faded blue eyes brightened as they soaked up her smitten face. He completed her, filling up the empty cracks from her childhood, convincing her that marital bliss could be hers, that happy endings were possible.

Oh, how times had changed. As MJ drifted off in the afternoon sun, the table wobbled and a hand skimmed up her bare leg, pushing back the soft fabric of her black skirt.

"What the hell!" MJ said, kicking out as her eyes sprang open, her foot making solid contact with an upper thigh.

"Ooof."

Clutching his leg in the chair next to hers sat Chris. He wore wrinkled khakis and a cream-colored Cuban shirt, pulled tight over his broad shoulders while hiding the small belly that had formed over once-taut muscles. They both had grown softer with the years — on the outside, at least. His short, brown hair, spiked from a day of running his hands through it, combined with stubble to make him look younger — if she overlooked the scattering of silver peppered among the darker scruff. His familiar blue eyes squinted at the sun, deepening the wrinkles at the corners.

Her stomach used to flip when she looked at him. Perhaps the alcohol and pie were weighing it down, trapping the butterflies that once zigzagged with glee. She still loved him — of course she did — but the wings had stilled. Missing their anniversary would do that to delicate insects.

"You know better than to sneak up on me," MJ said, tamping down the mild satisfaction of kicking her husband, but he really should have known better than to surprise her like that. She brushed away the last few pie crumbs still on the table, keeping secret her failed attempt at a romantic surprise. Their knees bumped beneath the cozy table and she tucked her legs under the chair to give him more space so they wouldn't need to touch. *When did I start doing that?*

Chris turned his head to look at her, setting a hand on her knee. MJ refrained from pulling back. That would start an entirely new discussion she didn't want to have right now. Best to just let his hand rest there.

"I suppose I deserved that," he said. "I'm so sorry I'm late. I didn't expect to get as deep in the tournament as I did."

MJ wanted to get angry, to wave her arms and shout or fold them and pout, but she couldn't muster the ire for more than a shrug. She reached for her drink, pulling her leg out of her husband's reach, then looked at him levelly over her sunglasses.

"And your phone doesn't work?" she began, but her words lacked the bite of accusation. Perhaps the brandy had burned off the edge, she reasoned.

He tilted his head down as his lips curved, showing his perfect teeth — a genuine smile, just for her — then squeezed her knee. Chris had two smiles. His polite smile, the I-don't-want-to-be-here-but-have-to-act-like-I-do one, was for when a smile was expected but not earned, like at work events

19

and extended-family gatherings. He would part his lips, crinkle his eyes, and keep them trained on whoever was speaking. But when he really meant it, when smiling was an uncontrollable instinct, he dipped his head and closed his eyes, almost as if he was trying to hide it — a secret amusement just for himself. And when he laughed he threw his head back, unable to keep his mirth inside, no longer caring who noticed. She once lived for those head-tossing moments, proud that she could draw the laughter out of him. It was his laugh she'd fallen in love with first, but that was a long time ago.

She wished he had laughed just now but was relieved to have at least earned a genuine smile.

A tiny butterfly flopped to life.

"I brought you something." His voice rose a bit at the end. He did that when he was hiding something. "Hopefully it will ease that line on your forehead."

Who didn't love a little bribery? MJ leaned forward while running a finger across her forehead, trying to smooth it out. Probably a lost cause.

"You did? What is it?"

From his pocket, Chris pulled a clear plastic bubble. Inside jangled a ring with a bright yellow smiley face. He popped open the container and slid it onto her finger, adjusting the cheap metal to fit. MJ held out her hand, admiring the new bauble for her ever-growing collection — though additions had been fewer in recent years. She'd always loved the bright colors and whimsical designs of the gum-ball machine rings, starting with the one he had given her on the night he had proposed.

"Lovely, as always," she said, the butterfly becoming more persistent.

"I'm assuming you ate without me?" he asked.

"I waited, but when you didn't show, I ate a big lunch."

"I really am sorry I missed our lunch date, Moon. Not much of an anniversary, is it?"

MJ's nerves began a low hum. He hadn't used that nickname in months, maybe even years. He'd given it to her after learning her full name (and her strong preference that it never be used), Margaret June, during one of Barbara's making-sure-my-daughter-is-still-alive visits during college. It had become their private joke, a mash-up of the despised name into a beloved nickname.

Chris twisted his torso while looking around the deck, taking in the view he'd been missing. "I got to the final table in the tournament, so I need to go back in an hour to finish. But I could win enough for a trip. Maybe something for the two of us?" He turned to her.

She knew what he was waiting for, what he wanted her to say. He wanted her concession that his poker playing wasn't ruining their anniversary. He wanted her permission to not feel guilty for abandoning her. Her heart thudded dully as she realized that she wasn't even mad or frustrated with him. She was . . . relieved? Tonight, maybe she'd finish her book and binge-watch the DVR with the kids before taking a long bath. She might even start another novel. A perfect Saturday evening — just, without her husband.

MJ smiled and squeezed Chris's hand.

"Go. Win big."

Chris squinted his eyes, trying to find hers behind the sunglasses. He could always tell when she was lying by looking into her eyes. Thank God for Ray-Bans.

"Really?" he asked.

"Sinceriously."

Chris's lips twitched at her word choice, his shoulders sagging with relief as he let out the breath that had held in all his spousal guilt.

"I don't deserve you."

"Obviously not."

He stood, then bent so his face was close to hers. His whiskers tickled her face before his lips found hers in a functional kiss. For an instant, she remembered a time when she fantasized about nibbling on his bottom lip for hours. Now she focused on the wintergreen taste of his kiss and waited for him to pull away so she could return to her peaceful solitude. Chris straightened with one final rote smile. MJ took another sip of her old-fashioned, erasing the mint taste.

His eyes moved from her to her drink; his lips opened to form words. Over her sunglasses, she raised her eyebrows and he closed his mouth immediately. After setting enough money on the table to cover her bill and a generous tip, MJ stood, swaying from the change in position. She wasn't just tipsy — she was drunk. *Dammit, I can't drive home like this.* Chris watched as she stabilized, knowing better than to help her. She estimated how long it would take her to walk the three miles back to their house and the number of blisters she'd get from doing so in her strappy wedge sandals. She took a sip from the previously untouched water and gritted her teeth against her lifelong hatred of having to ask for help.

But she swallowed her pride enough to

quietly request, "Can you give me a ride home?"

The car eased up the driveway to their cozy saltbox house, tucked among tall oak trees still clinging to their summer green while the towering maples down the street were already starting to turn. Chris coasted the car into the garage, and as soon as the car stopped, their Muppet-like dog, Daisy, danced outside MJ's door, waiting to greet her with kisses and dirty paw prints, as if she'd been away for days, not hours. MJ took a deep breath, trying to shake off the daytime-booze-induced fogginess. Chris turned his head to her.

"I don't have to go back to the casino." He thought she was sighing about him. How could she explain without triggering a fight? She fumbled for a benign response when two teenagers opened the garage door and raced out in stocking feet. MJ smiled, as she always did when she saw her littles, even though they were little no more.

"Mom, can we eat soon? Tommy ate all the food," said Kate. As usual, her long, dark hair hung in a wavy ponytail down her back. She wore her glasses, lending an air of studiousness to MJ's already-smart girl. Sometimes too smart. It was unnerving to lose arguments to your own child, and MJ had been losing them to Kate since she was eight. She had her father's height, MJ's earthy brown hair and eyes, and an attitude all her own. MJ never worried about boys getting the best of Kate. At seventeen, she loathed the teenage boys crawling the high school halls. MJ hoped that sense of superiority would last one more year until her girl was far away at college.

"Like you were even home, nerd. She's being lame, Mom. I didn't eat everything and I'm hungry." Tommy shoved his sister. MJ didn't doubt he ate most of the food, even in the few hours she had been gone. She'd heard about teenage boys and food, but the reality was more like the gaping maw of a black hole, sucking all edible matter into its void, never filling up. God help her when his friends came over, especially after baseball practice. Recently, Tommy was never without a baseball in one hand and food in the other. As tall as his sister, he had his father's brown, unruly curls, which he kept too long in Chris's opinion, but MJ liked the boyish mop.

"Fine, you left the edamame and brown bananas," Kate said.

"Shut it."

"Hey, guys. Can we at least get out of the

car before we have to listen to that?" Chris said.

"Way to go, dumbass." Kate shoved her brother.

"I went grocery shopping this morning, but I didn't have time to put it all away. The nonperishables are in the laundry room."

MJ walked through the door into the back hall, past the messy mudroom into the kitchen, the heart of her home — the home she could have sworn she'd left neat and tidy after breakfast. Now, dishes filled the sink and a stack of Kate's college brochures peeked out from under the crumbs and used paper towels dotting the island. Cereal skittered across the kitchen floor as she walked. MJ started strategizing the best plan of attack when Chris walked in behind her followed by the kids, crunching some of the cereal as they walked. *Nope, not this time.* She couldn't clean the kitchen a second time in one day. Chris disappeared into the laundry room.

"And now you two can clean up the kitchen," MJ said, pointing.

"It's all him." Kate glared at Tommy.

"Do I look like I care?" MJ said. "Tommy, you empty and load the dishwasher. Kate, you win sweeping and mopping. I'll handle the island counter later."

"I can do the counter, too," Kate said, shoving the brochures into her backpack.

"Did you have a good lunch?" Tommy smiled as he opened the dishwasher. MJ loved his smile. It was like his father's, but full of innocence and promise. He never could tell a lie, so you always knew where he stood. She worried that someday some femme fatale would crush her boy's joie de vivre, but that was far in the future.

Chris reentered the kitchen carrying the bottle of Hawaiian barbecue sauce MJ had bought that morning. Using a Sharpie, he wrote "Not for MJ" on it, then added it to the shelf containing a handful of similarly marked items — that's where he put all the food containing pineapple that she accidentally bought. If she ate any of it, her throat would start to swell shut. If she didn't take Benadryl in time, it could get dangerous. Chris paused to answer Tommy's question.

"Your mom did. My morning tournament went long, and now I need to get back for the final table." He kissed Kate's forehead and dashed out the door. He moved so quickly, he appeared blurred to MJ's brandy-fuddled brain.

MJ kept quiet, but Kate noticed and her

eyes flicked to the closed door.

"Mom?" Tommy asked.

"I enjoyed dessert." MJ smiled at him and left the room, the sound of clanking silverware following her up the stairs.

She slid the new happy-face ring onto her dresser-top elephant ring holder. It settled atop several dusty rings, the bottom one covered in chipped faux-gold plating with a clear-plastic center stone. She brushed at the dust, remembering when Chris had given it to her twenty-six years ago, on a bended knee with shaky hands. He had spent five dollars in quarters trying to get it from the machine; it was the one most similar to an engagement ring. At the time, they hadn't yet discussed marriage and certainly couldn't afford it, but that cheap ring had delighted her.

She picked up Chris's clothes from the floor in their shared bathroom and shoved them into the laundry basket. How was a man who so precisely lined up his toiletries on the bathroom counter incapable of getting his dirty underwear into the hamper?

Bending over and standing up had made her more light-headed. The room spun, replacing her fuzzy brain with a nauseous stomach. MJ sat down on the edge of their queen bed, willing the mountain of dirty laundry to shrink. That technique never worked, but she tried it at least twice a week anyway.

Lunch, complete with surprise anniversary pie, was supposed to bring them closer together, not the opposite. But here she was, alone, with the laundry pile. And her growing terror at the realization she preferred spending time apart from Chris.

There was a hole in her chest in the space where the caring was supposed to go. She could feel it — just under her breastbone, surrounded by a wall of bricks. When she took a deep breath, the to-be-expected tenderness and wifely warm-fuzzies tried to creep in, but the bricks held them at bay.

Distantly, she could hear Kate yelling at Tommy to get out of her way. She looked around at her empty bedroom. Other than a looming hangover, nothing was different after her apparently lame stab at romance. In fact, things might be worse. She needed to come up with a new plan.

CHAPTER TWO

The line of cars in the drop-off line stretched behind her and around the corner, the same as every day. A group of moms gathered in the nearby parking lot, chatting, with their perfect hair and tasteful makeup. This was their social time, but MJ couldn't understand the allure of standing in a high school lot. She looked at the license plate on the car in front of her — HOT MAMA. MJ had left the house early to avoid congestion, but this stupid white Escalade still beat her.

"Out of the car, you two," she said to Kate and Tommy. "Take the bus home today, okay? Love you!"

"Got it, Ma," Tommy said before slamming the door shut and joining a few of his teammates who stood near the school doors. Kate paused before leaving the car, just long enough that MJ thought she was going to say what was on her mind, but she mumbled, "Bye," instead. MJ would have to discreetly interrogate her later.

She checked her mirrors and prepared to zoom out of the drop-off lane but was confronted with the white wall of the SUV still in front of her. *What the hell?* This was a two-minute zone.

MJ gripped the steering wheel as a bleached-blonde mom — HOT MAMA herself, she supposed — got out and waved at MJ as she walked in between their cars to hand off a forgotten bag to the teenager who had jumped out moments before. It couldn't be. MJ squeezed her eyes shut, then opened them again, expecting to see someone else. Anyone else. No, that was definitely Tammie. Tammie Shezwyski, her college nemesis, had come to town and was holding her up in the drop-off lane.

MJ mustered a nod and resisted the finger. Tammie handed off the bag and sauntered back to the driver's seat, oblivious to the cars lined up behind her, just as a Nickelback song — the one about a rock star — started playing on the radio.

"I have died and am stuck in the eighth circle of hell."

MJ let her head fall onto the wheel, searching for an explanation to Tammie's sudden appearance in her world. She hadn't thought about her only rival in almost thirty years. Kate really needed to pass her driver's test so she could drive Tommy and herself to school. Or maybe they would need to start taking the bus, even if it meant everyone getting up earlier.

She flicked off the radio and resumed her glaring with renewed vigor. Her hand hovered over the horn as Tammie finally climbed back into her monstrosity of a vehicle. Honestly, if a teenager wasn't capable of getting into school, backpack included, without parental assistance, there were bigger issues at play.

"Don't use the effing drop-off lane if you're going to get out," MJ growled despite her lack of audience, finally able to drive forward.

The white Escalade turned off on a side street. Thirty years. But apparently the instant dislike born so long ago was just as strong today. Why did she have to pick MJ's town to live in? Or — here's hoping — maybe it was just temporary.

MJ coasted into a parking spot in front of This Great Coffee Place and hopped out — eager to dish.

"You'll never guess who moved to town," MJ said as Lisa sat down at her table. MJ gave her a moment to respond but couldn't keep it in long enough. "Tammie Shezwyski!"

Across the table, Lisa dropped her jaw in exaggerated horror. MJ looked around at the bustling coffee shop as she blew on her coffee, letting the news sink in.

This Great Coffee Place always lived up to its name. MJ and her coffee klatch had been meeting there once a week since their kids were in diapers. Sometimes, but not often, she missed seeing her kids mixing up plastic brownies and serving invisible coffee at the pretend kitchen in the corner — until one of the current little ones started whining or crying. MJ preferred her teenagers, even if they would soon leave her behind as they blazed their own paths to adulthood.

Photos and paintings by local artists hung on the terra-cotta walls, flyers for upcoming events filled a bulletin board near the cash register, and books by local authors sat next to the coffee urns. Even if the scones weren't the best in town — which they were — MJ would still choose here over the nearest chain. It also helped that one of her dearest and oldest friends, Lisa, owned the place.

Lisa's straight blonde-brown hair curved chicly around her chin, and her wrinkle-free, fair cheeks emphasized the highlights she spent so much on. Even during the day, she wore full makeup and bold jewelry. Everything about her sparkled from the inside out, and it always had. Lisa and she had met in college at Madison, where they'd become roommates and had shared late-night secrets over cheap pizza and cheaper wine. Thankfully, they had settled a few miles apart once husbands and children arrived.

"Ugh, I thought we were done with her," Lisa said.

"I hope you're not talking about me."

Ariana, the third member of their klatch, set down her mug and eased into her chair — her wavy, dark brown hair brushing against the lapels of her teal suit. Ariana had joined the group when their kids started four-year-old kindergarten together. She had moved to the area after divorce number two, and the three women had bonded in the back row of school events. When Ariana discreetly flashed her flask of Jack Daniel's during a showing of *The Muppet Movie* in the school gym, MJ and Lisa knew they'd found a kindred spirit. She shared their ambivalence for the PTA, but every fall, she bought coffee and scones for the entire school staff (from This Great Coffee Place, of course). Brilliantly, she had avoided being recruited for Room Mom duty all through elementary school. She often snuck out of her nearby office to join MJ and Lisa for coffee, a nice break from the drama of family law.

"MJ's college nemesis has moved to town."

"Ooooo. Tell me more. I can't imagine our MJ with a nemesis."

MJ flared her nostrils.

"She is *that* person. From day one, I couldn't stand her. Everything from her too-high-pitched voice to her fake blonde hair makes me want to punch her. She drives me crazy."

Ariana laughed, then paused when she noticed Lisa nodding along.

"No, it's true. She gets a little wacko around Tammie."

MJ took a big gulp of coffee.

"What did she do?" Ariana asked.

"Existed," MJ said. "We worked together at Bucky's, that bar in Madison. She's the worst. She'd spend the night in one tiny section behind the bar while I worked the remaining eighty percent, then split the tips fifty-fifty. Ugh, let's talk about something else."

"How was the anniversary?" Lisa asked.

Not exactly the topic I was hoping for. MJ slumped back in her chair.

"Chris spent the entire day at the casino." MJ's face melted into defeat. "I spent lunch drinking old-fashioneds and getting too much sun. And I ate our entire anniversary pie by myself."

Both her girlfriends were stunned, but Lisa found her words first. "He didn't." She set her elbows on the table and placed her chin in her hands, giving MJ her full attention. "I'm listening."

How could she explain — without sounding like a terrible person — the real problem: that she really hadn't minded Chris's absence? Being alone was just easier than being disappointed and angry. What bothered her most was the lack of bother.

MJ sipped her coffee, which didn't help the twisting in her stomach. She hated admitting things weren't perfect. Chris and she had everything — beautiful kids, a home in a quiet wooded neighborhood, and some retirement savings. They rarely fought about anything serious, and she did love him. She did. But the butterflies had disappeared somewhere between kids and now. Most days they seemed more like highly compatible roommates than husband and wife. But she wanted more than a roommate.

"Chris ditching me wasn't the worst part, though. The worst part was I didn't mind." Two pairs of eyebrows rose at MJ's unexpected confession.

"What are you saying?" Lisa asked.

"She's saying she doesn't want to spend time with him." Ariana reached over and squeezed MJ's pale hand with her tan one, her unpolished nails buffed to a shine. "Do you want to come back to the office with me? We can talk options."

MJ yanked her hand back. "No!" A few heads turned to look at her outburst, and MJ gave Ariana a reassuring smile. "No, thank you. I don't want to divorce him. I want to fix it."

She wanted the relationship she projected to the world, the vision of partnership they used to have, his earnest attempts to make her smile, and the thoughtful acts — like vacuuming the house before a romantic evening. She missed the wooing. But who got wooed twenty years in?

"So what are you going to do?" Ariana asked. The door jingled and she glanced toward it, then pulled her soft waves of hair away from her face. A youngish man in his late twenties looked toward their table and nodded. He had the lanky, athletic build of a swimmer, topped with short blond hair and startling pale blue eyes. He wore a college sweatshirt and running pants, like he was stopping in on his way to work out. Keys dangled from one finger; his other hand clutched a battered wallet.

"I don't remember guys looking like that when we were that age," said Lisa, letting her eyes roam freely.

"That's someone's son." Ariana gently shoved Lisa.

"He's not my son, so I'll look all I like."

This was why their weekly coffees were so crucial. Even in the midst of discussing her stalled marriage, levity never left the building. Lisa continued her blatant ogling until the young man left with his coffee, flashing them a quick smile as he passed.

"Whew," Lisa said, fanning herself with a napkin. "I wonder if he does yard work or clears pipes. I have something he can —"

Ariana chided, "Lisa. You are a married woman."

"Eh. Harvey probably wouldn't notice unless it interrupted his golf swing. Hey, MJ, maybe we can employ that young man while our husbands are off playing their respective games."

"I'm not sure that's the solution I'm looking for, but I'll keep it as a backup plan," MJ said.

"How are you supposed to spend more time with him?" Ariana leaned in and whispered, "If he's always at the casino, he doesn't have a problem, does he?"

MJ squeezed Ariana's hand, her sweet concerned friend, so well acquainted with how many ways a marriage can go off track.

"No, at least not the way you mean. We aren't in debt to some shady loan shark. But we do have a problem in that he'd rather play poker than be with me and that I'm finding it hard to muster up the strength to care."

"Why don't you just tell him not to play?" Lisa asked. "Seems pretty simple."

"You should talk. Once the snow is off the ground, does Harvey ever let go of a golf club?"

"That works for me. You don't hear me saying I want to spend more time with him. You, on the other hand, need to tell Chris."

"It's easier if I just fix it myself. I just need a plan of attack."

"You need to confront him," Lisa said. MJ opened her mouth. "I know you don't like talking about your feelings, but do it."

MJ frowned. "It's never that easy. Conversations come loaded with twenty years of land mines just waiting to explode with the wrong word choice."

"After two divorces and too many clients to count, trust me . . . you need to tell him, no games," said Ariana.

In the silence that followed, MJ tapped her mug with her short fingernails, a red so dark it was nearly black. The sound reminded her of casino chips clinking together, the plink of clay on clay. She sat up a little straighter.

"That's it, ladies. Playing games is exactly what I need to do." MJ smiled, relief flooding through her tense muscles. She had the perfect solution.

Tonight she'd share her idea with Chris over a rare family meal. In preparation, she was making scrambled eggs, bacon, and toast, one of the few meals she could cook without setting off the fire alarms. She hated having to come up with meals day after day after day. Chris was the one who could cook — her talent was eating. But it didn't make sense for him to work full time and then cook dinner every night, so she did her best, mastering a few simple dishes like tacos and barbecue pork sandwiches. If it involved more than one pot, forget it. Too many ingredients? No way. Scrambled eggs with cheese and herbs was her specialty. The family called them "Katie eggs" because when Kate was four, it was all she would eat for six months, ergo MJ's mastery of them.

The — as always — important first step was cleaning the kitchen. She put all the dishes into the dishwasher, swept the floor, and wiped the counters, but left Tommy's and Kate's bags where they had dropped them. Everything else unnecessary disappeared into cabinets. Now she could get out all the ingredients, cracking eggs and dumping spices into the mix.

Despite the routine, her hands fluttered with a nervous energy as she fretted about how Chris would respond. She didn't want him to think she was interfering in his man time, but she wanted to share something with him, like how they used to watch *Friends* and *ER* when the kids were little, or Saturday-morning sex before the kids were born. She may know he liked to get his hair trimmed every twenty-three days, but that didn't mean the magic had to be gone — they just needed to dig around to find it. And she might have found the right tool for digging.

Tommy and Kate thundered into the kitchen, stepping over their book bags and opening pantry doors.

"Hey, Ma," Tommy mumbled through an

apple he crunched.

"Since when do you guys leave your bags on the floor? Move 'em," MJ said. Tommy scooped up his bag, then rumbled up the steps to his room.

"What's for dinner?" Kate asked, kicking her bag into the dining room. MJ groaned at her least favorite question and the only one she was asked multiple times every afternoon.

"Katie eggs, bacon, and toast."

"Need help?"

MJ looked at her daughter — who never volunteered to help in the kitchen, often too busy with homework — in surprise. It would take twice as long to make dinner with help, but Kate waited for MJ's response, her brows furrowed with thought. She must need some mom advice, MJ concluded.

"I'd love it. You can do the bacon."

"How?"

MJ gave her bamboo tongs, a package of bacon, and instructions. They settled into a quiet routine, dodging each other in a culinary dance while MJ waited for Kate to spill what was on her mind. Tommy clattered back into the kitchen to toss his apple core and grab a glass of milk.

"So, what's for dinner?" he asked his mom

and sister.

MJ looked up from her herb chopping. "What does it look like?"

Tommy shrugged. "Food."

Kate looked down her nose at him. "You're such an idiot. It's Katie eggs and bacon." She gestured with the tongs, dripping bacon grease on the floor. MJ groaned and wiped it up before someone stepped in it.

Tommy nodded, gulped his milk, and said, "I hope it's ready soon. I'm starving," then went outside to throw his baseball against the roof, catching it as it rolled off. MJ watched him go, hair flopping about his head, then turned to Kate. She should get their conversation rolling with something safe.

"Did you get all your college applications submitted?" MJ asked.

"What?" Kate looked up at her. "Umm, yeah."

"You finished the application for Madison, right?"

"I think so." Kate poked at the bacon limply, her nonchalance fooling no one.

"Let me know if you want to tour any more campuses. I know it's a little late, but we could still squeeze in a few more." MJ whisked the eggs together until they were an even yellow, and Kate still poked. Something was definitely on her mind — usually bacon grabbed her full attention. Time for a more direct approach. "How are the girls? I know high school girls can get catty — I used to be one, you know."

Kate smiled and perked up a bit. "The girls are good. We're all too busy for drama."

She lifted an eyebrow and gave Kate the Mom Stare. She'd get it out of her. Kate looked up from the bacon she was absent-mindedly straightening in the sizzling pan.

"I had an appointment with the school counselor."

"What for?" MJ kept one eye on Kate as she dropped fistfuls of shredded cheese into the whisked eggs.

"Are you going to let me tell you?"

"Sorry, go ahead." MJ gave Kate a quick squeeze, then got back to stirring. Now they were getting to it.

"He wanted to talk about colleges."

Kate set the finished bacon on some paper towels and added more slices to the skillet. MJ pulled out the toaster and bread.

"And?" MJ tried to sound breezy.

"I told him I was a bit overwhelmed. There were too many choices." Kate looked up at her mom like she did when confronted with too many good books to read. "I don't

44

know where I want to go."

"What did your counselor say?" MJ worked to keep her tone calm and inviting.

"He said that was normal. It was a big decision and most seniors aren't equipped to make such big choices."

"That's absurd." MJ didn't notice she had pulled out every slice of bread until she held an empty bag in her hands. "You've known you wanted to be a doctor of some sort since you were five and performed surgery on all your stuffed animals." MJ smiled, recalling all the fluff surrounding her frustrated kindergartener when she couldn't sew up her beloved stuffed animal who had just received his new heart.

"Mom, it isn't funny. He wants a list of colleges ASAP. What am I supposed to do?"

"Oh honey, this is no big deal. You already have a list of schools where you've submitted early applications. Give him that list for now. You can let him know as you add more." Kate stiffened. *Right, right, you're supposed to let them make their own decisions.* Kate chewed her lip thoughtfully. "B-DIO?"

Kate rolled her eyes as she always did when MJ busted out the family motto: Boudreauxes Do It Ourselves. Over the years, the mouthful had melted into B-DIO —

pronounced bee-dee-oh. She may roll her eyes, but MJ had overheard Kate and Tommy using it with each other.

"I guess I can do that." Kate kept her eyes on the counter in front of her.

"Feel better?"

Kate offered her a lopsided smile. Perhaps she needed a bit more encouragement.

"You are at the top of your class and your test scores are great. Colleges will fight over you. All you have to do is let them know how awesome you are. Easy peasy."

MJ hugged Kate, hoping she found the fine balance.

MJ heard the garage door open and the soft shuffle of her husband's work loafers on the hardwood floors.

"Hi, hon."

Chris shuffled into the kitchen, saw Kate and MJ cooking, and smiled.

"I asked Tommy but he couldn't remember. So, what's for dinner?"

MJ — barely — tamped down the annoyance and let Kate answer the question.

MJ set the platter of eggs, toast, and bacon on the kitchen table, where her family already sat. Before she could slide into her seat, they started scooping food onto their plates. If she didn't hurry, they'd be done eating and off to their nightly activities before she could say a word.

MJ looked around the table at her family, their mouths chewing, and only the sounds of forks scraping and throats swallowing broke the silence. Chris flicked through e-mails on his phone with one hand while scooping eggs onto a fork with the other. Both kids watched the TV in the other room.

"Let's do Thankful." MJ eased the phone from Chris's grip and turned it off. "We haven't done that in a while." All three faces gaped at her break in the routine. They had become that family that doesn't talk. She remembered when all Tommy's Thankfuls ended with "and I love going down slides." She couldn't even guess what his Thankful might be, it'd been so long since they'd done it.

"I'll start," said Kate. "I'm thankful Mom let me help make dinner."

"Did I miss something?" Chris asked. MJ shook her head. "Fair enough. I'm thankful I have a wife capable of handling the day-to-day drama of teenagers, so I don't have to."

"I'm thankful Coach said I can be co-captain of the JV baseball team." Tommy beamed at his news.

"Honey, that's wonderful," MJ said, reaching over to run a hand through Tommy's hair.

"And good practice for when you make the varsity team," Chris said. Tommy frowned and MJ kicked Chris under the table. When he looked at her, she raised an eyebrow. Sometimes he could be so dense. He cleared his throat. "Good job, son."

Tommy smiled again.

"What's your Thankful, Mom?" he asked.

MJ finished chewing and swallowed.

"I'm thankful that your father is going to practice playing poker with me so we can go on a poker date this Saturday."

Three pairs of eyes looked up as one, mouths still chewing. MJ scooped another bite and put it in her mouth. She chewed, swallowed, and took a sip of the coffee she had made to go with the meal.

"You want to play poker with me?" Chris's face looked confused.

"If you want to. I know you love to play, so if you practiced with me, we could have date nights at the casino. Together." Bite, chew, chew, sip.

Chris pushed his eggs around the plate, his brows scrunched. "It doesn't have to be poker; it could be something you like. Or we could take a cooking class together. I've

48

been wanting to start cooking more than just pancakes on Sunday mornings. More like a real date."

MJ took a large gulp of coffee. She tried to envision a cooking class, chopping and sautéing like she spent every afternoon struggling to do. No contest with the exciting visions of dramatic bets and winning hands that she had spent that afternoon visualizing. She was trying to fall in love again, not relive her daily chore list.

"No. Definitely poker. I think it would be fun. Will you? Play with me?"

Chris's eyes squinted in thought, studying MJ. Would he insist on something else? Did he want to keep his poker world for himself?

"I would love to," he said. Chris smiled, his eyes never leaving hers. MJ sighed with relief.

"When should we start?" MJ asked.

"How about after dinner?" Chris said.

MJ beamed at him and waited for a flicker of warmth. Nothing. Apparently, falling in love with him again wasn't going to be as easy as the first time.

CHAPTER THREE

The kids retreated to their rooms for the evening, which was good — MJ didn't need witnesses if this experiment disintegrated. MJ lit a candle so the room filled with mango and coconut, then dimmed the lights. She took a deep breath, committing to the plan. Perhaps love was like any other habit: practice it enough and it becomes a part of you. She ran her fingers through Chris's hair as she walked past, then slid into her chair.

"Well, this certainly beats the air freshener and cheap nacho smell at the casino," Chris said. "And the players are better looking, too."

"We aim to please at the Boudreaux Casino." MJ winked, playing along. Yes, this levity was what she wanted. "So, let's get this party rolling."

Chris dealt the first hand.

MJ picked up the cards. It was all coming

back — the smell of beer, whiskey, and the cherry-flavored pipe tobacco the Gents would smoke.

She'd been bartending since she could reach over the wooden counter, her mom watchful, making sure MJ was treated with respect from the mostly male clientele at Gone Fishing. The core group of regulars rallied to this cause, shutting down trouble before it began and earning themselves the affectionate nickname of "the Gents." To help her with math, the Gents taught her card games like blackjack and sheepshead. When she showed a knack for cards, they moved on to poker — not just hold 'em, but seven-card stud, Omaha, and almost every other variation. Playing for peanuts and pretzels, she learned how to bet, how to get the feel of a table, and how to read what the other players might have. When she started winning most of the pretzels and peanuts, the Gents let her play with real money, pennies and nickels. They'd set up a small game at the end of the bar so MJ could still serve drinks between bets. The feel of the shiny, coated paper in her hand, even without the smell of pipe smoke in the air, rattled these old memories.

MJ picked up her cards, raised her eyebrow at Chris, and made her first bet. She had a jack and queen of different suits. Chris matched her bet, then put down the first three shared cards — a king of hearts, a nine of hearts, and a four of spades. She almost had a straight and with two cards left to share, she had a decent chance of getting the one she needed. She bet again; Chris called again. The last card was a ten of hearts. MJ had her straight.

"All in."

"Really?" Chris tilted his head to one side. "The first hand and you're going all in?"

"I've gotta play the cards I'm dealt." MJ smiled.

"Fair enough. Then I suppose I need to do the same. Call."

MJ frowned. Why would he call? He must be humoring her since they would just re-divvy the chips and start over. She flipped over her cards, showing her straight. Chris did the same. He had an ace and a three of hearts. He flipped over the last shared card — three of clubs.

"Why did you call me on that?"

Chris studied the cards and looked at MJ's face.

"Um, I have a flush; you have a straight. I win."

MJ stared at the cards. She hadn't even thought about a flush — she was so focused on her cards. Admittedly, it had been a while since those games with pennies and nickels.

"To refresh your memory, here's a list of what hand beats another hand. I wrote it while you were doing the dishes." He slid a piece of paper he had ready and waiting for this moment. While she was up to her elbows in suds, he was already assuming she would need his guidance. If he wanted to be useful, MJ thought, he could have been in the kitchen with her. Her lips pressed into a thin line.

He's just trying to help, MJ reminded herself. *You wanted this.*

She set one finger on the list and pulled it closer to read.

Royal Flush (A, K, Q, J, 10 of same suit)
Straight Flush (in numerical order, all the same suit)
Four of a Kind
Full House (three of a kind + a pair)
Flush (all the same suit)
Straight (all five cards in numerical order, ex: 2, 3, 4, 5, 6)
Three of a kind
Two pair
One pair
High card

The Gents had once scribbled a list like this for her on a bar napkin. It had been slow for a Saturday afternoon. Fall sunlight painted yellow-white rectangles across the dingy pool table and empty stools. They were Gone Fishing's only customers, so her mom, Barbara, worked on the accounts at her desk, a metal monstrosity she had salvaged from the junkyard and painted a vibrant spring green in hopes of brightening up the windowless closet she used as an office. With the door open, she could keep one eye on the bar in case MJ needed her help. Through sheer will and exhausting hours, Barbara kept the office spartan, except for a vintage French poster for *Jailhouse Rock* — a gift from a grateful bar patron and fellow Elvis devotee. Papers were filed immediately, stock was shelved, and anything unnecessary went out to the Dumpster. Only one cup of cold black coffee and the accounting book sat on the desktop.

Her eyes crinkled as she soaked up her only child, deepening the creases to match the smile on her face. Her thinning, curly dark hair was threaded with silver and piled atop her head with a red scrunchie stolen from MJ's room. She looked tired from working longer hours since they'd been short-staffed. She refused to let MJ work too much, saying her grades came first, so Mom had been working every night until close, her only break when MJ covered the bar for a few hours after school. The weekends were all hands on deck — they both needed to work.

MJ turned her attention back from her mom to the Gents. She studied the cheat sheet they had made her, nodding as she committed each of the possible hands to memory, unaware when the bells on the door rang, signaling someone had entered. She didn't notice until the long screech of a chair being pulled across the floor caught her attention. At the other end of the bar sat Joey St. Clair, the town drunk — and MJ's father. He wore a white tank top under his beaten black motorcycle jacket and faded jeans. A chain ran from a belt loop to the wallet in his back pocket that MJ knew was empty. Greasy shoulder-length dark hair fell across his face, hiding watery, bloodshot eyes. MJ worried he'd set it on fire as he lit his cigarette. The Gents quieted their banter and MJ glanced over her shoulder to see if her mom had noticed yet. Barbara was emptying boxes and hadn't seen Joey arrive. No reason to bother her. MJ could handle this.

"Hey, Joey." MJ walked down the bar to stand in front of him. "I can't serve you."

Joey flipped his stringy hair out of his face as he sucked on his cigarette, already hollow cheeks deepening with the inhale.

"I ain't lookin' for a drink." He blew smoke out the side of his mouth. "I'm almost outta gas and I need to get to a new job."

MJ knew he was lying, at least about the job part. She didn't doubt he wanted money. MJ looked over her shoulder to where her mom was bent over the filing cabinet, still oblivious to his presence. That wouldn't last long; maybe MJ could get him out of here before she noticed. No reason to ruin Mom's day, too.

"I'm not giving you money. We both know it's for brandy."

"Look here, Margaret June . . ."

"Don't call me that."

"I gave you that name; I'll damn well call you that when I want." Joey squinted at her, this time blowing smoke right into her face.

MJ's stomach turned at being reminded that half of her was from him. Why couldn't he just leave them alone? She and Mom were fine — they took care of themselves.

"Fine." MJ pulled a small wad of singles from the pitcher where she kept her tips.

MJ stretched to set the money on the bar, but her mom appeared at her elbow like a force of nature, using her iron grip to stop MJ. The hope on Joey's face washed away.

"Out. You will not now, nor ever, take money from my daughter."

Joey rallied for one more attempt.

"She's my daughter, too. If she wants to give me money, she can." He actually looked proud at this logic.

"Don't you act like you've done anything but make our lives difficult. She is getting out of here and away from you. She deserves better than you."

Joey's remaining spine crumbled when confronted with the immovable will of Barbara Olson. He stumbled off the stool and scurried out the door like a vulture chased off by a lioness. Barbara nodded to the Gents and they hopped off their seats as one to get Joey and his car home safely. Barbara watched them leave, then strode back toward her office, dropping a quick kiss on MJ's forehead as she walked by. MJ was left with the empty bar. She cleaned up the Gents' glasses and wiped down the counter. She hopped onto one of the stools and pulled the bar napkin with the poker-hand hierarchy on it. Instead of dwelling on her embarrassment of a father, she focused on memorizing that napkin.

Chris set more chips in front of her with a clink, the mango and coconut candle banishing the cherry pipe smoke of her memory.

"How much do you remember?" he asked.

MJ blinked away the memories that hadn't crossed her mind in years. She focused on Chris's face, his bright blue eyes reflecting that her wandering mind hadn't gone unnoticed.

"I guess I'm rustier than I thought. And I've only played with the Gents, so who knows if they didn't make up rules to give them an advantage." MJ smiled fondly at the memory of the old coots even as her heart thumped with the memory of her father.

"Okay. How about I start at the top?"

MJ nodded her assent. Chris looked surprised that his stubborn wife accepted so easily, but she needed the time to rein in her thoughts.

"Okay, so, you're dealt two cards." Chris laid two cards on the table for each of them, both facedown, while his eyes watched MJ. "Keep them facedown for hold 'em." He cupped his hand over the cards and lifted up just their corners to look. MJ copied him, her hands trembling a bit. She hadn't thought of her father much in recent years; he'd died so long ago.

"Then, the dealer will deal the shared cards. First three: the flop; then one: the turn; then the last one: the river." She nodded in acknowledgment as Chris laid these cards on the table, setting aside a card after the three, and the one. "These go in the middle of the table. Using the two cards in your hand and the five cards on the table, you want to find the best five-card hand."

To focus her attention, MJ squeezed her left wrist with her right hand while she looked over the cards on the table, two eights, a queen, a two, a ten. She nodded, taking in the two eights she already had in her hand. She squeezed her wrist tighter until her heart slowed to normal. Until she was back to normal.

"You ready for betting?" Chris asked, his eyes flicking down to her wrist then back to her face. She nodded.

"Bring it."

"All right: betting. If you have the best hand, then you want to eke as much money out of your opponents as possible. If you're bluffing, or don't have a very strong hand, then you need to trick the rest of the players into thinking you do. You don't say, 'I have the nuts.' "

"I sure hope not — that would be weird."

Chris rolled his eyes.

"The nuts is the best possible hand with the cards that are showing. If you have the nuts, no one could possibly beat you, but you would never tell someone you had them unless you didn't. Got it?"

MJ nodded. "Got it."

By the time they climbed the stairs to their room an hour later, the kids were nestled down into their beds, visions of teenage dreams dancing in their heads, and MJ — floating on the success of her reconnection plan — wanted to reconnect in their bedroom, too. She had won almost as many hands as she'd lost. Her plan was working.

She wiped off her makeup at the master-bathroom mirror.

"Do you think I'm ready for the poker room?" she called out to the bedroom.

Chris came up behind her and nuzzled her neck. "Sure, but I think you're ready for something else, too."

MJ tilted her head to one side. After so many years of marriage, she knew step one when it walked up behind her.

"How about Saturday?" she persisted.

Chris turned her around so he could press her into the counter; his hands roamed over her hips and waist. MJ could count down to the moment he'd move his right hand to her left breast. Three . . . two . . . one . . . contact.

"I don't want to wait until Saturday."

"I mean to go play poker." She shoved his chest a little, but he only pressed in closer. The sequence had commenced; there was no altering its order.

"Mrs. Boudreaux, are you asking me on a date?" Chris lifted her shirt off.

Time for step two. MJ grabbed his hands and pulled him into the bedroom.

"Why, yes I am, Mr. Boudreaux, and I think I'm going to need an answer to that question, 'cause I think I'm getting sleepy." She turned to face him and — step three — pulled off his shirt.

"It's a date," he murmured as he trailed kisses down her neck: step four.

The rest of the steps proceeded right on schedule.

Still naked, MJ nestled against Chris's bare chest and flicked on the TV. Despite the skin on skin, MJ didn't feel as close to him as she had anticipated. What was she expecting, literal fireworks? Chris kissed the top of her head and took the remote from her.

"Hey! I had dibs." MJ reached for the

remote that Chris held out of her reach.

"It's the final table at the Global Poker Finals. I want to see who wins. It should be over soon."

MJ scowled at him, then slid out of bed to put her PJs on.

"You really know how to make a girl feel special." She glanced at the TV to see a handsome dark-haired man. His strong jaw was covered with well-groomed scruff and he wore dark aviators over expressive eyebrows that rose and fell between hands. Unlike the other player, he wore a plain blue button-down shirt that lacked the advertisements for poker websites. Chips covered the table in front of him in piles and he grinned as he raked in more.

"Well, hello." MJ sat on the edge of the bed to watch him stack his chips with nimble fingers.

"Not so bad, is it?" Chris asked.

"I wouldn't kick him out of bed for eating crackers. Who is that?" MJ scooped up her pajamas and got dressed.

"Doyle Kane. And he's just about to be the new champ. It's just him and this kid from eastern Europe."

"Why haven't we been watching more of this?"

Chris's shoulders jostled from his quiet

chuckle.

"He's been unstoppable. He plays unpredictably and no one can figure out his style, but he seems to read everyone. He's a master bluffer."

Doyle flicked a chip across his knuckles, then back again. A smile twitched on his lips.

"Do you like him or is he an ass?" MJ looked at Chris, still naked on the bed. *I need to change the sheets tomorrow.* He ran his hands through his hair, ruffling it more.

"I think he's awesome. He helps new players, uses his winnings to take care of his parents in Ireland, and always has a different beautiful woman cheering him on from the sideline. Seems like a good guy, you know?"

"Sold — he's on the list."

Chris raised an eyebrow.

"Your list is getting longer than Santa's," he said.

"I like to keep my options open. But don't worry — I'm still your wife."

MJ climbed back into bed and snuggled up on her side, leaving a good foot between them. She was suddenly exhausted from trying to resuscitate their marriage. The game had been fun, and then there was the sex. What if mild amusement and the steps were as good as it got twenty years in? The worry wriggled in her stomach. She would see her plan through. She stared at the TV as Doyle Kane won the Global Poker Finals (GPFs). As the camera zoomed in, he took off his glasses to reveal dark lashes, so thick they looked like eyeliner, and crisp blue eyes that crinkled at the corners with his smile. He looked straight into the camera and winked.

CHAPTER FOUR

"Mom!"

"Hey, don't shout at me. You just need to ask." MJ looked at Kate in the passenger seat. She couldn't get used to seeing her all-grown-up daughter sitting in the front. If she could, she'd stuff her back in a booster seat and feed her Goldfish crackers and raisins. At least Tommy was still relegated to the backseat, where he rolled a baseball across his knuckles. Her stomach clenched at the thought of her and Chris tumbling around their house once the kids left for college. She took a deep breath; there were still a few years before they were both gone.

Out of the corner of MJ's eye, Kate looked grumpy.

"I've been saying your name for a minute and you've been ignoring me. Are you having a seizure?"

"No, just sorting out some thoughts." MJ checked the mirror as she changed lanes.

"Now, what did you want so badly you needed to shout?"

Kate wriggled in her seat and picked at her cuticles. MJ knew she was about to get asked about plans, plans that might be sketchy.

"Bree is having people over tonight after the game and I want to go. Can I?"

"Bree? You haven't hung with Bree in a long time. Are you friends again?" MJ waved to Lisa, who was pulling envelopes out of the coffee shop's mailbox. MJ would be back there in a few minutes.

"We never really stopped being friends. She had a boyfriend for a while, so she spent her time with him."

"Ahh, boyfriends. They do that. That's why it's important to not neglect your friends for a boy. Bree is lucky you aren't holding that against her."

"Can I go?" Kate was still working her cuticles relentlessly, so MJ reached out and grabbed her hand.

"You're going to make them bleed." After a squeeze, she put her hand back on the wheel. "Are her parents going to be home? Who else is going? What will you be doing? Will you —"

"Whoa! Relax on the inquisition. Yes, her parents will be home — you can call them.

It will be a small group of us girls. We'll probably go in the hot tub for a while, then order pizza and watch movies."

MJ smiled. "You can go, but I will be calling Bree's mom to double-check, because I know how you love it when I do that."

She pulled into the drop-off lane, eyes narrowing at HOT MAMA in front of her. Tammie had gotten out of the car. Again — this time wearing skintight jeans with patterned pockets and a spangled T-shirt, with precise hair and makeup. MJ looked down at her drab, faded black tee and — let's face it — mom jeans, her skin crawling from having not showered that morning.

"We're going straight there after school — then to the game," Kate said.

Tammie had approached a group of the moms in the parking lot. They stared at her, heads moving to eye her up from head to toe. MJ could see them close ranks, making it difficult for Tammie to join their circle. Schadenfreude kept her eyes glued to the scene as MJ continued her conversation with Kate.

"Okay, I'll text you once I talk to Bree's mom. Check in with me at the game, and I'll pick you up at eleven."

Kate and Tommy climbed out of the car,

but before closing the door, Kate turned to MJ.

"Can't it be midnight? Please?" Then Kate flashed the adorable face she had perfected as a five-year-old: pouty lip, tilted head, wide eyes, and batting eyelashes.

"Fine." MJ waved her off. She wasn't in the mood to negotiate. "I'll be there at midnight."

Kate gave a little yip.

"Love you," Kate said.

"Yes, yes, and I'm the best mom ever. Now get in school before the bell rings."

Kate closed the door and skipped off, smacking Tommy on the back of his head as she passed him. Tammie still stood on the edge of the circle. It was getting hard to watch, but MJ was trapped behind her behemoth of a vehicle because the drop-off-lane traffic had rerouted itself around their two cars. MJ blasted her car's horn until Tammie scurried back into her vehicle. *Twidiot.*

"I'm going to let Kate start driving, I don't care if she has her license or not. Harvey won't bust her, will he?" MJ said. Her mug clinked as she set it down next to a plate of scones and reached for one.

"Don't do it," Lisa said, breaking off a

chunk laden with blueberries and popping it into her mouth.

"I can't see that woman every day."

Lisa raised her eyebrow. "It begins," she said.

"What begins?" Ariana asked as she joined them, reaching for a scone.

"Get ready to meet crazy MJ." Lisa chuckled to herself. "One time when they were both working the bar, she dumped a pitcher of ice water over Tammie's head. I still don't know why you did that."

"That's because I'd been asking her for an hour to bring up some ice from the basement and she kept ignoring me on purpose. She brought the ice up the next time I asked her to do it." MJ shrugged. "And I was barely an adult back then. I'd hope I can control myself a bit better now."

"We'll see," Lisa said, waggling her eyebrows.

"Speaking of seeing." Ariana nodded to the door.

The door jingled in the background and MJ gave a low whistle. All three ladies looked up to see the young blond man walk through the door. He noticed them watching and grinned.

"Ladies." He nodded his carefree, mussed-but-probably-product-filled head as he walked by. MJ thought he added a little more strut to his swagger. Today he wore a fitted navy blue T-shirt and tight jeans, which made watching him walk away all the more fun.

"Damn, that is one sweet, sweet ass. We need to find out more about this guy," said Lisa.

"Why? He's not going to be interested in women our age, not to mention — you're married." Ariana pulled at a strand of hair.

MJ watched them volley back and forth while she blew on her hot coffee, still struggling with her decades-old annoyance at Tammie. Even though she claimed to have more control, her actions spoke otherwise. She hadn't needed to honk the horn quite so long, and her hands practically clenched into claws at the thought of that bouncing blonde head. She was an adult. She needed to act like one.

"Haven't you ever seen *The Graduate*?" Lisa's voice pulled her back into the conversation. "We are exactly what a guy like that wants. Experienced and horny, but don't want a commitment."

Ariana pursed her lips and tapped her coffee cup.

Mr. Hunk got his coffee and headed toward the door. MJ prepared to watch him walk away again when Lisa spoke up.

"Hey, blondy, come here a sec."

He stopped and pointed at himself.

"Yeah, you. Get over here."

"Lisa, you can't say that," Ariana whispered.

"Of course she can." He had reached their table and his full lips expressed his clear pleasure at being there. "Anyone as beautiful as her can make all the demands she wants." He leaned over the table between Lisa and Ariana.

"Oh, I like you, darling. Do you have a name?" Lisa asked. Ariana leaned in for a sniff and gave MJ a thumbs-up, making her chuckle.

"Kyle."

"Well, Kyle, what brings you to our neck of the woods? I haven't seen you before, and I know I would have noticed."

"I'm the new counselor at the high school."

"Lordy, we are going to need to lock up our daughters with this one around," Lisa said.

MJ sat up straighter in her chair. "My daughter, Kate, might be one of your students."

Kyle turned to look at her, tilting his head to the left in question.

"Kate Boudreaux?"

MJ nodded.

"Kate's on my list. She's really bright."

"That's my Kate." MJ bit her lip, wanting to ask about college applications. "She says you had a meeting."

Kyle frowned. "I hadn't gotten any school records requests for her. Usually colleges have started requesting transcripts by now. She really needs to start applying or all her preferred choices will be full — even for a great candidate like her."

That didn't make sense. MJ opened her mouth to ask more questions but Lisa cut her off.

"Now, off you go so we can gossip about you. I'm sure you need to get to school." She waved her hand to send him on his way.

"Yep, my free hour is just about done. Have a lovely day, ladies." Kyle winked, then walked away, the bells signaling his exit.

"Well, damn," Lisa said, before noticing MJ's perplexed frown. "What's up?"

"Kate has submitted all her first-choice applications. Something's not right."

"You are not going to interrogate the young, handsome counselor about your daughter," Ariana said, as her lips parted in a sly smile. "But maybe I will." She looked at Kyle's car as he pulled away.

"It's weird but don't worry about it." Lisa pulled back her hand and wrapped it around her coffee cup. "Now, back to the business at hand. MJ was going to tell us all about last night."

MJ looked up from her coffee to see her two dear friends staring at her.

"It started out great. We laughed a bit, played some poker, but then it descended into the same old, same old."

"Ahh, the married-couple routine," Lisa said. "Touch part A, rub part B, insert part P into part V. Harvey and I can get things done in six and a half minutes. It's better timed than a Navy SEALs mission."

MJ and Ariana stared, mouths agape.

"Oh, come on — are you telling me that's not what you meant?" She set her chin in her hands and blinked at the other two.

Ariana pointed to herself. "Between hubbies, remember."

"Pretty much," MJ admitted. "But we are going to the casino this weekend."

"So, date night?"

"That's all I'm asking for. I'm hoping it's just a matter of time, enough date nights to make some sparks. What about you ladies, any hot plans?"

"Oh, Harvey is golfing most of the weekend in Kohler. I think I'll tag along and take advantage of the spa. I might get a good dinner out of it, too," Lisa answered. "What about you?"

Ariana rolled her eyes. "Well, the kids have a soccer tournament, so I'll have to see Jason. We'll probably grab a bite with the kids after."

"I love how you always do things as a family. You aren't even married to him," MJ said. "You spend more time together than Chris and I do."

"It works. Though I sometimes think he's just grateful I didn't take everything he had in the divorce." She shrugged. "So, are you going to wear sunglasses and a hoodie when you play poker? That's what I see the players on TV doing."

MJ snorted.

"Not on your life. I think I'd look like a wannabe. No, I was thinking something comfortable. Jeans and a T-shirt. Maybe a sweater if it's cold."

"Oh, honey, that's not gonna do at all. You want to give those boys something to look at. You need to show the girls."

MJ blinked.

"You know, the girls." Lisa grabbed her chest and lifted.

"I'm not sure my girls will get me much

mileage with a table full of twentysome-
things."

"MJ, you are not giving yourself enough
credit. Wear something low-cut and sparkly,
do your hair, put on some makeup. Those
kids will be drooling and you'll rake in the
chips."

"I can't pretend to be something I'm not."

"Bull pucky. Just pretend to be me and
flirt shamelessly with the cutest boy at the
table."

MJ sipped her coffee. "I don't know. What
do you think?"

Ariana pulled a loose thread from her
suit's sleeve.

"I think it can be good to pretend to be
someone else for a while. It makes you appreciate what you have."

MJ studied Lisa's generously cut V-neck
sweater and chunky necklace that matched
her vibrant personality, but her own black
T-shirts and simple blue jeans could never
give off that vibe. She circled the inked tree
on her wrist, imagining herself as Lisa,
charming and welcoming, chatting with a
poker table full of strangers. She sighed.
She may not be ecstatic with her life right
now, but she didn't see a reason to escape
it.

■ ■ ■ ■

MJ put the phone on speaker so she could keep folding laundry in the master bedroom — two chores at one time.

"So, how was the anniversary?" Barbara's thick Wisconsin accent drew out the vowels in each word, reminding MJ how far north her mom lived.

"It was fine, Ma."

"Fine? No one ever uses 'fine' and means it."

Leave it to Mom to read into the tiniest of details — and be right. She tossed all her underwear into the top drawer, shoving them down to close it.

"But we are fine."

And they were. MJ couldn't think of a single person she'd want to trade places with. That must mean things were fine. She just wasn't sure if she adored her husband the way she used to, but that's not exactly something to tell your mom while cramming underwear into a drawer.

"If you're having trouble, you could see someone, ya know. Talk about it?"

"Ma, we're okay."

"As long as you're sure, Margaret June."

"Why do you call me that? You know I

hate it."

"I know it reminds you of Joey." Barbara's legendary BS-o-meter worked overtime, which was probably to blame for her solitude, but it was one of MJ's favorite things about her. "But it reminds me of the best day of my life — the day you were born. So, are you going to 'unfine' your 'fine' marriage?"

MJ smacked the phone on her forehead.

"Chris and I are good. Really."

"Okay." Her vowels stretched to new lengths, conveying her skepticism. "Besides, that's not why I was calling anyways. I wondered if I could bring a guest to Thanksgiving."

MJ halted her sock pairing and sat down on the bed. Her mom had never once brought a friend or date to any family celebration. Ever since Barbara had sold Gone Fishing to some Illinois couple who turned it into a brewpub, her social circle had shrunk considerably.

"Who did you want to bring, Ma?"

"Remember Gordon VanderHouse? The orthodontist?"

"Mike's dad. Yeah, I remember him." MJ tilted her head to consider the ramifications of her mom dating her high school prom date's dad. Was she too grown-up for *ew*?

"Well, his wife passed on a few years ago, and we started bumping into each other on the lake. So we started fishing together, make the time more pleasant. He's nice. He doesn't talk too much and likes Elvis almost as much as I do."

"I thought you hated him."

"I never hated him. I didn't like the way he defended your dad when he showed up at the bar that day. I've set him straight. He's a good man."

MJ tried to envision her mom dating. She could only remember the strong, stern woman who could quiet a bar with one glare, or manhandle a drunk biker out the door. It didn't compute. Mom and Dr. Van-derHouse. Her mom and Mike's dad. She turned the same sock right-side out, then back again four times before she could speak again.

"Dr. VanderHouse?"

"Honestly, you should be happy I've met someone."

"I . . . I am. I'm just caught off guard is all."

"Well, can he come?"

MJ plastered a smile on her face, hoping it would transmit warmth through the phone.

"Of course."

"And, honey, don't worry about fixing a room for us; we'll get a hotel room."

MJ dropped the sock in her hand.

After she hung up the phone and stared at it for a while, MJ remembered the one and only time she'd seen her mom and Dr. VanderHouse together. It didn't go well. Prom night 1984 . . .

The peach lace had scratched her inner arms each time she dealt a round of poker to the Gents, the satiny fabric under the lace shushing when she moved. She'd spent the afternoon at the local salon getting thirty-eight bobby pins to hold her thick brown hair on top of her head in bouncy curls. Out of consideration for her finery — and at Barbara's vocal insistence — the men refrained from their usual smoking. MJ glanced at the clock every other minute in anticipation. As if on cue, the door opened and haloed Mike's golden hair, a stark contrast to his dark clothing. As he came into the bar, the ruffled shirt took shape, framed by a peach tie and cummerbund.

"I suppose we need pictures," Barbara said from behind the bar. She looked at Mike. "Your dad outside?"

Mike nodded and MJ hopped off the stool and stumbled, still wobbly in her heels.

Mike cupped one elbow and pulled her waist to his, steadying her against him.

"I've got it, but thank you," she said, unwrapping his arm, nervous from the contact.

"Outside, you two. Let's get this over with. I have customers who need drinks."

Barbara herded them outside, walking past Dr. VanderHouse with a nod.

"Hello, Dr. VanderHouse," MJ said. She liked the tall, slender orthodontist. He had light, thinning hair cut so short that he looked bald from a distance, but it worked on him, and he spoke softly, in a gentle tone.

"You look lovely, MJ," he said.

Barbara snorted and posed them in front of the one flowering tree near the bar, a scraggly thing with a few pink-lavender spring blossoms. Every spring, MJ was amazed it managed to come back to life, but it did, her doubt making the small blushing blooms all the more beautiful. Her mom called it the iron tree — a bit rough around the edges, but indestructible. MJ loved it, had grown up alongside it.

A rumbling noise, screeching tires, and sliding gravel sent the small group scattering away from the tiny tree, and the massive hood of a rusty tan Oldsmobile appeared where her tree had stood. MJ willed the moment to rewind. Out of the giant car appeared her dad, staggering a few steps after he slammed the car door shut.

"Good. Didn't miss you." He looked back at the flattened tree, then stopped in front of MJ, pressing a malt liquor–scented kiss on her forehead. "Well, I guess I did miss you." He laughed at his own joke.

MJ stepped away from the smell and sight of him and looked to her mom for an explanation as to why he was here. The loss of her demolished tree morphed her sadness into disgust and anger. Everyone in their small town knew her dad was a drunk, but she didn't need it to be paraded in front of Mike before the only dance she'd ever been asked to. Barbara stepped between her and Joey.

"Get in the bar, MJ." She turned to Joey, pointing at his car. "And you can leave before you completely ruin the kids' night. Or any more of my trees."

MJ tried to pull Mike into the bar, but he wouldn't move. He was watching as his dad approached her parents.

"I was invited," Joey said, sliding his hands into his leather jacket's pockets.

"By who?"

"Him." He thrust his arm toward Dr. VanderHouse. Barbara's head blurred as she whipped around to face him.

"You did this? Why?"

"I just mentioned — he's her father; I assumed he would be here." Dr. Vander-House's voice weakened as he spoke, his final words a mumble. "He has a right."

This could go on for a while and she didn't need to see any more. MJ grabbed Mike's hand and yanked him toward the parking lot, her heels wobbling on the loose gravel, but she refused to let it slow her down.

"Bye, Ma," MJ shouted above their voices. She gave one last look at the fallen iron tree, her heart clenching. She wouldn't let her dad ruin this night.

MJ loved the electricity of a crisp fall night at the high school football field, with the marching band playing loud but mediocre versions of Michael Jackson and Katy Perry songs. Harvey and Chris walked in front of Lisa and MJ, Harvey's bald head towering above everyone else's. Rather than making him look old, his lack of hair gave him the air of a retired Hells Angel, complete with trimmed beard and flinty eyes. Built like a Packers lineman, he had broad shoulders and tree trunk–size arms, which explained why their son was a star linebacker on the varsity team. Even without his sheriff's uniform, Harvey radiated authority and order — at least until he looked at Lisa; then he turned to mush. He was putty in her hands and Lisa returned every bit of his adoration.

Tommy had run off from the four adults to meet some of his friends as soon as they paid their admission. Cozy in her jeans, black wool sweater, and a quilted black vest, MJ scanned the crowd for signs of Kate. She'd brought an extra sweatshirt in case Kate wasn't dressed warmly enough, but she didn't see her daughter. Instead, her eyes caught on a light blonde head on course to intersect their group, and her body tensed as if she'd been poked with a cattle prod. Tammie Shezwyski. Maybe it was because she hadn't eaten since the morning and was still processing the intel about her mom and Dr. VanderHouse. Maybe menopausal hormones raged through her body, wreaking havoc. Maybe thinking about her dad had actually caused something to snap in her brain. But her mind blanked to everything except for one clear thought: Chris and Tammie must not see each other.

Her heart pounded as she grabbed Chris's arms and turned him toward her abruptly, disrupting the flow of traffic behind them.

"Can you run out to the car and get the blanket, please?" The words tumbled out in a near shout.

"Why didn't you grab it when we were there three minutes ago?" Chris continued walking to the stands. Why did he have to be so difficult? She gripped his arm tighter. Tammie was closing the gap and she needed to get Chris away.

"Please, Chris?" She never begged. She picked up her foot to show him her heeled boots. "These are tricky on the gravel, and it'll take me twice as long as you." Then she actually fluttered her eyelashes at him. The tiny remaining rational part of her brain threw up its hands in disgust at her.

Chris's shoulders slumped in an annoyed sigh; MJ noticed Lisa raising an eyebrow.

"Fine, okay; I'll find you in the stands." He backtracked through the crowd behind them as Harvey resumed their progress toward the bleachers. MJ saw Tammie looking through the crowd, and their eyes met, so MJ turned away as if she needed to say something to Lisa. When she glanced back a moment later, Tammie was gone and the absurdity of her own behavior over the last minute smacked MJ in the face like a wooden paddle.

"You want to explain what that was all about?" Lisa asked.

"I'd rather not," MJ said, her face flushing with embarrassment.

"When you were in labor with Kate for twenty-five hours and you wanted some ice chips, you tried to get them yourself. Now you're blaming your shoes for not wanting to go back a hundred feet?"

"I would have succeeded if I'd been able to feel my legs. Damn epidural." MJ tried to smile to lighten the mood, but wiping away her ridiculous panic wasn't working. She hadn't felt out of control like that since college. Lisa still waited for an explanation, but it would take just one word: "Tammie."

Lisa nodded, as MJ knew she would, and patted her arm.

She hated herself for feeling insecure, for not feeling in control of her life. All it seemed to take was Tammie and her too-tight jeans to remind her of everything she was not. She told herself she'd feel more in control after tomorrow's date night at the casino, when she and Chris were in a stronger place. She couldn't let Tammie make her crazy. She needed to fix her marriage and fast. The stakes had been raised.

Cheerleaders led the crowd in chants of "Go, Hawks, go," while a beach ball bounced around the bleachers. The air swam with possibilities. Players hoped to score the winning touchdown, students hoped for a first kiss in the dark behind the stands, and parents hoped their kids would stay out of trouble for one more night. As for MJ, all her hopes hinged on Chris.

CHAPTER FIVE

The clang and din of the casino flashed around MJ and Chris as they wound their way through the slot-machine maze to the escalators. The dinging and flashing of machines amped up her excitement so that she almost bounced along as she followed Chris to the escalator. She tried to look everywhere at once, as lights flashed and people cheered. It seemed like everyone in the Milwaukee area had decided to come to the casino on this Saturday night, or maybe it was like this all the time.

In the center of the floor stood the blackjack, Pai Gow, roulette, and craps tables. Dealers dealt cards and swept away chips with a practiced ease, as if they did it as often as breathing. People lined up to take their turn with Lady Luck, and smoke wafted in wavy columns, combining in a hazy cloud above the cacophonous room.

Relieved to emerge from the maze, MJ

and Chris rose up the escalators to the second floor, which housed restaurants, the bingo hall, and their destination: the poker room. Once in the large, rectangular room filled with twenty tables, most of which were full at this time on a Saturday night, she and Chris registered at the check-in counter. When a seat opened up — Chris explained — they would head to their table. They stood side by side, and Chris leaned close to talk to her. Warm fuzzies skittered across her skin. Success.

He wore comfortable jeans and an untucked, striped button-down shirt — typical weekend attire, but it looked better on him than normal. When he moved his arms, the sleeves pulled across his shoulders and biceps, a reminder that he did still work out. As he studied the screens, he ran his hands through his hair, leaving it to defy gravity. She stepped closer to him as he started to explain how a poker room worked, savoring his presence in a way she normally didn't.

"So this is how it works. That's a list of games currently running." Chris pointed to a screen on the wall. "The games are broken into categories — limit and no-limit, and the amount of the blinds."

"What do the different dollar amounts mean?" MJ asked, pointing to the "$1/$2" next to one of the listed games.

"Those refer to the big and small blinds for that game. Since this is your first time here, you should play a limit game. In limit, those numbers also indicate the starting bets. Players can't go all in, so it makes it more difficult to bluff. It will give you a chance to feel more comfortable sitting at a table without getting bullied around like you would at a no-limit table. Make sense?"

MJ nodded.

Chris led her to the cages, where they each purchased a rack of chips — she, a hundred dollars' worth, and he, four hundred. MJ winced as she looked at their chips.

"Do you really need so much?" MJ asked. They could feed Tommy for almost two weeks with five hundred dollars. She knew it was her idea, but was this excessive?

Chris bumped her arm. "It's entertainment money. We don't take expensive trips, have over-the-top cars, or wear designer clothes. Hell, a nice dinner, a couple of drinks, and a movie can be almost two hundred dollars. Here we have a few hours of fun *and* could win some money back. You even get all the free coffee and soda you can consume."

"That sounds like a whole lot of excuses."

"That's why I don't do it every day." Chris

kissed her nose, but it seemed like the way he would pet the dog, habit with no heart.

At least he had a point about the money. As she clutched the heavy tray, MJ's stomach twisted with anticipation. She and Chris were finally spending time together. This is what they were missing, quality time and a shared interest, shaking up their habits. She envisioned nights playing together, raking in the chips, inventing some new poker words.

"Chris B., table ten," said a voice from the speakers. Chris started toward his table, MJ on his heels. He turned and put his hand up firmly, like he was telling Daisy to stay. "You need to wait until you get your table assignment. I'm sure it'll be soon."

MJ stopped. Disappointment flooded her mouth and pursed her lips. "We aren't playing together? But I thought —"

Chris put his hand on her arm. "I play no-limit, and you aren't ready for that. You need to get used to playing the game first."

"But can't you play limit with me tonight so we can sit at the same table?"

"Oh, I thought . . . Limit is boring to me. I can't sit there for a whole evening — I'll be bored out of my mind. You'll do great; you always do when you have your mind set on something. See you after." With that, he turned and walked to his table, leaving MJ hugging her chips for comfort. She looked around and saw a roomful of strangers, every single one of whom knew more about poker than she did. Her breath became shallow as her hands lost all warmth. Tears welled along her carefully applied eyeliner, about to be obliterated just like her carefully made plans. It wasn't too late. She could turn her chips in and go sit at a slot machine.

"MJ B., table nineteen."

She swallowed, her throat dry. Why had she decided to do this? She didn't want to be here with a table of people she'd never met. She wanted to sit by her husband. This was how the magic died, good intentions ending in disappointment — like their anniversary lunch. Why waste time being upset? *Get it together, MJ.* On autopilot, she wound her way through the tables to number nineteen, where an empty seat waited for her. She craned her neck, hoping to at least be able to see her husband from her chair, but she couldn't even find him. So much for date night.

She sat down and set her chips on the table, then looked around at her tablemates — all men. A mix of young and old, but no one as welcoming as the Gents. The young men slouched in their chairs, wearing faded hoodies and sunglasses on the backs of their heads. The older men seemed to know one another; a few nibbled nachos and sipped the free drinks brought around by the waitresses. The dealer was a man in his forties with pasty skin and long, dark hair pulled back into a ponytail. He turned to MJ and said, loudly, "You need to take them out of the rack."

"Huh?"

"You need to take your chips out of the rack, ma'am." He swept his hand to the rest of the players, all with neat little stacks in front of them. Her face exploded with heat. She'd been *ma'amed* by this middle-aged hippie. And why hadn't Chris told her about taking the chips out of the rack? That seemed like a good tip. Jerk. She carefully stacked them according to color as the cool chips slipped from her fingers, not wanting to stay in neat piles. Each clank drew attention to the fact that she hadn't known to unpack them right away.

"Sorry. Sorry," she mumbled, sliding the now empty rack under her chair.

I can survive anything for one night. It helped that she wore her usual uniform of blue jeans and a dark top — tonight was a black peasant shirt with silver stitching that glinted when the light hit it. Her hair bounced around her shoulders. Still flushed with embarrassment, she wished she had a rubber band to slip her hair back. She pulled out her bartender face from so many years ago, letting ice run through her to freeze out the discomfort.

Next to her sat an older gentleman. With his right hand, he flipped a chip over his knuckles as if it were a Slinky going down the stairs. In his other hand, he rubbed the belly of a small Buddha statue. He smiled at her when he noticed her watching.

"First time?" he said.

MJ half nodded. "First time with people I don't know."

"Nothing to worry about. Nobody bites, and they'll all happily take your money." His smile reminded her of Bruce, the friendly shark from *Finding Nemo* — he'd be your friend until he smelled blood; then you better run for your life. Tonight, MJ was the fresh meat. She took a deep breath, tasting the faint chemical smell of cleaning solutions and air freshener covering the funk of so many warm bodies in one room. She could do this. The worst thing these people could do to her was win her money.

Stomach swirling as her first cards slid across the table to her, she tried to remember all the casino rules Chris had drilled into her mind. She waited until the dealer dealt both cards, cupped her hands, and peeked at the corner, the cards stiff and reluctant to bend. A seven of diamonds and an eight of hearts. Two people bet two dollars and two people folded by the time it was her turn. All eyes looked at her. She peeked at her cards again.

"It's only two dollars. That's a cheap flop," one of the hoodied young men said.

MJ flushed again, but took two chips and tossed them into the center. The dealer laid down the flop: six of clubs, eight of diamonds, ten of clubs. Her heart beat a little. She had a pair of eights. Another round of two-dollar bets went around the table and MJ added hers. The dealer set down the turn: the eight of spades. She had three of a kind! Her heart beat a little faster. She could win this hand, her first hand at a real table. The betting went around again. This time everyone who was still in added four dollars to the pot, and one person folded. Now it was just her and two men.

The dealer laid down the last card: a nine of spades. That didn't do anything for her, but it was okay: she still had three of a kind and the other player — she had named him Slump for his poor posture — had to bet first. He bet four dollars. She raised the bet to eight dollars. Slump countered with twelve dollars. MJ called. They both flipped their cards over at the same time. He had a pair of tens, giving him three tens when combined with the shared cards, a higher hand than her three eights. MJ's heart dropped as she looked at the mini-mountain of chips in the center of the table and realized how many were hers.

"Damn," she said. Every man — including the dealer — looked at MJ as if she had morphed into a gelatinous slug.

"Ahem, you won," the man sitting on her left said.

"But he had tens; I only had eights."

Very gently, as if he were telling a little girl her bunny just died, he explained, "You had a straight, six through ten."

"Jesus Christ, they should have training wheels on this table." Slump scowled. The dealer started pushing the chips in her direction.

MJ burned with shame. How could she miss that? "Sorry. I didn't see it."

"That's okay, honey. We've all made mistakes. And if people can't handle playing with new players, then they should pony up the cash to play at the higher-stakes tables."

"Thanks." MJ nodded at the nice man.

MJ stacked the chips carefully, avoiding

eye contact with the other guys at the table.

Her new friend leaned in and whispered, "Don't forget to tip the dealer. A buck or two is good for this table."

"Thanks," MJ whispered back, and tossed a chip at the dealer, who nodded his gratitude — another helpful hint Chris neglected to tell her. Another thing she had to figure out for herself.

She folded the next few hands, barely looking at her cards. Her disappointment at not sitting with Chris had formed the first layer of dread in her stomach. Her mortification at making such a dumb mistake comprised the second. She didn't want to play any more. She should leave.

"Playing like a drum after that straight, eh?" one of the hoodie-clad young men said derisively. She named him Unabomber.

Rattled, she bet the next five hands in a row and lost all of them, forfeiting all of the winnings from that first hand, and then some. At this rate, she'd be done in a few more hands, and she'd be done with this failed experiment.

MJ was furious at herself for wanting to crawl away — she was stronger than this. She gritted her teeth and searched for her "date."

She found Chris's head between two older

men a few tables over. His rumpled hair stood out from all the baseball hats and hooded sweatshirts. Many covered their eyes with sunglasses, too, hoping to hide any tells their eyes might give away. Why would anyone go to such lengths to pretend to be something else? She was pleased to see Chris looking like his normal, open, and friendly self. He didn't look like a guy who would bluff. Maybe that was how he got away with it.

He glanced up, saw MJ looking, and gave her a thumbs-up and gleaming smile. MJ sighed. He looked so happy. Maybe this wasn't an absolute failure. She could manage a few more hands, maybe do something to make the table like her more. It was time for a little B-DIO. MJ signaled a waitress, who sauntered over to the table.

"What can I getcha?" the waitress said.

"I'll take a coffee with four creams and I'd like to buy the table a round of drinks from the bar. Whatever they want. They've been patient with me during my first time." MJ eyed Slump at the end of the table. He shrugged his shoulders and looked sheepish. The rest of the table murmured their thanks and named their drinks. The man on her left leaned in again.

"Well played. I'm James, by the way." He

held out his hand.

"MJ." She shook it. Now that she really looked at him, his watery, smiling eyes reminded her of the Gents. His gray hair curled tightly to his head, and his wrinkles hinted at abundant laughter. She pointed to the tiny Buddha. "For luck?"

"Partially, but I also set him on my cards if I'm staying in a hand so they don't accidentally get swept up by the dealer. He's my card protector." MJ nodded. "A word of advice: Fold for a few rounds but still pay attention. Watch everyone as they play. Look for tells. You'll be surprised what you pick up."

"Thanks, James. But I don't even know what I'm looking for."

"If you know how someone acts when their hand is crap — which is most hands, statistically — you'll notice when something changes. For example, our young man over there." He pointed to Slump. "He slouches back in his chair all the time. It's driving me nuts. But when he gets a good hand, he sits up straighter. If he bluffs, he hunches forward over his cards. Just watch."

MJ nodded again. Peeked at her cards and folded. She watched as Unabomber and a few others folded. Slump straightened and called. James peeked at his cards and matched the bet. MJ couldn't discern anything different in his play. After the flop, Slump hunched and bet. He must not like his cards anymore. James winked at her and bet. The turn. Slump curved even more, but bet. James raised. Slump grumbled, but called. The last card. Slump checked. James bet as much as he could. Slump chewed his lip, eyed James. MJ could feel James's left foot vibrating under the table. Slump folded. James showed his two cards. He didn't have a hand at all. He had bluffed Slump because he knew he hadn't had a good hand. And now MJ knew both their tells.

Perhaps poker was more interesting than she remembered. It wasn't much different from guessing which customers at a bar would cause trouble if she kept serving them shots of Jack Daniel's, or the exact moment when a five-year-old Kate would lose it in the grocery store — always near the yogurt because MJ wouldn't buy the ones with candy mix-ins. She didn't have to wait for the right cards; she just had to assess the table and work it to her advantage. It was the ultimate B-DIO situation. She was back in the game.

MJ watched the players for ten more hands, then joined back in, this time feeling much more equipped. She used her new-found information to win a few hands. After she called James's bluff — his leg had been vibrating like a jackhammer — he leaned in.

"I'm thinking you didn't need any advice. You've been playing us."

"Yes. That's my shtick — I pretend to be clueless, make an ass of myself, make everyone think I'm stupid, then take all your money."

MJ smiled, and James raised his eyebrow.

"That's actually a pretty good plan, isn't it?"

James nodded. "We all have our reasons for being here and most of them have little to do with money."

Her brow scrunched. She turned to find Chris. He wasn't in his spot but heading her way with empty hands. He stopped behind her chair.

"You ready?"

"Ready for what?"

"I'm out. Are you ready to leave?"

MJ blinked and her shoulders slumped a bit. Well, there went her earlier hopes to capitalize on his good mood. She really wasn't ready to leave but knew that taking a stand would only result in an argument, and that's not how she had envisioned the night ending.

"I guess." She racked her chips, tossed another one at the dealer, and gave James a squeeze on his shoulder. "Thanks for your help."

"I hope to see you again soon." He smiled. "Me, too."

And MJ meant it. She liked winning the game, the camaraderie with James, gaining her footing. Perhaps she'd be back soon.

She cashed in her chips and had only lost fifty dollars — not bad for a first time. On the way home, Chris relayed why he had none: a bad beat. She'd heard it before. But, like James said, maybe it wasn't about the money. Why did Chris like to play? It's true, they didn't spend frivolously, so they had some fun money, and he did win almost as much as he lost. So what was her husband searching for on the felt?

CHAPTER SIX

"I can never go to the Piggly Wiggly again," MJ said, swinging her damp black fleece jacket onto the back of a coffee-shop chair.

"This should be good." Lisa was already sitting at the table with Ariana.

"Let me guess: Tammie?" Ariana said, her wavy hair pulled into a polished ponytail that swooshed elegantly with her every movement. MJ nodded. "I'm starting to look forward to these stories."

"Okay, I went in for groceries and saw her by the butternut squash. Then, of course, I bumped my cart into a mountain of apples, which toppled all over the floor. So I did the only thing I could do: I grabbed my purse and ran." Lisa and Ariana didn't even try to not laugh at her, and she didn't blame them. She was acting like an idiot. "And the worst part is that I still need to go grocery shopping because I abandoned my almost-full cart amid the apple wreckage."

102

Ariana wiped a tear from the corner of her eye. "I need a better understanding of why this happens. This isn't like you at all."

MJ paused to collect her thoughts, trying to explain the temporary insanity brought on by the mere sight of Tammie Shezwyski.

"Imagine a young me, leaving her tiny town in northern Wisconsin, where she didn't have a lot of friends and spent all her time in a bar with her mom and a few kind, but much older, men. College was my big start in the world. My chance to leave all of the isolation and reinvent myself as someone else. Someone else who didn't have the town drunk for a dad.

"I needed to work, so I played to my strengths and got a job working at one of the busiest bars on State Street. Tips were exceptional, especially for a college bar. The owner was excited he wouldn't need to train me at all and immediately paired me with his daughter, who also would be working there. Tammie.

"Tammie is everything I am not. She's pretty —" Both Ariana and Lisa moved to protest. MJ held up her hand to pause them. "I was eighteen-year-old MJ, not the paragon of self-confidence I am now." MJ waved a hand at herself and took a deep breath before continuing. "So, she was pretty, and perky, and knew everyone. People, specifically boys, seemed to fight over who could do something for her first. She had everything, yet she treated everyone around her like subjects who were there to make her life easier. She couldn't do anything for herself. Every night we worked together, I would have to close all alone because she would make one of her doting followers take her home right at bar time. No one ever walked me home."

"That's because you carried a switchblade in your pocket," Lisa said.

"It's the one useful thing my dad ever gave me." MJ shrugged.

"Your dad gave you a switchblade?" Ariana asked.

"And showed me how to use it. Father of the Year." MJ took a sip of her rapidly cooling coffee. "Anyway, back to Tammie. We never got along very well, but we tolerated each other. And then she started treating Chris like one of her subjects. I didn't like it and things escalated."

"Is that when you dumped the ice on her?"

MJ chuckled as she remembered the shocked expression on Tammie's face as the icy water found its way down her spine. That had been very satisfying.

"I thought I was going to get fired, but

her dad told me I was too good of an employee to lose and he stopped scheduling us together." Her eyes flicked to Lisa. "After that, we mostly kept our distance."

Lisa cleared her throat, obviously picking up MJ's topic change. She didn't really want to get into the rest of the story right now.

"So, how did poker date night go?" Lisa asked.

"It sucked. Mostly." Maybe the girls could help her sort out the next step. "I made an ass of myself half a dozen different times, but then I found my groove. A nice man sat next to me and I ended up having a little fun. But Chris and I didn't sit anywhere near each other, so it didn't really count as a date night."

"What are you going to try now?" asked Lisa.

"I don't know. I kind of want to keep with the poker."

"But if you're not even near each other . . . that's not going to solve your reconnection issue," Ariana said.

MJ clucked her tongue as she searched for the words to express her curiosity at finding a hobby that was just for her. Playing poker, when it was going well at least, was like putting herself behind titanium — nothing could get to her.

"Last night, sitting at the table with strangers, once I got past the nerves and over the assholes, I liked it. It made sense. It was me against the table. I used parts of my brain that had been dormant for years. I felt more like *me* than I have in a long time. Besides, maybe the problem isn't the lack of time with Chris. Maybe I need to do something for myself. I can't rely on him to make me happy. I need to make me happy." MJ noticed the concerned looks on her friends' faces. Perhaps they didn't understand. "And if I get good enough, Chris and I can play at the same table — then it would be more like a date night. Plus, there are some nice restaurants there. It could work." But that last part wasn't it at all. MJ wanted to explore the thrill of discovering the other players' tells. The thrill of playing the people, not the cards. The thrill of leaving her repetitive days behind. The thrill of relying on only herself.

"So, you're going to keep playing poker?" Ariana asked in her usual slow, measured cadence. She formed her words carefully. When she would get flustered, her *r*'s would start to roll, which MJ found endearing but Ariana avoided.

"I think so. I was thinking about going down again this week for a few hours while the experience is fresh. I'm worried if I wait too long, I'll get intimidated again." Plus, she wanted to feel the rush.

"Kind of an expensive way to spend the afternoon, isn't it?"

"Not really. We played for three hours last night, and I only lost fifty dollars. And that was my first time. We spend more than that on a Friday fish fry. But enough about my boring marriage." She waved her hands in front of her. "Have we seen our hunky counselor yet today?"

She noticed a red flush cover her friend's face.

"What is this?" MJ pointed at Ariana, who turned even more red.

"What is what?" Ariana said.

"Oh. You look like a radish," Lisa said. "Why are you blushing at the mention of Hunky Kyle?"

"I'm not red." She trilled her *r*, hiding something.

"You're blushing like a Victorian virgin in a whorehouse," Lisa said.

"Is that even a thing?" MJ said.

"I'm sure it happened sometime. But don't get distracted." Lisa turned back to Ariana. "Why are you blushing?"

Ariana was rotating her coffee cup between her hands when the door jingled and the women turned. In walked Chris, cheeks flushed from the cold air, and big flakes of snow from the early-October flurry clinging to his windblown hair, making him look ten years younger. MJ's chest thumped like a sledgehammer against a wall. She attempted to still it through force of will.

"Hey, honey!" she said.

Chris looked over at her table, then scanned the room. He smiled, walked to their table, and leaned over to kiss MJ on the cheek. Her pulse switched gears and it felt great. Maybe she was making progress after all.

"I didn't know you were going to be here this morning," he said.

"It was a last-minute plan. Ariana is stalking Hunky Kyle, and we know he comes in most mornings."

While Chris asked, "Who is Hunky Kyle?" Ariana mumbled, "I'm not stalking him."

Lisa and MJ laughed.

"He's the new high school counselor. Kate's been talking to him about college apps. What are you doing here?"

"Thought I'd swing in for a coffee on my way to a meeting."

The door jingled again when an attractive blonde walked in wearing a fur vest and large sunglasses. She glanced at their table, paused, then continued on to the counter. MJ's hackles rose.

"Where are you meeting out here? Aren't most of your clients downtown?" MJ asked, keeping an eye on Tammie as she waited her turn in line. There was no way to keep Chris and her separated without being obvious. MJ eyed the fire alarm. Lisa noticed her line of sight and kicked her under the table. MJ conceded. They lived in a small town. She couldn't keep them separated forever.

"Prospective client in the new industrial park. If you'll excuse me, ladies, I should get my coffee so I'm not late."

After one more dutiful-husband kiss, he got in line behind Tammie, who turned and said something to him. Neither, MJ noticed, acted as if it had been almost thirty years since they last spoke. Perplexing or disturbing, one of the two.

"She's talking to him?" Lisa asked. "A bit ballsy."

MJ tilted her head and watched Tammie smile at something Chris said, then take her coffee and leave without glancing at MJ's table. She slid into her HOT MAMA Escalade and zoomed through the right turn out of the small parking lot, almost knocking over an elderly couple. After paying for his coffee, Chris waved from the door. "I'm off," he called. "I'll see you for dinner tonight." The door's bells tinkled cheerfully as she watched him drive away to the right, even though she could have sworn the new industrial park was the other way.

The weekday casino crowd seemed more subdued than the Saturday night group. Rather than a lively, excited vibe, a subtle desperation for a lucky break hung in the filtered air along with the guilt of people shirking their daily responsibilities — or maybe that was just her. Crossing the casino floor, MJ listed everything she should be doing: grocery shopping, scrubbing the kitchen cabinets, obsessing about Tammie talking to Chris, pairing socks. With each list item, her anticipation grew, like skipping history class when you knew there would be a pop quiz. The poker room, though quieter than her last visit, still had that work-like atmosphere MJ remembered. Minds calculated odds, estimated opponents, and tallied up wins and losses. The room itself seemed to project both boredom and intensity all at once.

MJ took a deep breath, trying to calm her excited nerves and get her enthusiasm under control. Ever since seeing Tammie whisper to Chris, her mind whirled with possible explanations. It was a constant buzzing, like a mosquito she couldn't see but knew would eventually bite her.

She could do this without Chris to guide her. Besides, he hadn't really guided her last time anyway. And on her own was the only way to learn. She dressed simply again — black jeans, black T-shirt, black boots. She let her hair fall around her shoulders, a veil she could place between herself and the other players. She put her name in with the host and looked over the room while she waited. Half the tables had games going; most were filled with men, though there were a few women scattered around the room.

"MJ, you can go to table twelve," the host said. She nodded, bought her chips, and settled into her seat. Unracking the chips and looking over her table, she saw no familiar faces. Good. Today was about learning, not small talk. She tapped the iron tree on her wrist for luck and folded the first few hands, watching her opponents for twitches and tics, giveaways and tells.

Hours passed and she found her little stack growing chip by chip. Players left, others arrived, dealers changed. She had almost hit the felt an hour ago, but a string of good cards and bad players had pushed her ahead. MJ listened to the room, the chips clinking, the cards snapping, and the low rumble of players as they ground through hand after hand after hand. In a room full of people, she was alone and loved it. Here, there was only one job: to play cards. Here, she didn't worry about anything else. Bliss. She still wasn't sure why Chris came to the tables, but MJ had found her reason.

Then, over the speaker, she heard, "Tammie S., table nine."

No, it couldn't be. MJ turned to see a perfectly coiffed blonde head slide into a chair a few tables over at the no-limit game Chris liked to play. Yes, it was. She met Tammie's eyes as the other woman settled into her seat, but MJ coolly turned back to her game and started racking her chips. Perhaps she had found Chris's reason for playing, too. She had gone almost thirty years without thinking of Tammie Shezwyski and now she kept seeing her everywhere, letting her get back under her skin. This coincidence was just too weird. As she walked to cash out her chips, she glanced at the back of Tammie's head. Her hair formed the perfect halo above her slim shoulders and unnaturally tan arms. Maybe, MJ thought, it wasn't a coincidence at all.

CHAPTER SEVEN

The blue light on the coffee pot darkened. In practiced motions, MJ poured in a generous amount of half-and-half while dodging the island and walking to the table that took up the far end of the kitchen. Golden morning light streamed in the window above the sink, casting a soft glow on the pine cupboards. As MJ propped open her book on the pumpkin centerpiece to read and enjoy her cup, Chris entered the kitchen dressed for work in his usual white shirt and dark suit, two ties draped over his shoulder — one blue striped, one purple dotted — ready for her daily opinion. Puffs of Daisy's hair tumbled with his steps. She would need to sweep. She wondered whether they would grow to the size of tumbleweeds if she didn't. Maybe then someone would notice them and take a turn at sweeping.

Sigh.

With barely a glance, she pointed to the

purple, which he quickly tied, no need for a mirror. They did this dance every morning. She should ask about Tammie, but as soon as the thought entered her mind it wafted away. No reason to start a big conversation when he was about to go to work. They could talk about it later.

"I'm glad you're up. When I ate breakfast this morning, I heard some weird scratching from the mantel. I think there are mice in there." His hair tamed into a professional side part, Chris stole a sip of coffee from her mug, making a face at all the cream she used. "When will you start drinking coffee that tastes like coffee?"

"When coffee comes with cream in it. And don't try and sneak that mouse thing in like you aren't dumping it on me."

Chris shrugged. "I have to get to work; otherwise, I'd help."

"I could wait until you get home tonight to tackle it."

"You could, but I have a dinner. And we both know you won't be able to leave it alone."

"Coward."

"Yellow to the core." He paused on his way out the door and pulled her into an unexpected hug, her face smushing into his armpit. Chris flashed her a guilty smile —

he knew he was ditching her to handle the problem solo — and left for work. She got up to inspect the mantel. It'd serve him right to wait until he could help her. She always got the crap jobs because she didn't have a real office to go to every day. She should call an exterminator to handle it, then go play poker instead and escape this mess for the day. But as she turned to go upstairs, she heard it — a faint scritch-scritch. MJ's shoulders sagged as she resigned herself to a day of pest control, knowing she wouldn't be satisfied until she had handled it herself.

The yellow rubber gloves made MJ's hands sweaty as she wedged the crowbar between the pieces of wood that made up the chest-high mantel stretching the length of their fieldstone hearth. She wore ratty red sweatpants tucked into her flowered rain boots with a formerly fluorescent pink sweatshirt. Her hair slipped out from a shower cap, a ridiculous topper to her ridiculous outfit. The only element missing was a face mask, or maybe a hazmat suit. *Oh, and the supposed man of the house,* she thought bitterly.

MJ yanked the crowbar harder and an inch-wide crack opened. Using her flashlight, she peeked in, worried she might see hundreds of beady eyes staring back. But no, just a lot of mouse poop. The earlier visitor must have scampered off. With a bit more maneuvering, she removed the front panel of the mantel, revealing the horrific diorama within — a pink insulation mouse condo, blessedly minus the residents.

She gritted her teeth and assessed the situation, ignoring the pungent smell of rodent waste. Half of the mantel's inside was crammed with pink insulation, while the other half was blackened with urine-stained wood and pellets. A few acorn shells varied the landscape. She could see gaps in the brick on the back wall that led to the chimney — the entry points. The little bastards had found the perfect place to spend winter, cozy-warm and safe from predators. Their free ride ended today.

With more cringing and squealing than MJ would ever admit to publicly, she slid the insulation into the blue recycling bin from the garage with a broom handle, careful not to look too closely in case any of the inhabitants were still in residence. She hated Chris a little bit for letting her handle this alone. To be fair, though, she never asked for his help.

With the insulation out of the way, she

could see all the damage left behind. If it hadn't been for the scratching Chris had heard, they never would have known this was happening. Given the amount of fecal matter and the extensive mouse nest, this arrangement had been going on for a while, right under their noses. What else might she be missing?

MJ's phone rang with Chris's ringtone. She glowered at it, then answered.

"You are not my favorite person right now," she said.

"Ah, you've cracked it open?"

"You owe me. It's mousepocalypse in there."

"Nice one. Any critters?" His voice sounded guarded — as if he wasn't sure of her mood.

"Not that I've seen, but I'm not looking too closely." MJ covered her nose with her sleeve to block out the odor.

"Probably wise."

"Are you calling to check on me or is there something else?" Her voice clipped the words, like she was trying to bite off the letters.

"A little of both. I wanted to remind you I have a dinner tonight. I might be late. Will you be home?"

"I'm not sure. It all depends on how long

this takes to sanitize. It's possible I'll have to burn the entire house down." MJ walked into the kitchen to get some clean air.

"Please don't do that."

"I make no promises; you aren't looking at this dioramic hellscape."

Chris laughed.

"This is not funny," MJ said. She didn't want to discuss the mice anymore. She wanted to discuss Tammie and why he didn't seem surprised that she'd appeared at This Great Coffee Place.

"It's a little funny."

MJ sat at the kitchen table, her skin itching with disgust and irritation and uncertainty. She *wanted* to laugh with him, forget that they hadn't done that much anymore, forget about the insecurity blossoming in her chest. "I might play poker after I feed the kids dinner. So . . ." She wanted to ask about Tammie. She should just ask. "Who are you having dinner with?"

"Um, a possible client."

"The one you met with the other day?"

"Yeah." Chris's voice was tight, and it spread to MJ. He wasn't telling her something. MJ's stomach dropped. She returned to the living room, decided she didn't want to ask more, not with a hole in her wall.

"I gotta go. I want to get this done so I

can shower."

Chris paused. "Okay."

"Later." MJ hung up and stared at the mess.

After making a quick dinner for the kids, she left them doing their homework and headed downtown. The casino air caressed her face as she stepped into the circuslike entrance. She took a deep breath and left worries about Chris and irritation at the mice behind her. Heading straight to the poker room, ready for the thrill, her heart beat faster with each step so she was breathless as she stopped to study the boards. She'd been back at least once a week since that first night with Chris, usually during the day when the kids were at school. This was the first time she'd come at night by herself when the room was more crowded. Invigorating.

The wait list for her usual limit hold 'em game was four people deep, but there was an open spot at the no-limit table. A shiver of excitement danced down her spine. She hadn't played no-limit since the Gents.

She claimed the open seat.

She set her chips on the table, triple her normal stack, but she'd been winning enough that she had a small bankroll to fund her trips to the casino. The entire sum, though, was sitting in front of her. Anything less and the more experienced players would shove her around. Her table was a mix of businessmen after work (Suit One, Two, and Three), young men (Punk, Opie, and Frat Boy), and one older gentleman with a giant stack in front of him (she called him Scrooge).

Tonight, she decided, she'd play it serious — no talking. Per her usual, she folded the first few hands, letting herself watch her opponents. She settled into a game of "what's his story?" with herself — guessing at each of the player's backgrounds. While she studied them, they glossed over her, dismissing her as a nonthreat. This was a different kind of table; these players weren't afraid to go all in. They wouldn't expect her to bluff on her first play. They'd expect her to tiptoe in. They expected her to be easy prey.

She flipped up the corner on her fourth hand. Ace of hearts, ten of spades. Not a bad hand to bluff with. She could get lucky, lots of options. She tripled the previous bet, causing all but Suit Three to fold. He called. The flop hit: five of clubs, six of hearts, jack of spades. She had nothing, but he didn't know that. She held her hands clasped in front of her, something she tried to do on every hand, and stared at the cards as Suit Three waited for her to make her move. She had to bet first. MJ gave her tattoo two quick taps for luck, then bet fifty dollars. She went back to clasping her hands and waited for her opponent to call or fold.

MJ could feel her pulse pounding in her neck, so hard she was sure he could see it. She focused on her breath and keeping herself still. Suit Three was talking to her, but she zoned him out. Years of working in bars followed by years of boisterous children had trained her to ignore unwanted noise. She wouldn't be intimidated by this man, but the longer he waited, the more intensely her neck veins throbbed. There may as well be a flashing neon arrow pointing at her throat. Hands together and neck pulsing, MJ waited and stared at the pot, where the mountain of chips waited for her. With a disgusted growl, Suit Three finally tossed his cards in the pot.

"Did you have pocket jacks?"

MJ slid her cards out, facedown, as the dealer pushed the stack of chips toward her. She tossed him a generous tip with a smile.

"I don't remember," she said sweetly, stacking her chips slowly so her neck could return to normal. She'd just bluffed her first pot! With the adrenaline zooming through her, she could probably lift a car. On the outside, she piled her winnings with the boredom generally reserved for diagraming sentences. Where else could she get this? She looked around the table, studying the other players. This time, they studied her back. She was a mystery — and she loved it.

When she left a few hours later, her bankroll had doubled. She folded the six hundred-dollar bills and slid them into her pocket, where the roll buzzed against her hip, wanting to play some more. She gave it a little pat — she'd be back, and soon. As she practically floated out of the poker room, she noticed a new poster for an upcoming tournament. The winner would win a trip for two to Vegas, entry in a satellite to the Global Poker Finals, and a poker lesson from Doyle Kane. The tournament took place after Christmas, the prize trip in April.

A nearby host noticed her reading. "Would you like to register?" he asked.

MJ shook her head without thinking. She would get slaughtered in a tournament, everyone out for blood. She needed to get better, to play more before she could do that.

Regardless of that worry, though, she

heard herself saying, "I'll think about it."

During the drive home, MJ thought about that tournament. How deep could she go? Could she make the final table? Would she even make it past the first round? She wanted to know the answers. But the tournament would take up an entire day, at least, meaning she would have to miss some of Kate's and Tommy's events. When she got home, she pulled out a notebook and began to write.

Events I'd miss:

Lego Robotics competition day — Tommy
HS musical — Kate's in the pit orchestra

Events I made:

323 baseball games
23 orchestra concerts
9 tae kwon do belt testings
11 class parties
6 years of co-leading Girl Scouts
2 years early-morning flag football
Room mom for 3 years

She continued the list for two full pages without scrounging in the corners of her memory. All the sports, rehearsals, and concerts she had clapped and cheered and coached her children through. It looked like an application for Mom of the Year; yet she knew she'd probably forgotten the majority of the classes and activities she chauffeured her kids to. MJ was exhausted just looking at the list. In the suburbs, parenting was a competitive sport.

With such clear evidence of her years of dedication, MJ didn't think missing one day for a tournament would be the end of the world. She smoothed the pages onto the counter, as if that might help brush away the lingering guilt she still felt.

The ball smacked into the well-worn baseball glove, stinging the palm of MJ's hand and nearly causing her to drop it among the scattered leaves in their yard. She scooped up the ball and tossed it to Kate, who then tossed it to Tommy, who then rocketed it to her, stinging her hand again.

"Twenty-two," MJ said, declaring the current count for their game of catch. Their record was fifty-six before someone dropped it. "Okay, Yount, lighten up on the speed. Your ma isn't going to last long if you keep doing that." Tommy grinned at the compliment and reined in his arm on the next throw.

They'd taken a break from raking and burning leaves in their front yard to play catch. Since Chris had to work, she recruited the kids to help her, with promises of Thai takeout and hot fudge shakes from Le Duc's, their favorite frozen custard stand. It would be one of the last nice days before the snow began to fly in earnest, so MJ was taking advantage of the weather. A pile of smoldering leaves sent wispy smoke to the sky and hinted at the winter to come.

MJ caught the ball and threw it to Kate, who interrupted their game of catch.

"Twenty-nine. So, mice in the mantel? That sounds like a bad picture book," she said, her hands curling around the ball, then shooting it to Tommy.

"It was a nightmare. I'm still considering burning the house down."

"Please don't, Mom." He caught the ball. "Thirty-three. I'd lose my baseball card collection."

"Thirty-four. That's what you're worried about." MJ smiled, appreciating that her growing teenage boy still treasured something from his childhood. "So, I'm thinking about entering a poker tournament. The winner gets a trip to Vegas to play in a satel-lite. What do you think?"

Both Kate and Tommy looked up at her.

"What's a satellite?" Kate asked.

"It's a smaller tournament where the win-ner gets the entry fee paid for a bigger tournament. In this case it would be the Global Poker Finals. And a free poker les-son with Doyle Kane, the reigning champ."

Tommy nodded. "Are you going to enter?"

"I'm considering it. If mousepocalypse taught me anything, it's that I need to broaden my horizons a bit — get off the hamster wheel."

"Forty-seven. When is it?" Kate asked.

"It's the second weekend in January."

Kate's face scrunched as she ran the dates in her mind. "That's the musical weekend."

"Forty-nine. And Lego league," Tommy said.

The ball flew toward MJ, who reached out her glove and closed it too soon, causing the ball to flop into the leaves. Why was she even discussing this? Of course she wouldn't choose poker over her kids.

Kate walked over to her and hugged her from the side.

"Mom, you should go. We'll be fine."

"Do you think you have a chance at win-ning?" Tommy asked, scooping up the ball from the ground and tossing it up in the air to play catch with himself.

"I've been doing really well lately, but I don't expect to win. It's mostly for the experience. But you never know. I know it doesn't make a lot of sense, but I really love playing. And I'm pretty good, good enough that I win more than I lose."

"What does Dad say?" Kate asked.

"I haven't talked to him about it yet. I wanted to touch base with you two first."

"What do you like about it?" Tommy stepped back to catch the ball, stepping in dog poop. He didn't even notice. She made a mental note to pick up the yard before the snow hit — otherwise it would be a mess in the spring — then filed it away to deal with later. Tommy had paused playing catch as he waited for her answer, then continued once she started talking.

"When I'm sitting at a table with nine people I don't really know, I only have my wits to keep my chips safe. They don't know me, I don't know them, but we both want to take everything from each other. There's no subtext, and we all have the same goal. Each hand is a new battle and new opportunity. Every game is different and challenging. I learn something new every time I walk into the casino. And this tournament is the next logical step."

"We're fine with it, Ma," Kate said, nodding her head toward Tommy, who had finally noticed he had doggy doo on his foot and was scraping it off with a stick.

"I haven't completely made up my mind. I'm still waffling a little. It's a lot of money to sign up."

Kate rubbed her arm.

"Ma, it's like Nike — just do it."

MJ laughed and looked at her kids. When did they get so grown-up? They were right, though, and just like that, her mind was made up.

CHAPTER EIGHT

The Thanksgiving dinner, made with love by a local caterer, reheated in the oven in shiny aluminum pans. MJ would transfer everything to her special Thanksgiving serving platters before they sat down. This twenty-year standing charade was perpetuated by adding a few last-minute touches to further the illusion — a sprinkle of parsley here, a dash of salt there. Alone in the kitchen while everyone else watched the parade on TV, she poured herself another glass of Riesling. If she made it through today without screwing up one of the dishes — her family made bets each year on which course she'd ruin, even though she only needed to reheat them — she would reward herself with a day of poker tomorrow, or maybe even tonight.

She opened the oven doors, dodging the blast of heat, and took the turkey's temperature: 150 degrees. Dammit. The instructions said to reheat to 160 degrees, so she needed another ten before she could pull it from the oven. This would set back the entire day, pushing back dinner, and pushing back the time it would take to get everyone out of the house.

She walked into the living room. Her mom and Dr. VanderHouse sat on the love seat with a cozy six inches between them. Her mom's shimmering white hair was pulled back into a curly and casual updo. She looked younger despite all the white. Perhaps it was the unstoppable smile on her face every time she looked at Dr. Vander-House. He got up and filled a plate with cheese, sausage, and crackers, then handed the plate to her mom. She beamed up at him. Yep. They looked adorable. MJ clenched her teeth.

The kids and Chris sprawled on the floor playing Monopoly while flames flickered in the fireplace, complete with new mantel. MJ had insisted it be done immediately so she spent three weeks making phone calls and harassing contractors to make sure it was complete by Thanksgiving. She'd only gotten to the casino twice. Blerg.

"Hey, everyone, the turkey is taking longer than expected. Dinner will be closer to two thirty," MJ announced.

"No worries, Margaret June." Barbara squeezed Dr. VanderHouse's arm. "We're enjoying the excellent company."

The two smiled at each other. Chris and Tommy were absorbed in the parade on TV, pretending the giant balloons were carrying on a snarky commentary of the chaos below, while Kate gave a haphazard thumbs-up, busy plotting her hostile takeover of Park Avenue. MJ blinked and turned back to the kitchen, taking a long swig from her dwindling wine supply. It was a bit much to see her mom cozy with someone. In MJ's fifty years, she'd never seen her mom affectionate with anyone other than her. She pulled another bottle from the fridge and had her glass full in a matter of moments.

"You okay?" Chris leaned against the counter and crunched a cracker, leaving crumbs stuck to his lips. Minus the crumbs, she had to admit he looked good. His long-sleeve T-shirt skimmed his now flatter stomach. He'd probably given up eating fries last week and dropped ten pounds. MJ pulled out her smile.

"Of course. It's good to see her happy." MJ could feel her own lip threaten to crack from the tightness — she should probably drink some water.

"I know you better than that. It's bothering you that your mom is dating Mike's dad. And honestly, it's a little weird." And still those little crumbs dangled.

She didn't really care about Mike or his dad. The Facebook grapevine had informed her that Mike went to med school, recently got married, and now practiced as a surgeon somewhere in Minnesota. What had her so upset was seeing her mom soft and googly-eyed after years of lectures on how important independence was. This indoctrination was rule number one in their house, well, number two after "no serving underage customers alcohol." For goodness' sake, when she'd called to tell her mom she was engaged to Chris, Barbara's first words were: "Don't get used to him taking care of you. And make sure you keep your own checking account." And now she was letting this soft-spoken orthodontist fill her plates of schnibblies. What was next? Rubbing her feet? Doing her taxes? It was like finding out your math teacher thought algebra was overrated. It didn't make sense.

"Don't be silly. We so rarely have the family all together. I'm only worried they'll start making out in front of the kids," MJ fibbed, and squeezed his arm. "You should get back to the game before our darling children start cheating."

MJ watched the crumbs on his lips quiver as he breathed. Would they fall? Spray into her face? How could he not notice them? She reached up and brushed them off, her fingers lingering a bit on his lips. She leaned up to kiss them. Instead, Chris kissed her on her nose and took a sip from MJ's wineglass. MJ closed her eyes in annoyance or possibly disappointment — she wasn't sure which.

"Do you want me to bring up a couple more bottles?"

"No, I can do it. Now go out there and keep everyone entertained so I can get dinner done."

When he left, she took another gulp of wine. The sound of the TV from the other room nearly drowned out the buzz of Chris's phone on the kitchen island. Automatically, she picked it up and started walking it to the living room, but then . . . the screen said the call was from T. Just T. She looked at Chris through the doorway, but he still didn't notice the phone. She clicked the top button to ignore the call, set the phone back down where it had been, and started chopping parsley into infinitesimal bits.

It had been a busy night for a Tuesday.

133

Bucky's A-Team Drinking Bingo was more popular than expected. Scattered on every surface were laminated bingo sheets with squares describing events like "Face kisses a girl" and "Someone calls Murdoch crazy." When a customer had the action on his card, he marked it with a peanut and took a drink. Five in a row, he won a pitcher of beer. MJ had thought the game up a few weeks ago to improve her tips on Tuesday nights and it had finally paid off. Word had spread and the bar was full of people glued to the six TVs scattered around the large room. Not only was she busy, but the patrons were mostly quiet, with scattered cheers when they peanutted a square.

At the end of the bar sat Mike Vander-House, former prom date and sole friend from back home. After the dance, their tepid romance had cooled to a comfortable friendship. Turns out MJ wasn't his type; in fact, all women weren't his type. Neither of them made friends easily, so at a big university like Madison, it was nice to see a familiar face, someone she didn't have to make small talk with.

Tammie Shezwyski appeared on the empty bar stool next to Mike. Even though MJ and she didn't work the same shifts anymore, she often came in when MJ was working —

throwing her I'm-the-owner's-daughter weight around and irritating the heck out of MJ by her very presence. She delighted in it the way a younger brother would torture an older sister just to see her crack.

She worked her way down the bar, collecting empty glasses and refilling pitchers. She plopped a fresh beer onto the smudged wood in front of Mike, jolting the two's attention to her.

"Hey," MJ said. Mike gave her his please-help face, then eased it into a smile.

"Hey," he said. "MJ, you know Tammie, right?"

Tammie giggled and put her hand on his arm.

"You're so silly. Of course she knows me. My daddy owns this bar, so she kind of works for me." Her falsely high voice scratched at MJ's ears. "You two used to date, right?"

MJ set a cranberry and Absolut in front of Tammie, a wedge of lime perched on the rim, just the way she liked it.

"Barely. Turns out I wasn't his type."

Tammie pressed her perky boobs into Mike's arm. Mike rolled his eyes and scooted to the far end of his stool, trying to put some distance between them, but she followed.

"Well, I imagine you're an . . . acquired taste. Some of us are more universally appealing." Tammie sipped her drink, then pushed it toward MJ. "You didn't use the good stuff."

Without a word, MJ grabbed the drink, dumped it, then made her a new one, this time using the rail vodka. Tammie sipped it and closed her eyes like she was tasting the best chocolate.

"And maybe some of us are more oblivious than others," MJ said, winking at Mike.

"Bingo!" A guest at the back of the bar yelled. MJ looked at Mike and he handed her the master bingo sheet that marked all the possible phrases. She didn't have time to make sure people didn't cheat, so Mike kept track for her in exchange for free beer. She confirmed it was a valid bingo and poured the winner a pitcher of Augsburger beer. As she topped off the pitcher, Mike went to the bathroom, mouthing the word "help" as he passed her. MJ glanced to her left, where Tammie was shaking her empty glass.

MJ made another just like the last and set it in front of her.

"I'm taking Mike home with me tonight," Tammie said.

MJ contained her smile.

"Good luck with that," she snorted. "Word of advice, Tammie. Don't waste your time on him. He isn't for you."

Tammie narrowed her eyes and pursed her lips, clearly working up her next nasty thing to say, assuming MJ was jealous. MJ almost felt sorry for her. When Mike returned, her scowl smoothed into a too-bright smile, and she twirled her hair around a finger. MJ went back to filling beers and washing glasses as Tammie batted her eyelashes at Mike. It was like watching a cow bumping into a barn door; she wasn't going to get anywhere. The more Mike seemed unaffected by her wiles, the harder Tammie pushed — literally: her free-range boobs squashed against his arm.

MJ couldn't let this go on. As much fun as it was to watch Tammie fail, it wasn't fair to let her friend suffer for her enjoyment. She set a glass on the rail in front of Tammie and filled it with Sprite, but when she went to put the soda gun back in its holster, she let it keep spraying, soaking Tammie with the cold, sticky liquid. Her squeal of protest turned every head in the bar.

"Sorry. The button got stuck." MJ shrugged and threw her a dry bar towel.

"My daddy is so gonna fire you." She

rushed out of the bar, probably to call her daddy.

MJ watched her go, then got a rag to clean up the mess. Mike smiled like an idiot. Problem solved.

MJ glanced back at the phone on the far side of the island. Who was this mysterious T? She didn't want to play the jealous, suspicious wife, but she needed to know. Was it Tammie? How could she find out without Chris knowing how insecure she was? His phone whistled. The caller had left a message. She could listen. She glanced into the living room, where Chris was still on the floor with Kate and Tommy, and looked at his phone again. One new voice mail. Her hand floated toward the device. She had to know. It wasn't that she didn't trust him, but she was going crazy.

"Did I hear my phone?" Chris said from behind her. MJ picked up the phone and turned to him.

"Yeah, I was going to bring it to you. I couldn't get to it while it was ringing because I was parsleyed up."

"Good call. You never want to mix parsley and phones. That's like crossing the streams." Chris picked up his phone and took it to his office. A few minutes later he stepped out, grabbing his keys and coat off the rack.

"I have to run out. I'll be back before dinner."

MJ's stomach clenched like she'd slammed a glass of cheap malt liquor.

"What happened that you need to leave the house on Thanksgiving?"

Chris's eyes flicked to the parsley she had been hacking to pieces.

"A client has to get me some paperwork. They're visiting family in Pewaukee so they brought it along rather than send it overnight. I won't be gone long." He opened the garage door and left her with the family and a lukewarm turkey. MJ stared at the door, willing him to come right back and say it wasn't important enough to leave on a holiday. He hadn't even given her a chance to say anything. She wanted to say something, though she wasn't sure what. Instead, her mom entered the kitchen.

"Are you sure I can't help?" she asked.

MJ blinked and pulled herself back to the tasks at hand.

"No, Ma. I can handle this."

"Can you?" She looked meaningfully at the door Chris had gone through.

Lips tight, MJ tapped her tattoo silently and started cleaning up to make room for the turkey, which she prayed would be warm enough soon. "It's an unexpected work thing. He'll be right back," she said, faking her nonchalance. God, she really needed to get out of here. Her mom watched every motion she made. Nerve-racking.

"I believe that, but do you?" Barbara's laser gaze, the one that would send under-age customers scurrying for the door, cut through MJ's bluff. MJ kept her lips closed. "He's a good one, MJ. I know I spent a lot of time telling you not to rely on anyone, especially men, but I was young, too. You're smarter than me. Don't make the same mistakes I did."

MJ nodded. She didn't trust herself to speak.

After yesterday's uncertainty, MJ woke with a start. The day after Thanksgiving had always been the first day of the Christmas season in the Boudreaux household. MJ would normally pull out all the boxes, unpack the ornaments, set up the prelit tree, and work all day until the house looked like Santa's elves had gotten punch-drunk with holiday cheer. But this year, after the stress of the day before and the mysterious phone call, MJ was inspired — or desperate.

She was doubling down on poker strategy.

She waited in the kitchen, making her favorite post-Thanksgiving breakfast of leftover stuffing and gravy on toast. As she finished off her second piece, Chris shuffled in, running his hands through his hair until it looked like it was trying to escape his head.

"Morning," she said. He nodded and poured himself some coffee. As he sipped from a chipped Tigger mug, MJ decided it was now or never. "So, since you don't have to work today, I thought it might be fun if we play some poker. At the casino. It's been a while since you've gone."

MJ stood and put her empty plate in the dishwasher while Chris waited until the coffee jolted his brain awake. He started nodding. This was a good sign.

"Sounds like a good idea. Don't you usually decorate?"

"I'll get a little done this morning and finish later this weekend. I'd rather have a day with you at the casino." MJ's smile spread to take over her face.

"Great. Let's try to beat the crowds."

Once the kids were settled in the basement with a *Harry Potter* movie marathon, and she and Chris headed downtown, her happiness jolted her like twelve cups of coffee. Not even her heavy breakfast could hold her down. She had let herself get distracted by her enjoyment of the game itself. She'd lost sight of her goal — her husband — but no more.

They weren't the only ones that thought playing poker on the day after Thanksgiving was a good idea. Most of the tables had waits. Only the higher stakes, no-limit tables had immediate seating, so that's what they put their names down for.

MJ handed in her players card to the hostess when her name was called first.

"You can head to table ten," the hostess said.

MJ gave Chris a quick kiss, then approached her table, already analyzing the players. Most were young men, with a handful of middle-aged men. Still several feet from her seat, she turned to see Chris sit at his table . . . next to a blonde head . . . next to Tammie. God, that woman was everywhere! A steady buzz filled her mind, blocking out the rational voices. She wanted to yank Chris away from her and drag him to safety. But then she would have to explain herself. And how do you explain crazy? It would probably lead to an argument about how she didn't trust him, but it wasn't him she didn't trust. It was that woman.

MJ needed to pull it together. She was about to sit down with more money than she had ever played with before at a higher-stakes table than she had ever played at before. She turned her back on Chris and tried to forget about Her.

She'd try something new today. She pulled her hair out of the clip holding it up and slid on her new glasses. They were thick framed and lent her an air of sexy librarian. She pulled off her black cardigan to reveal a low-cut, black sequined T-shirt. As she pulled her arm out of the sleeve, her wedding ring caught a loose thread. She untangled it, careful not to pull the thread further. Her simple wedding band held a small diamond, nothing fancy or flashy. On a reckless impulse, she slid her large teal octopus ring off her right hand and put it on her left ring finger, easily hiding the small circle.

Giving her hair a shake, MJ stood taller and closed the last few feet to her table, pausing before she sat to give every player a chance to look up and take her in. More than a few eyes skated over her left hand. MJ's lips curled into a smile; her edginess faded a bit. This is what she needed.

"Gentlemen."

She slid into her seat and smoothed her

shirt down, then unracked her chips, taking her time so she could make eye contact with a few of the men, giving them names as she went: Junior, Nose Hair, Shaggy. She folded her first few hands, barely looking at her cards, watching the other players with wide eyes and a vapid smile. The older man on her left, Pops, seemed amused when she peeked at her hand and folded for the fourth time.

"You play at the big-boy table often?"

MJ turned to him. He was maybe ten years older than she was, handsome, with salt-and-pepper hair. He smelled nice and had straight white teeth. She caught his eyes flitting toward her hands. The ring check.

"Oh, darling, don't you worry about me." She patted his arm.

He smiled.

"Something tells me I need to worry about my chip stack."

"No. Now, him." MJ pointed at the young man across the table with mirrored sunglasses and baseball cap — Sparky. "He should worry about me."

Pops raised his eyebrows. "He's been trying to push around the table for an hour and doing pretty well."

"Well, our young man hasn't been pushed around by me."

Pops looked at her again, closer this time, his eyes grazing her low V-neck. Under normal circumstances, MJ would scold him for his wandering gaze, but instead she sat up straighter, rolling her shoulders back and meeting his eyes.

A new hand had started and MJ peeked at her cards. Finally! A hand she could work with. She licked her lips and let the real play begin. Maintaining a new persona and the higher-stakes game kept her focused on the present. Chris and Tammie faded into nothing. All that mattered was the next hand, the next bet. Could she bluff a few more chips from the table?

Each time she won a pot, a new thrill ran through her. Sometimes she bluffed, sometimes she had a great hand. When she lost, she replayed the action in her head to figure out what she had missed. Completely in the zone, she felt invincible.

Then her Zen mood exploded into shards at the sound of Tammie's piercing giggle. It carried across half the room and stabbed right through her spine, tensing all her muscles at once like an electric jolt. Her laugh was a wireless taser. Rational thought became impossible. She needed to get away from that sound before it zapped her again. She needed this hand to end, a hand that a few seconds ago she was convinced she could win. She folded, leaving half her chips in the pot, basically giving them to Sparky — but she couldn't stay there. She collected the rest of her chips and her cardigan and scurried to the cage to cash herself out.

As she waited for her cash, she found Chris's tousled hair. He hadn't noticed her movement; instead, he laughed with his table, with Her. Maybe her marriage wasn't fixable — he hadn't laughed that freely for her in . . . she couldn't remember how long. This wasn't the life she wanted, standing alone, listening to her husband laugh with another woman.

But what *did* she want? MJ looked at the money in her hand. Even though her play tonight ended poorly — thanks, Tammie — her bankroll was still significantly bigger, five hundred dollars bigger, to be exact. MJ read the sign for the upcoming tournament again. She should give it a try. She had the money, the kids were in support. It was six weeks away and selling out fast. She stepped up to the counter, excitement taking over — *this* was what she wanted.

"Hi, MJ, what can I help you with?" the host said.

"I'd like to sign up for the tournament."

CHAPTER NINE

The words "When did you start talking to Tammie?" flew out of MJ's mouth in a reckless tumble, so fast that she had no hope of stopping them. Now they were out, hanging between her and Chris. She already lay in bed. Chris had just come upstairs after spending an hour responding to e-mails that had come in while they were at the casino. He was digging in the basket of clean laundry and stood once he found the T-shirt he was looking for.

She had held in all her thoughts and insecurities during the long walk from the poker room to their car, during the twenty-minute ride home, and during the short walk into the house. But it hovered over her like a dark cloud, pressing down on her, making her feel smaller. Making her feel needy.

More than anything, MJ hated to feel needy.

"I thought you were going to sleep." Chris stood still, trying to find her eyes in their dark bedroom. He gave up and went into their walk-in closet to change clothes and set out his suit and tie for the next workday, even though it was Saturday. Habits were habits, and Chris didn't like to change them.

"I am." MJ spoke a little louder so he could hear her. "And you didn't answer the question."

Chris walked back into the room, now wearing his pajamas. A part of MJ wanted to drop this conversation and pull him close, maybe nuzzle the spot where his ear met his neck, help them both forget she had even asked that question.

Moonlight shone through the window, illuminating his face enough that she could see his frown. He didn't want to have this conversation either.

"I've bumped into Tammie a few times. We've been catching up. You know we were friends in college."

" 'Were' being the operative word." The words came out harder than MJ had intended. Chris tensed.

"Is there something you want to say to me?"

MJ swallowed, hoping the right words

148

would come out to explain her reaction.

"You know how I feel about her. I don't understand why you need to associate with her."

"Am I supposed to ignore her when I see her at the coffee shop? We're not in college anymore." Chris paused as if he was going to say more, then closed his mouth.

"And the poker room."

"Is that why you've been playing so much poker?" Chris slipped under his side of the covers. "You're spying on me?"

"I'm just trying to understand what you're thinking."

"I'm thinking this conversation is ridiculous. We're adults. If we're talking about trying to understand what each other is thinking, I'd like to know why I have to scrounge through baskets of laundry to find clean socks."

"I'm not a maid."

"Anyone who walked in our house would know that's true."

MJ bit her lip and her eyes started to sting and water. That was the thing about arguing while married — the arsenal was unlimited. If an argument wasn't going the way you wanted, just reach in and grab a missile. Or if you really want to stop it, use precision warfare. Chris had pulled out their own personal Manhattan Project of spousal argument grenades.

"I guess we're done here. Sorry I tried to have a conversation about something that was bothering me."

Chris scowled and turned over. MJ looked at his back. Despite the hurt from his cutting comments, her hand twitched to rub his broad shoulders, ruffle his hair, and dispel the tension. Instead she rolled over to the very edge of the bed and squeezed her eyes shut.

MJ spent the next week cleaning, hoping that would appease Chris's disgruntlement. They hadn't spoken much since their blowout. Instead, they moved around each other like two magnets repelling each other. Just as they would get close, an invisible force would push them apart. One of them needed to flip so they could come together.

MJ was hoping she could get him to flip. Maybe if he didn't have to search for matching socks in overflowing baskets, they could have a conversation about Tammie. She even had dinner waiting in the Crock-Pot for the family. For the first time in a few months, the house was organized and she felt on top of everything. She had certainly earned her time at the felt that afternoon.

With her recent routine of cleaning then cards, she'd been spending a lot of nights in the poker room, so much so that the attendants and dealers knew her by name. She currently sat with Joe, a lovely man who grew up in northern Wisconsin not far from her hometown but had moved to Milwaukee to work in a brewery. He'd been downsized in the nineties and learned to deal at the casino when it started expanding. He'd worked there over twenty years and had two high schoolers.

While Joe flicked cards to each player, his eyes darted to MJ's neck as her left hand rose to brush the blue and green stone necklace. MJ was trying on her sexier persona again, this time in a black sweater and chunky jewelry to draw attention to her neckline. As she peeked at her cards, a new person sat to her left. MJ's nostrils flared. Tammie. She folded her cards and waited for the next hand to start.

"Hey, MJ. I was wondering if we'd ever play together." Her voice was sweet and slightly lower than she remembered, but still MJ clenched her teeth.

"Tammie." Somehow she spoke without unclenching her jaw. "Today's the lucky day, I guess."

"I like your ring." Tammie pointed at her

octopus, the one covering her wedding ring. MJ and Tammie hadn't spoken in more than twenty-five years, their last conversation hadn't been cordial, and now she was full of compliments?

"I call it Mari."

"I get it." Tammie unpacked her chips, lining them up in even stacks. "It's part of your poker strategy to be someone else."

Joe shuffled and dealt the next hand, an eyebrow raised at the two women. If Tammie kept yammering like this, she'd have to put in her earbuds.

"Hm?"

"Like how the guys use hoodies and sunglasses so people have a harder time reading the real them. You're wearing sexier clothes and that big ring."

MJ narrowed her eyes as she peeked at her cards. Pocket pair. Eights. She bet.

"Yes, I'm in disguise. You aren't supposed to recognize me."

Tammie giggled, zapping MJ's nerves, and called MJ's bet.

"I've never understood the need to be someone else when I play. I guess I'm just honest that way," Tammie said. MJ nearly choked on her annoyance. She'd never disliked anyone before, not like this. She wanted to pluck her bleached-blonde hair out like dead grass.

The flop came and MJ bet again. Tammie called. It's like she knew her very existence put MJ on edge. There was no way Tammie was winning this hand. The turn came, giving MJ three eights. She bet big, doubling the size of the pot. The table quieted. Tammie called. MJ looked at the showing cards and swore. There were so many hands that could beat her trip eights. She had let Tammie get under her skin and throw off her game. She knew before Tammie even flipped her cards that she was beat. Dammit — a straight! How could she even think about playing in the tournament if she couldn't keep her shit together in the face of an annoying player?

"Nice hand." MJ tossed her cards face-down, not showing what she had. She didn't want Tammie to know how stupidly she had played. Tonight's lesson was apparently a reminder to ignore emotion and keep her focus on the game. MJ did a quick count of her stack of chips and Tammie's, who had her beat by at least three to one. She wasn't leaving this table until that ratio reversed itself.

"So Tammie," she said. "What got you hooked on the felt?"

"It's a great way to meet men, don't you

think?" Her eyes flashed down to MJ's ring finger.

"Why would I need to meet a new man when I have one at home?"

"Is he?"

MJ barely stopped herself from sucking in a breath and giving her the reaction she was clearly seeking. Now she was just goading — easy enough to ignore.

The deal came around again. *Focus on the cards. Do not get distracted.* MJ folded and Tammie called. Good, now she could watch her. Tammie kept a slight smile on her face as she played, like she had a secret she wanted to share but couldn't. Her forehead was smooth, probably the result of Botox. She didn't seem to have any exceptional blinks or twitches. If it weren't for the calm rise and fall of her ridiculously perky boobs, she could have been a figure in Madame Tussauds museum. She didn't lick her lips or pick her nails. She was still . . . too still. That was it! MJ cracked a smile. Tammie's incredible stillness was her tell. Now she just had to find out if it meant a good hand or a bluff.

MJ let a few hands go by without playing, keeping her attention on Tammie. At last she knew. When Tammie had a good hand, a hand she felt could win, she went still.

Gotcha. On the next good hand, MJ bet and Tammie called, wiggling just slightly in her seat and fiddling with her cards. After the flop, MJ checked, Tammie did the same; a few more players stuck around, but no one raised. The turn didn't help, but MJ bet, Tammie called, and the rest fell off. It was just them. Based on the cards displayed, there were only a few really good hands and MJ knew Miss Wiggly next to her didn't have any of them. Joe dealt the river; it didn't help either. MJ tapped her wrist and bet big, keeping her hands clasped in front of her. Tammie looked at her as she toyed with her cards.

"What do you have?" Tammie murmured, playing with a stack of chips.

MJ stayed still, reciting the lyrics to "All That Jazz" in her head to keep her mind focused on something else. Let Tammie sort it out on her own. MJ almost got to the end of the song as Tammie chewed her lip, counted out chips, and peeked at her cards one more time. With a breathy "damn," she tossed her cards into the middle of the table.

"Did you have me beat?" she asked.

MJ pulled in the stack of chips the dealer was shoveling her way, leaving a nice tip for him.

"Oh, I never give anything away for free. I suggest you try it."

Tammie's eyes narrowed. "What are you suggesting?"

"Only giving some helpful advice."

"Me-yow," Shaggy said from the other side of the table. MJ and Tammie both turned toward the young man.

"Can we step away from the table and talk?" Tammie said. MJ nodded and followed Tammie to a quiet corner of the room.

"You know, when I saw you here, I got excited, like maybe we could be friends because we shared an interest in poker. Let bygones be bygones. I thought you might be less judgey than the rest of our fun-filled community of hypocrites. But you're just like the rest of them. All you see is a nice pair of boobs and a pretty face, and you feel threatened."

"Should I feel threatened? Because based on the last few hands, I have control of the situation."

Tammie huffed. "You're pretty good at reading people, but you're really blind when you want to be."

"Then what are we talking about?"

"Does your husband know you hide your wedding band when you play?"

MJ stared at her.

"I didn't think so," she said. "Take a good look at your own life before you start slinging mud at mine. At least I'm not trying to be someone I'm not."

Tammie walked away, leaving MJ to gape at her. Heat radiated from her face as she realized the table was staring at her, waiting for her to return. She shook her head no when Joe asked if she wanted to be dealt in. Checking her watch, she saw it was only five o'clock. If she hurried, she could be home in time to eat dinner with the kids. And maybe find out more about where Chris might be. MJ had thought he was the one who needed to flip over, but thanks to Tammie's prodding, she felt the magnetic pull toward home, her family, and her marriage.

CHAPTER TEN

MJ massacred romaine for dinner, hacking it into jagged pieces, while Kate and Tommy did homework at the dining room table and classical music played in the background. She chewed her lip while she chopped. During the car ride home, her eagerness to be with her family was replaced by insecurity. Why had Tammie acted like she knew something about her husband? Paranoia welled. She checked the clock for the third time in ten minutes. Chris wouldn't be home from his meeting for an hour yet. She went to the computer, her hands hovering over the keys, an invisible line holding her back from immediate action. She shouldn't look. She should just ask. But Tammie's words tickled in the back of her mind. She had to know, so she mentally erased that invisible line and logged onto his computer to open his calendar. In a few days he had a 10:00 a.m. appointment labeled "Meeting with T." T didn't sound like a company. It sounded like tight-jeans-clad, expensive-sunglasses-wearing, big-haired college arch-enemy.

She closed the calendar and the laptop and went back to the lettuce, holding the knife with white knuckles. He was meeting with Tammie — she knew it. Or she was pretty sure she knew it. She let go of the knife and banged her fist onto the wooden cutting board. Kate looked up at the loud sound.

"Ma, you okay?"

MJ looked up at Kate's concerned face and instantly felt snapped back to reality. She smiled. Perhaps she was overreacting and reading into Tammie's comments. That's what Tammie wanted her to do. She had wanted to throw her off at the table, cause strife between MJ and Chris. She always had been a troublemaker and that's all that was happening here.

"Totally fine," she lied. "The lettuce was acting up. It needed to know who was boss."

Kate rolled her eyes. "No one else has a weird mom."

"Consider yourself lucky, then."

Tommy laughed. "I don't think you're weird, Mom." She heard Chris's laughter in their son — saw his floppy dark hair. MJ took a calming breath. She was being ridiculous. Chris would never cheat. Why risk all this? But still, she picked up her phone and in a few swipes had made a new calendar that synced with his. Insecurity made her twitchy, and the only thing that helped lately was the solitude of the poker table. She needed to get back, and soon.

MJ stepped out of the shower, the steam fogging the mirrors and clouding the air like an evening in London. With the holidays behind them and the tournament almost here, she'd settled into a daily routine finely balanced between family and felt. She filled the fridge with sandwich meat on paper plates every week so they didn't need to dirty dishes. The entire family was living out of their laundry baskets in their rooms, but at least the clothes were clean. In the mornings, she'd see the kids off to school, go back to bed for a few hours, then arrive at the casino around three in the afternoon to play until one or two in the morning. When MJ got home, she'd take a quick shower, then slip into bed with as little movement as possible to not wake up Chris. She hadn't seen him awake in nearly a week.

But tonight she wasn't alone in the bathroom. Chris leaned against the door frame, hair rumpled to match his T-shirt and Captain America pajama bottoms, eyes half-open against the sleep as the steamy air swirled around him.

"Was I being loud? I didn't mean to wake you." MJ wrapped a towel around her body, then retrieved a second from the bathroom linen cabinet.

"No. I haven't seen you in a few days, so I set my alarm to wake up."

"That's sweet. You woke up just to see me?" She rubbed the towel down her legs, careful to keep the other securely wrapped around her. The foggy air thinned and disappeared through the open door.

"And talk."

MJ's stomach dropped. Of course his seemingly romantic gesture was not. There was a time when he would have set an alarm just to see her. But then, this was the first time he'd ever needed to. Guilt bubbled up in her throat. She'd gotten so far away from her goal of bringing them closer together. She finished drying off and wrapped the towel around her hair.

"About what?" She rubbed lotion onto her exposed arms and legs.

"How about the fact that I need to set my alarm to see you in the middle of the night? That doesn't bother you?"

"Of course it does, but that's what happens when two people are pursuing their passions." Chris crossed his arms.

"Poker is your passion now? You just started playing a couple months ago."

MJ put her lotion away and slipped her nightshirt on over her towel-covered body, letting the towel fall once her shirt covered her hips.

"So I can't be passionate about something I just started? Or is it because I'm doing something you wish you could be doing?" As soon as the words came out, MJ wanted them back. "That didn't come out right." But it was too late; she'd dropped the bomb and now she had to deal with the wreckage. She braced for what was coming.

In a tight voice, Chris said, "We have responsibilities, a family, a life, MJ. You seem to have dropped it all for a card game."

"So what you really have a problem with is that I'm not waiting at home every night when you finish work with a freshly poured cocktail and a warm meal."

MJ walked past him into the bedroom. She knew she'd been a less attentive wife and mother since she had started playing poker. But why couldn't he be supportive of her? She didn't give him grief when he wanted to play or when he had a late night for work. She smiled and took care of the family in his absence. Why did he have to make her feel bad when all she wanted was for him to give her the same courtesy? Besides, it was just until the tournament. Then everything would go back to normal.

"You know that's not what I'm saying."

"For the first time since we met, I'm doing something just for me. Why can't you be supportive of that?"

"I want to be, but does it need to come at the cost of our family?"

"Are you saying it is? Is there something you aren't telling me?" MJ recalled the mysterious appointments with T. Chris opened his mouth to speak, then closed it again.

"I guess not." His shoulders slumped. "I support you." He turned and crawled back into bed. MJ watched him, hands shaking. He couldn't tell her the whole truth but still expected her to sacrifice her interests for him.

Not anymore.

■ ■ ■ ■

Chris: Can we go out for dinner tonight?

After last night's contentious conversation, she didn't expect a date to be Chris's next approach. Maybe he was sorry about not being more supportive. Maybe he realized she needed this right now. Or maybe he wanted to talk more.

MJ: Of course. Where and when? I'll meet you there.
Chris: A Simple Twist. Reservations at 7. See you then.

■ ■ ■ ■

As soon as MJ slid into her seat at the table, her nerves eased. She clicked her phone to silent, still puzzling over Chris's invitation, and her whole body melted into the chair. As she set out her chips with precision, she enjoyed the smooth arced edges, cool to the touch and with a satisfying heft. Without even counting, she separated her stacks into towers of twenty. Before she could turn to look, a waitress had brought her a glass of ice water and a coffee with four creams. She gave the woman a dollar chip and set the drinks on a small side table to her right. Now everything was ready. She nearly moaned with pleasure as she trailed her fingertips over the worn green of the table-top, waiting for her first hand of the day.

This was the distraction she needed. If she had stayed at home, she'd be a nervous mess waiting for their reservation time. Now she could while away the hours honing her play, then take the shorter drive directly to A Simple Twist for dinner. Noticing her own spirits lifting, MJ remembered she'd been meaning to try the new restaurant out for a while, and began to look forward to a delicious, romantic dinner. Maybe she and Chris could even come back to the casino afterward for a nightcap and an hour or two of cards. She could pull a few strings to make sure they were seated at the same table. Yes, this could be a great evening.

She lost herself in the rhythm of the game, the quick shuffle of cards in the machine, the precise dealing, each dealer's signature toss. Her body settled into a zone, muffling the ambient sounds to a low hum. She matched her play to the even and controlled breaths she took. If she were a yogi, she might wonder if she'd achieved nirvana. This was bliss.

Time suspended itself. She guessed a few hours had passed since she'd started, when the first dealer she'd had returned to her table. MJ looked at the number of tables in play and did a quick calculation, knowing they rotated every half hour. Could she have been here six hours? She pulled out her phone: seven thirty. She missed her dinner with Chris and he hadn't called or texted.

She sent a quick message.

Just saw the time. So sorry. I'll be there in 20.

Cashing out her chips and hustling to her car, she tore through the casino parking lot and almost crashed into a slow-moving Cadillac. All the earlier tension had rushed back in spades. Chris was going to kill her. She should have set an alarm. Or he could have texted — never mind, she wouldn't have gotten it. He wouldn't forgive her for this, and why should he? But then again, she had no problem forgiving him when he missed their anniversary lunch, so he sort of owed her one.

She zoomed through the Milwaukee streets, running only one red light, and managed to find parking only two blocks from the restaurant. As she jogged down the street, she girded herself to face Chris's upcoming anger. She yanked open the door and was greeted by a bustling restaurant decorated in black, white, and a fresh kelly green. It smelled amazing, reminding MJ that she hadn't eaten since breakfast.

She found the hostess, who appeared

startled at MJ's whirlwind entrance and heavy breathing, and asked for the Boudreaux table.

"I'm sorry, but that table left thirty minutes ago. He said his date couldn't make it."

MJ's shoulders slouched and she shook her head, peering past the hostess stand into the dining room.

"Are you sure? That doesn't sound like Chris."

"Yes. He was quite apologetic. I'm sorry."

The hostess turned her attention to a ringing phone, leaving MJ to digest what had just happened. She'd never blatantly let Chris down like this before. Why hadn't he called her? She checked to make sure her phone worked, but there were no new messages from him. She stumbled outside the restaurant and leaned against the giant front window, her breath coming in shallow bursts. She had lost track of time — surely Chris could understand that, if anyone could. He'd spent plenty of evenings at the table. He'd have to understand once she explained.

She held the phone to her ear, listening to the rings. One ring. Two rings. Three rings. Voice mail. MJ never got his voice mail. This was the first time she heard his outgoing message.

Now he was just being petty. If he wasn't going to allow her to apologize, then screw him. She wouldn't. If poker had taught her one thing, it was that you needed to adjust your play to the players. If he didn't want to talk, she could do silence with the best of them.

CHAPTER ELEVEN

MJ pulled her car into the garage, disappointed that Chris's wasn't already there. The empty spot echoed the feeling in her stomach. Her anger had ebbed as she drove the thirty minutes home from downtown, replaced by an ache she didn't want to acknowledge. She hung her keys on the hook where they belonged, ignoring the bare one beside it.

She looked in on both the kids, who were hunkered down in their rooms, gave them kisses, and went to the master bedroom. She paused in the doorway, taking in the vacant room. She pulled on her pajamas and crawled onto the center of their bed. Determined to wait up for Chris, she sat and crossed her legs.

MJ woke the next morning curled in the middle of the mattress with a blanket on top of her. The kids — most likely the noise that woke her — opened doors and poured cereal in the kitchen. With five hours until the tournament began, she needed to shower. She needed coffee. She needed to talk to her husband. She flew through a shower, tossed on a bathrobe, and went downstairs before the kids left for the bus.

"Hey, Ma," Kate said. She stood at the island, buttering toast. Her long hair shimmered in the morning light. Kate shoved her toast in her mouth, sending crumbs onto her shirt. Tommy walked in the kitchen, wearing track pants and a Brewers T-shirt.

"Mom, you're up early." Ouch. He was right. She hadn't been getting up that early recently. Or grocery shopping. Or cleaning. Or doing laundry.

"I know, sweetie. But I wanted to see you both before you left. I have the big tournament today that I'm hoping to do well in, remember? If I do, I won't be home until late."

"Don't worry, Mom. Dad's got this," Kate said.

The words slapped at MJ's already wounded pride as she recalled Kate's musical she would be missing.

She just needed to get through the tournament today; then she could get her focus back on Chris and the kids. Then she'd find a balance. For the first time MJ had purpose when approaching the table. Before, it had always been about escape. Now she wanted to win, to get the trip, to reconnect with Chris. Today was for him, not her. Show him that she still wanted him in her life, that he was more important than poker.

This was it. Hope and focus filled her as she smiled and took her seat at the table, nodding to Joe the dealer. It was a good sign, starting off with a dealer she knew well. She checked her phone — five minutes until shuffle up and deal.

Chips already sat in front of each chair — five thousand chips to be exact. Five thousand chances to beat the other players, five thousand chances to win. Players around her queued up playlists, stretched their backs, and tucked sunglasses onto collars to pull on during important hands.

MJ smoothed her ponytail and swiped on some lip gloss. She had dressed for comfort today, her favorite jeans and a simple black T-shirt. She wore no other jewelry besides her wedding band and the smiley-face ring Chris had given her on their anniversary. It was her luck today.

The tournament host announced, "Shuffle

up and deal." A bell rang and the room's energy became palpable, building on itself like a snowball rolling down a hill. MJ struggled not to get swept up in it; she needed to keep her focus. The first two cards arrived in front of her before she could settle in. A few weeks ago, she may have looked at them immediately. Instead, she took some calming breaths and simply watched as everyone around the table assessed his or her hand. As each player looked, she gauged their reactions. Slump — her old friend from day one — sat to her right and bet, tripling the pot. MJ waited until the bet came around to her and she finally peeled back the corner of her cards: pocket queens. She called. Everyone else fell away, too early to gamble so many chips. MJ would have done the same if she hadn't already played with him. She knew his tell and his slouch was screaming "Bluff." The flop came — queen, ten, three. MJ focused on breathing in and out, not moving. Slump hunched farther over his chips and echoed his first large bet. She could call, fold, or raise. She knew she had him now, but he could catch a lucky break on the turn or the river. *Could he beat me?* MJ wondered. He could have a possible straight if he had a king/jack or jack/nine. The suits were a jumble, so a flush was unlikely, but any two pairs could lead to a full house. Anything else she had beat. He wasn't acting like he had any leads. He was acting like he was bluffing, and she had the cards to beat a bluff.

MJ called.

Slump stared her down. Would he back off, or would he remain committed?

The turn came — a six.

That wasn't going to help him. If he backed down, he would know that she would think he had nothing. He wasn't going to admit this early that he'd been shooting blanks. He was slumped so far over the table, his chin practically touched the padded edge. MJ knew before he said it what he would do. And she knew her reaction and she knew the outcome like it was fated.

He went all in. She called. She won with her three queens.

In the first hand MJ had already knocked someone out and doubled up. As she stacked her new chips, the happy smiley ring grinned at her, almost as if Chris were there cheering her on himself.

As players dropped out, the remaining ones were moved to open spots in an effort to keep each table as full as possible. She had survived three table reshufflings and several hours of play to make it to the final table. MJ studied each of the players sitting with her. She had played with at least half of them during her regular games, so she knew a little about their play. Her butt and back hurt from hours of sitting, her shoulders twitched from holding the same position, and her brain dulled to the flashing numbers and suits on the table. Hands started to blur together. This was how she consciously chose to spend a weekend?

As players became more aggressive and chip stacks either multiplied or dwindled, bluffing became the tactic of choice. She was getting sick of faking it, of pretending to have stronger cards than she had, of keeping all the emotions hidden from the other players. She could feel the cracks in her facade starting to give way, but she was so close now. The discomfort of her cramping back muscles cleared her mind to focus on what really mattered. Looking back over the past few months, she saw that her mistakes were so obvious, like someone had taken a neon yellow highlighter and circled them. This place was never going to fix her marriage. She had used it as an excuse to break out of her daily routine, but now she was risking her entire family's happiness.

No prize was worth that risk.

Players busted out, while MJ stayed. With two lone survivors in the tournament, MJ began to get excited, focus returning. *On the other hand,* she thought, *the trip to Vegas would be an opportunity to really focus on me and Chris.* She could even give the prize to him, letting him have the private lesson and the tournament entry. She was in too deep to give up now — the final hands of the final table.

She'd watched her opponent as she and he took turns knocking out the other players; he liked to take risks, so she called him Kenny Rogers. They parried back and forth, feeling each other out. Playing heads-up was an entirely different game. You could win a pot with a pair of twos or an ace. They took turns exchanging the escalating blinds preflop. At last, they both had hands they liked enough to pay for more cards. MJ had pocket eights — a pair of snowmen. The flop: ace, jack, eight. She had triple eights. Kenny Rogers could have a lot of hands that could beat hers. She couldn't read him, so she had to test him. MJ had to bet first; she would normally triple the pot — a sign that she had a decent hand. But would he have something better?

He studied her as MJ ran all the possibilities in her head. She didn't want to see a king, queen, or ten on that board. She should get rid of him while she could.

"All in." Her voice squeaked the words.

Kenny kept his eyes on her. On the one hand, she wanted him to come with her. She was up right now and could knock him out. On the other hand, since there were so many possible outs that could give him the better hand, there was a good chance she'd lose if they saw the turn and the river.

"Call," he said.

MJ's breath whooshed out. This was it — the whole tournament. They both flipped their cards over and stood. He had ten/nine and was a queen or seven away from a straight, but she had him for now.

The turn: seven.

Kenny Rogers pumped his fist. He'd gotten the card he needed. The only way she could beat him now was with a full house or a fourth eight appearing on the river. She was so close, one card between her and the trip, the chance to make things right with Chris. Without it, all those hours in this dark room were for nothing. Sure, she would take home some consolation money for finishing second, but winning would make all that time away from her family worth it. She clutched the back of the chair as the dealer flipped the final card.

A jack. A beautiful, gorgeous jack of spades for her full house.

Kenny Rogers stared at the table and nodded his head solemnly before he walked around and shook MJ's hand.

"Nicely played."

"You, too."

MJ turned to the person presenting her with the winnings. A camera flashed, blinding her with spots. She had done it. She'd earned this victory with her wits and, yes, a little bit of luck, but all for herself, by herself. Her body ached, her eyelid twitched, and she couldn't wait to take Chris to Vegas.

CHAPTER TWELVE

MJ stood by the island in her kitchen, pulling ingredients for eggs from the fridge. Daisy gave a low woof and she heard the garage door open. Chris was home, finally. She had woken up alone to an empty house. She let the fridge door close as she stood still listening for every noise, gauging his progress into the house. Her fingers drummed a staccato, the only outward sign of her anxiety. The whole drive home she had played the scene of her telling him about the trip, about her tournament win, over and over in her head. Sometimes she left playful notes leading up to the bedroom, sometimes she shouted as he walked in the room, unable to contain her excitement anymore. Every iteration ended in kisses and mended hearts.

She stopped tapping her fingers when Chris, Kate, and Tommy walked through the door, Kate carrying a box of doughnuts from their favorite bakery — dense glazed crullers, perfect for dunking in a hot cup of coffee. Chris paused when he saw her standing there, then kept walking, lining his shoes up in the closet while the kids kicked theirs off and left them in the middle of the hallway. The kids tore open the box, barely acknowledging their mom's presence. She knew better than to get between them and Sunday-morning sugar.

Chris opened the fridge and drank from the open milk jug. MJ sighed.

"Can't you get a glass? Tommy has started doing that, too." Tommy managed to look sheepish with half a cruller hanging out of his mouth.

"My house, my milk. No glass."

"Lovely." MJ studied his face for any sign of emotion, but it was blank. "I won. I took down the entire thing."

"Way to go, Mom!" Tommy said, wrapping his gangly arms around her shoulders. Kate gave her a thumbs-up as she left the room with her breakfast for the quiet of her room. MJ's eyes stayed on Chris.

He filled the cups sitting on the counter, then twisted the cap back on the milk and set it back in the fridge. MJ wanted a response from him. Anything. This indifference was too much. If she could get a reaction, then she knew she could reach him. She had to reach him. Tommy followed Kate out of the room, two doughnuts in his left hand and a full glass of milk in his right.

"I won a trip to Vegas in April. It includes poker lessons with Doyle Kane and an entry to a tournament with only forty players. The winner of that gets entered in the Global Poker Finals."

Chris looked at her blankly.

"It's a trip for two. We're going to Vegas!"

Chris blinked at her.

"I don't think so. Take Lisa. Have fun."

Chris walked out of the kitchen. She could hear his measured footsteps on the stairs. MJ grabbed the counter. He didn't want to come with her. His words had scooped out everything in her chest and thrown it across the kitchen floor. What had just happened? She sunk to her knees, still clinging to the counter edge, a part of her brain registering that fur balls tumbled under the edges of the cabinets. It hadn't occurred to her in a single one of her daydreams that he would say no.

Daisy's nails clicked on the floor as she walked toward MJ, putting her nose on MJ's nose before attempting a sloppy kiss.

"You still love me, don't you, girl?" MJ scratched behind her ears and down her back as Daisy wriggled with canine glee. Daisy gave her one more puppy kiss, then wandered off to slurp water from her bowl, most likely thinking her work was done.

"This is fudiculous." MJ shook her head and stood up, wiping away the tears that had collected in her eyes.

MJ didn't want to fight. They had gotten too good at poking each other's soft spots. But he couldn't stop communicating. She wasn't giving up yet. She followed him up the stairs into their bedroom, where he was pulling a shirt over his mostly firm stomach. Her stomach twisted with a yearning to wrap her arms around him. This time, she couldn't tamp it back down. She needed to tell him how she felt, that she didn't like the distance between them. That she wanted to touch him, and hold him forever. But when his eyes met hers, her resolve fled. They weren't cold or angry or hateful; they were ambivalent. He may as well have been looking at a parking lot or an empty field.

"When do you leave?" Chris asked.

"I don't want to go alone."

Chris stared at her, burrowing into her eyes. She tried to put all the emotions she couldn't speak out loud into her face. He had always been able to read her. He had to know how important this was to her. He exhaled.

"You shouldn't miss out on this. You earned it. Lisa or Ariana will go with you."

He walked past her, careful not to touch, and went to the basement to watch whatever sporting event happened to be on TV. Numbness washed over her. She had failed. She had lost Chris and had no idea what to do next. There was no backup plan. She'd reached the end.

"What's with the schmoopy face?" Lisa slid a still-warm cinnamon roll in front of MJ. MJ pulled off an edge, then swirled it in the melting frosting only to set it back down uneaten. "Spill," Lisa said.

MJ looked into Lisa's dear, concerned face. She remembered meeting Lisa for the first time on a rainy afternoon. She had taken one look at MJ and known how to get her to talk.

Bucky's had just opened for the day, so it was MJ, an empty bar, and reruns of *Family Ties* on the muted TV while rain poured down outside. She'd finished her preshift setup, so she had planned to get some studying done when the phone rang. The phone never rang. It was probably a wrong number, but now she was curious.

"Bucky's. MJ speaking."

"MJ, it's me," said her mom. "Sorry to call you at work, but we need to talk. Do you have time?"

What Barbara really meant was, "Any customers?" If even one customer was in the bar, she'd set a time to talk to MJ later. The customer came first — always.

"It's empty. I won't have anyone for a few more hours. I'm even caught up on my side work."

Barbara paused before she began speaking.

"I don't know how to tell you this . . . Joey is dead. He was driving too fast on the Zig-Zag, that switchback road out past the Nelson farm, and went off the edge. He was on his motorcycle and didn't stand a chance."

MJ drooped against the bar and closed her eyes; the image of her dad zooming off the side of the cliff, still believing he was living life to the fullest, played on her eyelids.

"Was he drunk?" she asked.

"He'd been at Jimmy's all afternoon. I'm sure he didn't feel a thing."

Joey had never been a father to her. He'd been an embarrassment, a hassle, and a burden, but he'd never been a father. Now she had a big, dad-shaped gap in her life where that idiot had taken up space. Fuck gaps.

Tears squeezed out of her closed eyes. God, why was she crying over him? This should be a relief — one less complication in her life. She wanted so much to hug her mom, but they were four hours away from each other.

MJ heard the tinkle of chimes, the sound of rain, then the door closing.

"I gotta go, Ma. Customer," she choked out, and grabbed a bar towel to scrub the tears from her face, but her chest still heaved as she turned to face the patron. Already propped on a bar stool sat a drenched young woman, her shoulder-length hair hanging in sad, permed curls around her face. She wore a simple jean jacket over an oversize, torn T-shirt. They were wet, too. Despite her bedraggled appearance, she flashed MJ a welcoming smile, then scanned the wall of bottles behind MJ, until she pointed to the Jack Daniel's.

"There, that's what I need." She looked at MJ's rosy cheeks and wet eyelashes. "Pour one for you, too."

MJ took a shaky breath, intrigued by this soaked, happy Jack drinker. And as long as the girl was going to ignore her obvious tears, she was game.

The two shot glasses clinked on the counter. She poured the brown liquid with efficient skill, stopping at exactly one ounce, though only she knew that. She slid one to the newcomer and lifted her own glass. They clinked and both tossed back the shot. With practiced ease, MJ gulped it down and clapped the empty glass back on the bar. The woman finished swallowing her shot after MJ, shaking her head as the liquor burned. She pushed her empty glass toward MJ.

"Again," she croaked.

MJ poured two more shots and a glass of water. They picked up their shooters, clinked, and swallowed; the other girl chased the fire with the water. MJ let the Jack burn off her tears from the inside out. She put the bottle back in its spot without taking her eyes off the stranger.

"So, what brings you in?" MJ asked.

"The rain." Drenched, she smiled at her.

"And the shots?"

"Are you saying you didn't need a little Jack right then?"

MJ's brows furrowed.

"But why did you order them?" MJ asked.

"I came in to get out of the rain and you

were crying. Like really crying. Seemed like a good time for some shots with a friend."

"But I don't know you."

She stuck her hand across the bar.

"I'm Lisa. Now, tell me all about it."

That same face still sat across from her. A few more wrinkles and pounds, but even more perceptive.

"I screwed it all up." There, she'd said it. And it felt better to get it out. She kept going. "I was worried I didn't love him. I should have been worried about if he loved me. I really thought this would help bring us together. That we could wrap up my foray into poker with a fun trip to Vegas. He was like a different man, so cold and far away from me. What do I do?"

"So, are you talking?"

"Sort of. It's all very polite and sterile."

"And what are you feeling?"

"Guilty for all the time I spent away, but pissed that he isn't even a little impressed that I won that tournament. I've gotten quite good at something for the first time in years and I can't even share it with him. It's like it's not real without him."

"You did forget about your date with him because you were playing poker. I imagine he's sore about that."

186

"Of course he is. I've tried to apologize. He acts like he's over it, but he's so distant. And let's not forget, Lees: this whole thing started with him ditching me on our anniversary — to play poker."

"What about the trip? Are you going to go?"

MJ sighed. Her well-laid plans were blazing to bits, but she did have a wonderful friend who would make the perfect travel companion.

"What are you doing in early April? Could you get someone to fill in here?"

Lisa grinned.

"Are you kidding? I've been dying for a girls' trip. My staff can handle it. What about Ariana?"

"What about me?" Ariana plopped into a chair next to them, her normally neat ponytail falling out around her face. She slumped in the chair, using an outstretched arm to swipe some frosting off the abandoned cinnamon roll.

MJ pushed the plate closer to her.

"Want to come to Vegas with us in April? Free room."

Ariana drooped more. "I wish. I just took on a new case that might kill me. Brutal, and there is no way it'll be done by then.

I'll be lucky if it's settled before April next year."

"Oh no. Well, maybe we shouldn't if you can't come," MJ said.

"Don't even think about not going. Just have enough fun for me, too."

The three of them smiled at one another. At least she had another goal to work toward. If Chris wasn't going to be proud of her poker success, that didn't mean she had to stop. She could spend the next six weeks keeping up her game, preparing for the trip. That way she wouldn't make a fool of herself. And getting away from this entire mess might be just the thing. So why did she feel disappointed?

CHAPTER THIRTEEN

"Do you really need to leave, Mom?" Tommy asked as he rolled a baseball across the back of his hand. With baseball season ramping up, MJ was sure he only let go of it to shower. She shook her head as she carefully wrapped her highest heels and tucked them into her suitcase.

"I do. But I'll only be a text away. We can FaceTime, too. You'll barely notice I'm gone. And it's just for a few days." She ruffled his hair and smiled at him.

"I bought several meals and put them in the freezer. They have instructions if you need them; just don't eat them all at once. There's enough down there to feed your baseball team for a week."

"I guess." Tommy chewed on his lip.

"Stop that — you'll make it bleed. Just say what's on your mind." Half of her parenting with him, it seemed, was preventing loss of blood.

Tommy stopped and licked his lip.

"Why do you have to go?"

MJ grabbed her son's hand and pulled him into a hug. Even though he was taller than she was, and had become so seemingly overnight, he was still her little boy.

"You know how you spent that summer trying different sports, hoping to find the one you really loved?" Tommy nodded. "That's what I'm doing. You and Kate are growing up, and I need to find something I really love." She brushed his slightly fuzzy cheek. "I'll miss you while I'm gone." She didn't need to say, though she thought it, that she and Chris needed some more physical distance after two months of living around instead of with each other, and she was hoping to do some soul searching with Lisa to come back with a new approach on how to win him back.

"You, too, Mom."

MJ squeezed Tommy's arm and returned to packing.

"Where's Kate? I thought she was going to be here."

"She went home with Bree after school. And she didn't do her chores this morning. Her dirty clothes are still in the laundry room."

MJ frowned. She wanted to say good-bye

to Kate before she left. This wasn't like her to not check in about her plans. She checked to confirm she hadn't missed any e-mails or texts on her phone, but none appeared, so she sent off a message and waited for a reply.

MJ: Where are you? I'm leaving for the airport soon.
Kate: OMG. I forgot that was today. On my way.
MJ: Grab the mail, too.

They had entered college acceptance season and MJ expected acceptance packets to start flooding in any day. It would be nice if a few arrived before her trip. She was getting nervous that none had appeared yet, even though Kate seemed unperturbed. MJ finished packing and carried her suitcase downstairs. She checked her purse to make sure she had some cash, ID, and credit cards. Part of the prize was a limo picking them up at the airport. Even at fifty, MJ smiled at the thought of such pampering. She double-checked her list of chores the kids needed to stay on top of while she was gone: dishes, laundry, vacuuming, and sweeping. There was an envelope with some money in case they needed to buy more food or wanted to order pizza.

Tommy looked at all the notes.

"You know, Mom, Dad is still going to be here."

"I know, honey, but his work schedule might get crazy, so I want you and Kate to have everything you need." And, she again refrained from adding, left to him, she would come home to no food, piles of laundry, and filth everywhere except for his perfectly aligned toiletries and tidy office. It wasn't that he was a slob; he just didn't seem to notice any messes he hadn't created.

MJ heard the door open, and Kate scampered in, a handful of envelopes and flyers in her hands, but nothing large enough to indicate an acceptance packet.

"Sorry, Mom, I forgot you were leaving," she said.

"No college letters?" Kate shook her head in answer. "I should contact your counselor to see what he thinks." MJ pursed her lips.

For the briefest of moments, Kate's eyes widened, then she shrugged. Something was off. Daisy woofed to indicate an approaching car they couldn't hear yet. MJ wrapped her arms around her girl. "You two can text, call, e-mail me anytime. I'll always answer. Always."

"I know, Mom. Have fun."

MJ looked at the clock. Time to go. Her children stood side by side and she pulled them in for one more hug. She didn't know what would happen between Chris and her, so she wanted to savor this moment while everything could still be okay. Her heart split in two. One half staying back with her kids and the other eager for the distraction of the tables, the thrill of the game.

Lisa's SUV pulled into her driveway as Daisy foretold. Tommy carried out her luggage, and both kids waved as she and Lisa drove away. The trees were just starting to bud and a few bold daffodils brightened up her mostly barren flower beds. She memorized every detail, knowing that when she returned, things would be different. She just wasn't sure how different.

So much had changed already from when Chris and MJ first met.

Why did she let Lisa talk her into attending a frat party? She spent enough time with drunken dudes at Bucky's — she didn't need it during her off hours, too. At least this one seemed to be invite-only rather than the open-call meat market of most college keggers. As she weaved through the crowd, her wrist smacked against a nameless, faceless body. She pulled it in close and rubbed the sore spot, still raw and shiny from the tattoo she'd gotten yesterday.

She pulled out of the crowd and looked at her wrist. Rising above the tender skin was a tiny tree, no bigger than a dime, scraggly and windswept. Tiny pink-purple flowers burst from the branch, barely specks, but evidence of survival. It was her reminder, her motto. She had survived and she would continue to survive because she was strong, like her tiny iron tree.

Another body stumbled into her. She turned to yell at the offending idiot and was greeted with Lisa's already-rosy face. MJ's ire melted. She could never be mad at Lisa.

"Oh my God — you have to come with me. They have pie in the kitchen," Lisa shouted above the music.

Without waiting for MJ's reply, Lisa grabbed her arm — not the sore one — and yanked MJ through the crowd into the only-slightly-less-crowded kitchen. Standing in the corner was a tall boy with sandy-brown, floppy hair breaking into a curl on the back of his neck. He wore a faded blue T-shirt, jeans with holes worn in the knees, and ratty sneakers. His clothes hung off him, as if he needed a few years to fill them out. Lisa ruthlessly elbowed her way through the handful of girls surrounding him. When she reached her target, she turned back to MJ and pulled her up alongside.

MJ found herself staring up at him. His full bottom lip held a crumb in the corner of his mouth, which turned upward into a wide grin when he saw her, before he ducked his head down, keeping the smile to himself.

"Chris, you have to give MJ a piece of your pie. *Now!*" Lisa said.

He looked back up at Lisa and gave her a smaller smile.

"Who am I to refuse two lovely ladies?" He turned to the counter, where two pie pans sat, one empty and one almost. While he scooped a piece out and slid it onto a plate, Lisa leaned in to drunk-whisper, "Isn't he adorable?"

MJ could see Chris's mouth twitch upward. He had heard.

MJ whispered back, "Need me to be your wingman?"

"Not for me, for you." Lisa poked MJ in the chest.

Before she could respond, Chris slipped a paper plate and plastic fork into her hands.

"Saved by the pie," he said with a wink. MJ smiled back, appreciating the twinkle in his blue eyes. Maybe Lisa was onto something. It had been a while since she'd been on a date. But as the other female party guests clamored for his attention, MJ shook off the feeling. Why would he choose her?

"Thanks." She turned her head and was searching for a place where she could eat her pie in peace when Chris put his hands on her waist and lifted her onto the counter. In an instant, her heartbeat tripled and her face flamed. If she hadn't held the pie, she'd have punched him. Or kissed him. Or both. Her nostrils flared as she rallied her anger, though she wasn't sure if it was directed at him for touching her without permission or at her body's reaction to said touch. Lisa's eyes widened in alarm, recognizing the warning signs.

But before she could let loose her tirade on personal space and presumptuousness, Chris tilted his head and said, "Sorry. I should have asked first. It seemed faster to just lift you out of the chaos, and now you're there, so you might as well enjoy the pie. You can yell at me later."

He flashed another small smile.

Disarmed, MJ nodded. Lisa gave her a wink and disappeared into the crowd, probably looking for someone for herself now that she'd effectively thrown MJ at Chris. Chris turned his attention to the other girls fighting for the last few slices as MJ used her fork to cut off the first bite, having to force the meek utensil through the crispy crust. MJ was used to store-bought graham cracker crusts with instant pudding and Cool Whip. This was something else altogether. It was creamy and flaky and lemony and like nothing she'd ever tasted before. She closed her eyes to block out all the commotion around her.

"Sweet Jesus," MJ said.

She finished the pie, opening her eyes only long enough to carve off each taste, enjoying every bite in her solitude. After the last morsel, she opened her eyes to see Chris staring at her, a small smile tugging at his lips when their gazes met.

"Marry me," MJ said.

Chris's eyes widened; then he threw back his head to laugh. MJ's stomach fluttered. His smile made her heart race, but his laugh electrified her whole body. She hadn't felt like this . . . ever.

"It might be a bit early for a proposal, but I will accept the compliment."

"Probably wise; I'd only be marrying you for your pie."

"I get that a lot." He handed the last piece to a dewy-eyed, stumbling girl. Then hopped up on the counter next to her. His hand brushed against hers, warm and slightly sticky from the dessert. MJ pulled her hands into her lap, but he still sat close. Too close. She tried to scoot away without being obvious, but he just leaned in closer to talk over the party's noise.

"Does Lisa do that to you a lot?"

"Do what?"

"Shove you at seemingly eligible single men?"

"More than she should if she values her life," MJ said, then digested what he'd said. "Seemingly?"

She glanced at him quickly from the side of her eye, then returned to scanning the room. Now that the pie was gone, the partygoers were returning to the rooms stocked with booze. Only a few stragglers like themselves, craving a bit of quiet and space, remained.

"Let's say I'm in pursuit."

MJ's nerves relaxed. He wasn't interested in her.

"Ah, who's the lucky lady? Is she here?"

"Nah. She's in the marching band, so she's at a game this weekend. She works at a bar sometimes. I'm trying to figure out her schedule."

MJ nodded, envisioning a cute, bubbly band member she'd never met but still didn't like. She hated making small talk with people she didn't know. She scrounged the archives for a good question to change the topic.

"Where did you learn to make such a bliscious pie?" MJ asked.

"Bliscious?" Chris asked, raising his eyebrows.

"It's bliss plus delicious. I'm being efficient but you're slowing me down by needing an explanation."

"You can't just invent words."

"I refuse to be linguistically constrained by dictionary writers."

Chris laughed again and MJ couldn't help but share a smile. He had a great laugh that shook his entire body. It wasn't self-conscious or contained. She wanted to make him laugh more.

"I like that. I'm going to join your quest to throw off the yoke of definitional tyranny," Chris said.

"We can start a movement."

"The Frefinitions!"

MJ scrunched her face in confusion.

"Free plus definitions," Chris explained.

"Not bad," MJ said. "It's a start."

Lisa helped her once to find her true love.

Maybe she can do so again, MJ thought as they left her cozy neighborhood.

CHAPTER FOURTEEN

"Why don't we live like this all the time?" Lisa asked, lying like a starfish on their giant king-size bed. She moved her arms as if she were making snow angels in the fluffy comforter. They had arrived late the previous evening and already MJ felt ridiculously pampered. A limo had picked them up at the airport, and they were led straight to their room rather than having to deal with check-in. Chilled champagne and fresh strawberries greeted them in their spacious suite. They'd kicked off their heels and enjoyed the gift, leaving only the empty bottle and a plate of strawberry stems, giggling well into the night.

After sleeping late and enjoying a delicious breakfast of warm croissants and hand-poured coffee, the two treated themselves to mani-pedis. MJ loved her family, but this was the first time in twenty years when her only responsibility was to herself. No driving the kids to school or wrangling the dirty laundry into the laundry room. Nor guilt for not doing those things. The freedom was addictive.

MJ sat on a squishy armchair, admiring her newly polished fingers and toes, her relaxed feeling slipping away as the time to leave approached and her fingertips began to itch for the feel of cool clay chips.

"If we lived like this all the time, what would we do to pamper ourselves?"

"Duh, get more massages." Lisa sat up on the bed to see MJ's face. "Are you nervous?"

"Not too bad. When I start to feel anxious, I remind myself that none of this really matters. Who cares if they decide I'm a crap player? I'll never see these people again." MJ checked the time on her phone, then pulled on her boots. "I better go — time for my lesson with Doyle Kane!"

"Are you going dressed like that?"

MJ looked down at her dark blue jeans, black button-down shirt, and black boots.

"I always dress like this when I play."

"We're going shopping later. You need to sass it up a bit, Mrs. Poker Maven."

MJ rolled her eyes, but now she was kind of looking forward to it. Maybe spicing up her wardrobe would provide another coat of armor, another angle she could use to dominate the table. Besides, unlike at home, no one here would know the difference.

"Okay. I'll text you when I'm done."

She left Lisa to enjoy an afternoon at the hotel spa while she went to the poker lesson. MJ scanned the crowded poker room: mostly men of varying ages, but she could see the occasional female head. Some older and wrinkled, others young and big eyed. The consistent clink of chips mingled with the rumble of fresh air pumping into the room. Muted earth tones covered the walls, floors, and chairs, broken up with vibrant greens. The instructions had said to meet at The Fourth Leaf, but she couldn't find any signs pointing the way. The map in their room had indicated it was in the poker room, but she only saw tables.

A young man wearing a dark three-piece suit walked up to her.

"Can I help you, ma'am?" MJ forced a smile. Ma'amed again. This needed to stop happening. Not a great start to a day where confidence would be key. Getting lost didn't help.

"I'm looking for The Fourth Leaf. I have a lesson there."

The man's face smiled.

"You must be MJ. TFL is back there. We're still waiting for Mr. Kane."

He pointed to a door in the far corner. Frosted windows were broken by slivers of clear glass, giving glimpses into the private room. At the mention of Doyle Kane, MJ's heart added a few extra beats. How would she play poker while trying to ignore his face? She'd done a fair bit of Googling him. There were a lot of pictures of him with attractive women on his arms. Were she much younger — and not married, of course — she wouldn't mind being his arm candy for a night or two. But enough nonsense. She pulled back her shoulders and licked her lips. Time to pretend she was someone else.

"Would you like me to show you to your seat?"

"No, darling, I've got it from here." Darling? Where had that come from? Apparently, Vegas MJ addressed people as "darling."

MJ took off regally, using the quickest path between the tables, but pausing before the door to summon her courage. To the left, a few people were peeking in the windows, trying to catch a glimpse of who might be playing in the elite room. They wandered off as she gave herself a once-over, then undid an extra button on her shirt to show just a glimpse of the black lace underneath. If she was going to play a part, might as well go all in. She gave the girls a quick extra boost, took a deep breath, and pulled open the door.

The cozy room held two poker tables and a scattering of leather couches and chairs, with a bar in the far corner. Pictures of poker legends hung on the walls. The dim lighting added to the warmth. MJ wanted to kick off her heels and curl up with a book. The only other females in the room were the dealer and an attendant who was already making her way toward MJ. While the room allowed for twenty players, only eight spots were taken — the other regional winners, she supposed.

"You must be MJ. Can I get you anything to drink?" The attendant handed her a name tag to wear like the rest of the men already assembled. She slapped the sticker into place right next to her diving neckline.

MJ looked at the other players. All men, they were dressed similarly to her, comfortable and casual. Most had on hats and sunglasses — a few wore hoodies. One older gentleman immediately reminded her of James back in Milwaukee. He had a large, hooked nose and a bemused smile, just happy to be there. MJ would have to watch him. The rest already had their game faces on.

"I'd love a coffee, extra, extra cream, please."

There were two empty seats, one across from the dealer and one in the first spot to the left of the dealer. Her ankle wobbled a bit while her heartbeat thundered in her ears as MJ took a few steps toward the open chair opposite the dealer. The older gentleman sat to her left. He smelled like good cigars and Big Red gum — and that's what she'd call him: Big Red. To her right was a young man already wearing his sunglasses, shrouded in a gray hoodie with "Poker God" emblazoned on the back. She liked it when they made assigning nicknames easy.

"Gentlemen." MJ nodded to the table and smiled. A few nodded in return as the dealer gave her a big smile, clearly happy to see another woman in the room.

"First time in Vegas?" Big Red asked. MJ looked at him under her lashes. He wore a tailored dark blue button-down of thick cotton and dark pants. His hair looked well groomed; his skin looked soft and tan. He must moisturize. Gold glinted under his cuff. He was definitely different from the young bucks comprising the rest of the table.

"I'm sorry." She smiled. "I was distracted by your delicious smell. My grandfathers used to smoke cigars."

"Nice." He held out his hand. "I'm Jerry."

"MJ." She shook his hand. "And this is my first time in Vegas to play poker. You seem like you've been here before."

"I've seen my fair share of VIP poker rooms. This one's a bit higher stakes than I'm used to, but it's nicer, too. Fifty grand to get a seat."

MJ let out a low whistle.

"Ah, now we begin." Jerry pointed his chin toward the door as Doyle walked in with two tall blondes flanking him. Both wore skirts short enough that MJ could nearly tell their waxing preferences. He wore jeans, a dark sport coat, and a gray T-shirt with Kenny Rogers's face on it, circa 1980. He searched the room for his spot and a smile cracked through his scruff. He sent his blondes off to entertain themselves on the couches and walked to stand behind Poker God to MJ's right.

"I believe you're in my spot, lad. And there'll be no need for the disguises today," Doyle said, his Irish lilt adding charm to his command. Poker God rose and slouched to the seat next to the dealer while the rest of the table tucked their sunglasses into shirt pockets. "And don't look so glum. Samantha is a lovely woman." He gave the dealer a wink, and she blushed back. The room stayed silent, not knowing what would happen next. Would they all be expected to shuffle their places? Were they committing some unknown faux pas? Many fiddled with the chips already waiting on the table, nervous habits MJ hoped to use to her advantage later.

"Hello, lads and lovely lass. The lesson can begin." Doyle folded himself into the chair, giving a friendly nod to Jerry. He leaned into MJ's space and grinned at her pointedly. He set a pale green oval on the table in front of him. MJ wondered what that was for. "Isn't this cozy?"

Based on his choice of companions, she had expected him to smell like a cheap brothel doused in tobacco spit. But instead, hints of tea and fresh-cut wood wafted over her. She dug into the confidence of her sexier self and leaned back toward him.

"Really?"

"Really, what?" he asked.

MJ looked at the blondes giggling on the couch.

"Could you be more cliché? Models?"

"Of course." He smirked.

"How do you expect people to respect you when you act like a frat boy?"

Doyle blinked at her as the rest of the

table stared at her audacity. Jerry chuckled next to her. Then a grin exposed Doyle's white teeth.

"Methinks she doth protest too much."

"Darling, I never protest. Not when it's something I want."

Doyle grinned bigger.

"Then I'll just have to find something you want." His eyes shone through his thick lashes and he winked.

MJ's heart raced and the pulse in her neck jumped. She turned her attention to the empty green felt. The host settled a small table between her and Doyle and set down her coffee.

"Your coffee with extra, extra cream." She looked at Doyle. "Mr. Kane, can I get you anything?"

"Just water, please." The young woman went to retrieve the drink.

Doyle gave MJ another wink, popped a mint in his mouth, then turned to include the entire table.

"Lesson one: Fake it. Fake it like you've been there. Fake it like you know more than your opponents. Fake it like sweat isn't dripping down your back and the pulse in your neck isn't visible from space. Fake it like things are happening exactly as you planned.

Fake it like the Pope at a stripper convention."

The table laughed nearly as one. Instead of joining the nervous twitters, MJ took the lesson to heart, folding her hands on the table and rubbing her tiny tree with her thumb. Doyle noted her lack of laughter and folded hands, his lips twitching with obvious amusement.

"So, this is how this will go, yeah. You each have five thousand dollars in chips. We're going to play for three hours. If anyone can knock me out, I'll pay his — or her — entry into the Global Poker Finals."

The table straightened up. Now they were talking. MJ sighed softly while her brain danced in excitement at the prospect of this shortcut to the GPFs.

Doyle turned to her.

"Am I boring you?"

MJ licked her lips.

"You asked me to fake it like I've been here before. If that's the case, wouldn't beating you be run-of-the-mill?"

Doyle's eyes dipped to the name tag stuck on her chest. "MJ, love, beating me is never boring."

MJ couldn't help a quick intake of breath. He really was attractive, especially when his clear blue eyes were so focused.

The dealer shuffled the deck and dealt the cards with precision and speed — a machine couldn't have been more consistent. Everything in this room was more intense than at home — the pumped-in scent, the players, and the stakes. Hell, even the coffee was significantly better.

"There is one last difference between this and a regular game. Since this is a lesson, we'll talk about each hand afterward, right."

And the game began. Cards, bets, dissection of play. As they played, Doyle commented on what their moves revealed to him — telling them not only whether they had weak or strong cards, but what those cards were, explaining his thought process thoroughly. MJ absorbed it all, thirsty for the poker knowledge peppered with his outrageous tales of games past. MJ had dismissed Doyle as a poker playboy, but he really was a gifted teacher. She even learned what he used the pale green disk for — it was his card protector.

On top of the table, Doyle performed tricks with his chips, making them dance across his knuckles or pop from the palm of his hand, all the while keeping up a steady stream of banter. At the end of the three hours, Doyle held most of the chips, with MJ in a distant second. She had held her own and knocked out a few of her table-mates. Not too shabby, if she did say so herself, even though she was pretty distracted by the flirtation.

"Not bad. And you'll notice I didn't lose my bet. That's the final lesson — only make bets you know you can win. Now, if anyone has any last questions, hit me."

The young pups peppered him with questions about what to do in specific situations, what he was thinking during the last GPF, and asked for selfies with him. MJ didn't need to stroke his ego by asking for one, too, even if Chris would love to see a picture of his poker idol.

Doyle grabbed her hand as MJ rose to leave. His hand was warm and soft on her skin, while zapping electricity up her arm. His blue eyes stood in bright contrast to the thick, dark lashes lining his lids. Groomed scruff defined a strong jaw and framed full lips that curved easily and often. The man could charm the habit off a nun, and MJ was no nun.

"Perhaps you'd like a picture with me, too?"

MJ shrugged. *Act like you've been there before.* "Sure."

She pulled her phone from her back pocket, but he took it from her hand. "I have longer arms."

He positioned her slightly in front of him so she was pressed against his right side and his face was next to her left ear while his left arm held the camera aloft. She could see their image on the phone's screen. His lips were right next to her ear and his right hand settled on her right shoulder, pulling her in closer.

"Smile," he whispered.

MJ blinked. Click.

Before handing the phone back, he texted himself the picture.

She grabbed the phone back and stepped away to look at the photo. It was intimate. He wasn't looking into the camera, but at her, while her eyes were half-closed with a sleepy smile on her face. What game was he playing?

The two blondes sidled to him. "Doyle? We want to go to the pool." One pouted.

MJ turned from the threesome and saw that Jerry was getting ready to leave, too. She waved to him so he'd come say good-bye. He was comforting and good company, reminding her a bit of the Gents.

"You've been a pleasure to play with," he said.

"Aren't you a doll? If you're interested, I'd love it if you joined my friend and me sometime while we're all here." MJ kissed him on the cheek as he left.

"How do I get one of those?" Doyle asked.

MJ looked at him and his leggy models.

"You earn it," MJ said. She walked out of the lounge, letting the door shut behind her.

CHAPTER FIFTEEN

MJ leaned against a faux-stone wall near a replica of the Blarney Stone in the Castle Shops, waiting for Lisa to meet her for some promised shopping. She tried not to gag as tourists took pictures of themselves kissing the rock. It might make sense if they were kissing the real one, but this was a Vegas knockoff; the only luck they could hope for was to not get mono.

She checked the time: only one o'clock. The kids were probably home from their half day of school. Which one would answer if she called? Probably Kate, and she'd have a list of complaints about Tommy and food. She picked up her phone and dialed, a smile on her lips, excited to tell them about her poker lesson.

"Hey, I didn't expect you to call so soon."

MJ stood up straighter. His voice soothed her jangled nerves from the last few hours, even if it wasn't his normal playful tone, the tone she fell in love with. Her tough-girl poker act melted away.

"Chris! I didn't expect you to answer the phone." It was so good to hear his voice, and she was suddenly eager to share the lesson with him. She knew he could appreciate how awesome meeting Doyle Kane was. With how distant he'd been over the last few weeks, she was surprised he even answered her call.

"I came home early so I could be here when the kids got home."

"Are they around?"

"Tommy's outside throwing balls around and Kate went to Bree's." His answers were brusque, but at least he was talking to her.

"Do you know if any college acceptance letters have arrived for Kate? I can't believe we haven't gotten any yet."

"You want me to call over there?"

"No, I'll send her a text."

MJ couldn't believe they hadn't heard anything from all of those college applications Kate had submitted. She was smart, motivated, and an ideal student. Colleges should be fighting over her.

MJ picked at a loose thread on her sleeve, searching for questions to keep the conversation going. It hadn't always been like this. From their first meeting over pie so many years ago, conversation had always come easily. How could she find a way back to their effortless connection?

"So —" MJ began to tell him about the lesson when he interrupted.

"How was the trip?" Chris asked.

"Good. No glitches. The lesson was awesome and the room is really nice. I can send some pictures."

"No, that's okay."

MJ wanted to reach through the phone and touch Chris's face, look into his eyes and see whether the disinterest lived there, too.

"Mive you," she said.

"Uh-huh. I'll let you go, and I'll tell the kids you called."

She heard a click and her phone ended the call. She stared at the blank screen. She should call him back, make it clear that she missed him. That she loved him. Maybe he hadn't understood what she was trying to say. It was one of her lamer attempts, she'd admit. Another opportunity to fix things had slipped through her fingers. Her phone buzzed with a text alert. Maybe it was him.

But it was from an unknown number.

Hang at the cabana with me? — Doyle

He had attached a picture of himself lounging sans shirt by the pool, wearing snug blue swim trunks and a wicked smile. He held a drink toward the camera.

Sorry, my friend and I have plans.

It was just shopping, but she wasn't about to ditch Lisa.

Bring her.

MJ looked up to see Lisa walking toward her.

"It's like the Cliffs of More in here." She chuckled at her own pun while looking around at all the high-end shops. "I think I maxed my credit cards window shopping on the walk in."

She stopped in front of MJ, taking in her expression, then rubbed a finger on the crease between MJ's eyes.

"What's up with that?"

"Chris. But I don't want to talk about it."

Lisa nodded. "There's been something I've been meaning to ask you. What's the difference between what you did today versus tomorrow versus back home? Basically, I'm confused."

MJ had been so immersed in her poker world, she forgot it wasn't obvious to those outside. "There are two ways to play poker: a cash game or a tournament. A cash game is just that — you bring in as much money as you want to play with. At any point, you can decide to stop playing and leave with however much money you have left. I play that way the most, like at home. You can't win as much as at a tournament, but you have a better chance of leaving with some money.

"Tournaments are different. Every player pays the same fee to enter and starts with the same amount of chips. You play until you are out of chips or the last player left. You can win a lot more money, but you're also more likely to leave with none at all. Most tournaments pay out money to the top finishers — that number varies per tournament, so you can still earn something even if you don't take it down.

"I won a tournament in Milwaukee and the prize was a trip here for my poker lesson with Doyle and my entry fee into another tournament tomorrow night. Tonight I'll play a cash game just for fun and practice. Tomorrow's tournament is the real prize of the trip. The winner gets their entry fee for the Global Poker Finals paid for. That's like the Packers being told at the end of the season that they have a free pass into the Super Bowl. Make sense?"

"Cash game, tournaments. You really like this?"

"It has some positives. For example, how do you feel about hanging out at the pool for a few hours in the company of a handsome, charming man after we're done shopping?" She held up the phone so Lisa could see Doyle's text.

Lisa raised an eyebrow.

"You know I won't say no to that."

MJ laughed as she typed out a quick text. We're in. See you soon.

MJ made sure no one could see her as they arrived at the pool area before yanking her suit bottoms out of her backside. It was a tankini with a halter top, all in basic black. She shimmied her hips to make sure the adjustment would stick and caught up with Lisa, who had walked through the entrance already.

As they approached the private cabanas, MJ saw that Doyle had been watching for them. He waved them on.

"He's a tasty treat, isn't he?" Lisa said.

MJ couldn't agree more. He wore the blue shorts she'd seen in the picture. They were a cross between boxer briefs and running shorts. Smaller and more fitted than the typical swim trunks she saw at the lake, but not too tight. They accentuated his toned legs, and his chest was just hairy enough to shade the stomach muscles underneath. He wore dark sunglasses to hide his eyes and his scruffy jaw blended into his thick, dark hair. He greeted them as they entered the small enclave made private by potted palms and ferns. A white tent made up the back border, where she could see a bar and lounge chairs in the deep shade. In the sun, there were a table and a few more lounge chairs. Behind them was the pool. Doyle took off his glasses to reveal blue eyes that matched the sparkling water. MJ's knees wobbled a little.

"Well met, Wisconsin." He took her hand and turned it so her wrist was facing up, his lips parted slightly as they touched the pale, sensitive skin. He maintained eye contact to gauge her reaction. The unexpected intimacy caused MJ to inhale, trapped in his gaze. "Even lovelier than before."

She pulled it together and asked, "Wisconsin?"

He gave her a half smile. "I did some research."

He surveyed her from head to toe, appreciating MJ's black halter top. She liked it because it drew attention to her chest rather than her curvy hips and butt, and — based on Doyle's line of sight — it was working. MJ refrained from snorting at his over-the-top greeting. He released her hand, his smile revealing a chipped tooth and a wicked glint in his eye.

"Doyle, this is my best friend, Lisa." MJ nodded in her direction.

"I was wondering who this lovely lady was." He took Lisa's hand and raised it to his full lips to kiss it. Lisa squeaked, "I'm married."

MJ laughed. "Don't worry — he prefers blonde, leggy models. Speaking of, where is your arm candy?"

"I'm looking to upgrade."

Lisa looked back and forth between Doyle and MJ. "Well, kids, I'll be over here taking advantage of these comfy-looking chairs if you need me." She set her bag on the ground, lay down on the nearest chair, and positioned her floppy hat to shade her face. "Lisa out."

MJ set her bag on the next-nearest chaise and looked over the pool. Even though it was huge, only a few people cooled themselves in it. Midday in the desert stifled, so MJ planned to spend as much of it as possible in the water. A young woman in a nearly sheer white string bikini waved to Doyle as she walked by. He ignored her, keeping his gaze on MJ.

"Do you need anything before I get in the pool?" MJ said to Lisa.

Lisa waved her off with a hand. "No, hon.

I just want to soak up all the sun."

"You can't go into the pool. No one goes in the pool," Doyle said.

"Then why are we outside in this heat?"

"To get some color on our skin like Lisa, be seen, and enjoy the company of beautiful lasses, like you." He took a step closer to MJ. She backed up until her legs hit her chair, causing her to tumble onto it. Damn, he got under her skin. And where did he get off calling her a lass? Especially on the same day she'd gotten ma'amed by the poker host.

"This is going to be fun." Doyle reached out his hand to help her back up.

Lisa laughed from under her giant hat, and MJ looked at her, steel returning to her spine. Where did this laddie get off playing with her?

"You aren't helping, Lees." MJ turned back to Doyle. "If I can't go in the pool, then how do we stay cool under such heated circumstances?"

"We drink, of course." Doyle put his hand on MJ's arm and guided her back into the cabana. "I'll make you my specialty." He stepped behind the small wooden bar, setting his sunglasses on the counter and using his blue eyes to follow the wandering bead of sweat as it disappeared beneath the dark fabric of her swimsuit. Based on her rapid heartbeat, he may as well have traced the path with his finger. *Pull it together, Margaret June. You're a married woman.*

The cabana cut them off from everyone else around the pool. They could only see Lisa, lying on the chaise, like a lazy guard dog keeping intruders away. MJ was alone with a man she had just met. A sexy man with toned muscles and seductive eyes. A voice whispered in the back of her mind that maybe a married woman shouldn't be alone with a man like Doyle, but she brushed it aside. He wasn't a threat. Not really. And they were in a cabana — a very steamy cabana, yes — but not a bedroom.

"So, why did you really ditch Legs One and Legs Two?" MJ asked. She hopped up onto one of the wooden stools.

Doyle rummaged behind the bar, pouring juices, muddling berries, and slicing citrus.

"I told ya, I mean to upgrade."

MJ took off her sunglasses and deployed her best I-know-you're-full-of-shit look.

"Come on — two middle-aged married women isn't an upgrade from tall, lean, and willing."

He pulled a bottle of champagne from the ice, the cubes shifting into the now empty cooler. He moved with the same confidence as when he played poker. He reached for bottles and utensils without a second guess, like he'd done it a million times before. He probably had.

"I'm not often challenged. It's a lovely change of pace, right."

As he worked, he looked up at her and smiled. Each time she jumped inside, annoyed at herself for being thrilled that this handsome man noticed her. Perhaps she could steal a few cubes to cool down. With a pop, Doyle opened the bottle and poured it into the glasses behind the bar. He set the two drinks on the countertop. The cocktails were fizzy and pink toward the top, then became a dark red at the bottom of the glass.

"What's in this thing?" murmured MJ.

"I call it a First Kiss," Doyle said.

"Why?"

Doyle's mouth twitched into a saucy grin.

"Because it's sweet and simple with the first sip. But each sip after becomes more intense and irresistible."

MJ gulped for air. She reached for the glass, trying to hide her trembling hand. *What would Chris say if he could see me now? Would he care?* MJ shook the thoughts from her head. She was here because she needed to think only about herself, reboot herself. And right now she wanted Doyle to think she was a cool customer, used to witty banter and flirty drinks.

"I do enjoy a beautifully constructed cocktail." Her voice sounded rough with nerves. She sipped the drink, hoping the shade in the cabana hid the red flaring of her skin. The tingling drink tasted like cherries, a million little bombs bursting on her tongue. Delicious. She took another sip, still full of cherries, but with something darker, more exotic, more enticing. She wanted more.

Doyle watched her reaction, sipping his own drink. It was too tasty to waste even a single drop. She licked her lips, her champagne-cooled tongue sizzling from their heat. Doyle reached across the bar toward her, his fingers inches from her own hand. She had just begun to anticipate the feel of his skin on hers when Lisa walked in.

"I hope you made an extra one, handsome," Lisa said. "This heat is melting me."

MJ pulled her hand back from Doyle's and gulped the rest of her drink, hoping Lisa hadn't noticed anything between them. But her eagle-eyed best friend didn't miss a trick. And Doyle's frown made it clear he didn't appreciate the interruption.

"Oh my, I'm so sorry to interrupt." Lisa batted her lashes at Doyle as he half scowled.

Even as she smiled, MJ's throat tightened and her tongue began to itch. She used her teeth to scratch at it, but the itching spread down her throat as if she'd swallowed fire ants. When she tried to catch her breath, a ragged whistle escaped. Both Lisa and Doyle turned to her. MJ's hands went to her chest, trying to push in more air.

"Allergy," she wheezed. She looked at Doyle, who just stared at her, watching as her face splotched over and her lips swelled. Lisa punched him in the arm.

"Did you put pineapple in the drink?" Lisa said.

Doyle nodded. "Pineapple juice."

MJ's throat tightened. She needed to get to her pills before she couldn't swallow anymore, but Lisa was already moving. She grabbed MJ's purse from the lounge chair and dumped out the contents on the cabana's teak floor. Her wallet, tampons, and three tubes of lipstick scattered, but Lisa saw what she needed. She ripped open the pink and white box, tearing open the bubble packs.

"Water," Lisa ordered.

Doyle finally sprung to action and retrieved a bottle of water from the bar's refrigerator. MJ tossed the Benadryl into her mouth and drank the water, grateful her throat hadn't closed completely. The cool rush soothed the itchy, irritated flesh as it chased the pink pills down. Now she just needed to wait — everything would be okay. She lay down on the lounge chair and tried to take slow, even breaths as she waited for the reaction to stop. She looked up to see Lisa and Doyle staring at her, looking as rattled as she felt.

"I'm okay," MJ whispered. "Need to relax. Half hour." She gave a thumbs-up.

"I'm so sorry," Doyle said. He knelt by her side.

MJ waved him off. She tried to adjust her body to hide her curvy stomach and fleshy thighs. Lisa stood by her other side and squeezed her hand.

"Oh, hon. Thank God you had the pills. I'll go get your cover-up so you can be more comfortable." She left the cabana, and Doyle grabbed her hand and attention.

"I really am sorry. Let me know how I can make it up to you. Anything, really."

"My fault. Should have asked." MJ took a deep breath and smiled. Lisa returned and helped MJ into her cover-up. Now she at least didn't feel so exposed as the two looked at her like a misshapen statue. "Go enjoy the sun." She waved them off.

Lisa looked at her and nodded. MJ liked that Lisa took what she said at face value.

"You let me know if you need anything, okay?" she said as she left the tent again.

Doyle apparently didn't take MJ at her word. "What can I do?" he asked. He moved closer to her and still held her hand. His brow was furrowed with concern. He brought his other hand up to brush a strand of hair out of her face. MJ resisted the urge to lean into the touch. This wouldn't do. Doyle was dangerous. Chris and she may be having problems, but she had no intention of actually being unfaithful. She pulled her hand out of Doyle's and stood up despite her postanaphylactic exhaustion. Her throat had eased a bit, though her lips still pulsed from the swelling.

"Really. I'm okay. This isn't the first time. That's why I carry the pills with me. I just feel like a dork when it happens in front of other people." She started picking up her scattered purse contents. "I'm going to head back to my room and rest up for tonight."

"At least let me walk you back to your room." He reached to hold her arm.

"Not necessary." MJ stepped out of reach and strode out of the cabana, leaving Doyle alone to wonder what just happened.

Chris was always the vigilant one. He was the one who checked every sauce or fruit cup for stray pineapple. He never would have let her drink that concoction without an ingredient list. She didn't just miss Chris. She needed him. Losing him might kill her.

CHAPTER SIXTEEN

MJ's nerves still buzzed as she slipped out of her swimsuit and into a comfy robe. On the way back to the room, Lisa had peeled off to pick up some food. She curled up in one of the armchairs, looking back on all the times Chris had stopped her from eating something containing pineapple. It was a little thing, almost an afterthought to him, she knew. How many other ways did she need him that she didn't even realize? A knock disrupted her musings. She peeked through the hole to see shining highlighted hair.

"Took you long enough; I couldn't get to my key card," Lisa said as she swept in with an armload of food. She set it on the small dining table and started spreading out sandwiches, cookies, chips, and water. "Get over here and eat. It'll make you feel better."

"You're kind of bossy, you know that?"

MJ sat across from her as Lisa pushed a sandwich at her.

"No mayo, no tomato."

"Just the way I like it. You must really love me." MJ blew her a kiss, which Lisa returned.

"Always."

They nibbled in silence, though Lisa kept pausing as if to speak. After the third time, MJ had to know what was going through her mind.

"Okay, spit it out."

Lisa set down her sandwich and finished chewing.

"This Doyle guy. What's up with that?"

MJ took a long drink of water, letting the cool liquid soothe the lingering soreness in her throat and giving her time to gather her thoughts. "Nothing is up with that."

"It took you that long to come up with that bull pucky? I'm not new here."

MJ sighed. There was a downside to having such an astute friend.

"Truly. Nothing is up with that. At least not on my side. I'm flirty with him, because, let's be honest, it's been a long time since an attractive man I'm not married to flirted with me. It's nice."

"Be careful. He's not what he seems. I'm getting a vibe from him."

"It's poker — no one is what they seem. That's what makes it so much fun."

Lisa shook her head.

"No, Mr. Doyle Kane likes what he sees in you."

MJ swatted her hand at the air. "He's only teasing me, trying to get under my skin."

"I think he's trying to get under more than just your skin. Is it working?"

"No. I'm married to Chris. I want Chris."

Lisa bit into a chip and chewed slowly.

"Then why are we here?"

"I won a trip and you agreed to come with me."

"You know I love you and will support you in everything you do, but there's more going on than I know, and I think it's time you spilled."

MJ pushed her sandwich away and failed to control the hitch in her voice as she spoke.

"I think I'm losing Chris. I got so caught up with poker, it became my escape from what was wrong with us."

Lisa reached across the table to hold MJ's hand.

"What is wrong with you two?"

"Twenty years of forgetting how irreplaceable he is to me. I've spent my entire marriage pretending I didn't need him, because

I was strong, independent MJ who didn't need anyone." MJ gave a halfhearted chuckle. "When I tried to reconnect, it all backfired. I got sucked into the excitement of poker, and he's back at home with the mysterious T."

"And you're here. With Doyle."

"That isn't going to happen."

"I know that, and you know that, but he doesn't know that. Doyle is used to getting what Doyle wants. Now there's you." Lisa spread her hands wide toward MJ. "You are unattainable, a challenge. He can't snap his fingers and expect you to jump into his arms."

"He'd be wasting his time." MJ wrapped her robe tighter.

"Then make that clear to him before it gets complicated. And let's get out of this room. We didn't come to Vegas to look at each other."

The crowd around them was growing, a sure sign the water show was about to start, but MJ and Lisa weren't paying attention, much to the annoyance of the people next to them. They were focused on MJ's phone, where Ariana's face filled the screen.

Ariana had a floral print scarf wrapped around her head, as if she belonged next to

Cary Grant, cruising down a coastal highway in a convertible. Instead she sat in her own car, slinking behind the steering wheel.

"Are you going to tell us where you are and why you're in disguise?" MJ asked.

"At the Starbucks. I was getting out of my car and noticed Chris pull in. It seemed odd, so I thought I'd observe. It looks like he's waiting for someone," Ariana said.

"He knows what your car looks like," MJ said. "And why are you whispering?"

"Good point and I don't know." She raised her voice to a normal volume and unwrapped her scarf. Ariana looked at them through the camera. "Where are you?"

"In front of the Bellagio," MJ said, turning the phone so Ariana could see the lit-up Lake Bellagio in front of them.

"We're being tourists. The fountain show is about to start."

"I want to be there. Why am I not with you?" Ariana said.

"Because you're handling the War of the Roses," Lisa said.

"Ugh, they are the worst. I wish I could tell you about it. Just know that some people should not procreate. I wish I had never taken this case, and then I could be there, having fun with you." Ariana pouted into the camera.

"What's he doing now?" Knowing Chris was right there, MJ couldn't concentrate on Ariana's clients.

Ariana cleared her throat and moved her arm as if she was shoving something, or someone, out of the way.

"Is someone there with you?" Lisa asked.

Ariana blushed. "No one."

"Now I'm really intrigued. You have to tell us something."

She gave another shove and they heard a grumbled "I'm not no one."

MJ laughed, temporarily distracted at Ariana's failure to hide something.

"Yes, yes, moving on." Ariana craned her neck. A person appeared behind her, a male person, a younger, blond male person.

"Is that Kyle, the school counselor?"

Ariana moved the phone so he was out of frame.

"Oh, shit."

"Holy crap, Ariana."

"Now is not the time." She gave a stern look into the camera. "Do you want to know what Chris is doing or not?" She paused.

MJ looked over the phone at the lake. The water was still, like the calm before a storm. "So you're in a Starbucks parking lot. Has he noticed you yet?"

"Of course not. Honestly, do you know

nothing about tailing perps?"

"Chris is not a perp. What's he doing now?"

Ariana craned her neck to see over the steering wheel.

"He's checking his phone. Oh wait, he's getting out and walking toward another car."

"What kind of car?"

"Just shush. I'm watching. Oh." Ariana's face fell. "Oh my. I didn't really think . . ."

"What's happening? What didn't you really think?" MJ stood up straighter; Lisa grabbed MJ's hand and held it tight, preparing for the worst. Ariana took off her sunglasses and squinted as if trying to see better, her eyes moving as they followed Chris and whoever had gotten out of the other car. "Dying here!"

"Oh mamita, it's Tammie. They hugged and went into the coffee shop. She looks like she's lost way too much weight — like a walking skeleton. Terrible."

MJ's stomach plummeted. She didn't think it was true, not really. Maybe it wasn't what it looked like. Maybe it was actual business. But she knew it had nothing to do with work. She tried to swallow past the lump in her throat, but it wouldn't work. Why wouldn't it work? Lisa wrapped her arms around MJ.

"MJ, you okay? You want me to wait here and follow them when I'm done?"

MJ shook her head. All the nerves were wrapped in novocaine.

"No," she said. Her voice sounded husky and scratchy. "Thanks."

MJ blinked at the screen, hoping the dry Nevada air would take care of the tears threatening to fall. It didn't.

"I gotta go." MJ turned off her phone and wiped her cheeks as Lisa pulled her in for a hug. She hated crying, especially in front of other people. They always felt compelled to comfort you, to offer condolences. She didn't want that. The muscles in her face hurt as they squeezed out more tears, her breath making croaky gasps. The fountains blazed to life, dancing to "My Heart Will Go On." At the moment, MJ didn't think hers would.

The crowd scattered as soon as the fountain went dim. MJ did her best to wipe the tears off her face.

"Here, let me." Before MJ could protest, Lisa wiped a tissue under MJ's eyes to tidy up her smudged makeup.

"Better?" MJ asked, wishing she could look in a mirror to check.

"Better." Lisa nodded.

"MJ?" a deep voice said. MJ turned to see Jerry from the lesson walking toward them. She hoped the dark would mask the majority of her emotional wreckage. "I thought that was you."

MJ made the introductions.

"So this is the delightful friend you mentioned." He looked at Lisa.

"Whatever she said about me, it's all true." Lisa looked at her watch.

"You should get going. You don't want to be late for your blue dude show," MJ said.

"I don't want to leave you."

MJ squeezed her arm. "I'm good. Really. We'll catch up later."

"I'll make sure she gets back okay," Jerry said.

Lisa gave MJ a quick hug and turned in the direction of the show. MJ turned to Jerry. He had changed to a white shirt and dark dress pants for the evening. His hooked nose cast a shadow on his face, and he still smelled like Big Red gum, but now with the warmth of good scotch. Before she could say anything, he said, "You want to talk about it?"

MJ didn't, or at least she didn't think she did, but when she opened her mouth to reassure him, out came her entire story. Somewhere along the way, Jerry set her arm on his so they could walk back toward the Bonn Oir, the sparkling lights of the Strip glittering around them. He guided her around selfie-taking tourists and skeevy guys smacking stacks of leaflets advertising scantily clad women.

She told him how she and Chris met, how close they once were, their recent troubles, the poker, and Tammie.

He nodded and listened, and never interrupted. She found it refreshing to have to explain every detail because he didn't know any piece of her history.

"But why do you dislike Tammie so much?"

MJ sighed. "So many reasons, but mostly because she wasn't nice to Chris."

He raised his eyebrows, then guided her around a pack of fanny-packers.

"We'd become friends after he turned down my pie-induced proposal. We'd study together. He was good company. He didn't fill the silence with unnecessary conversation, and he always walked me home if it was past dark, even though he lived on the other side of campus." MJ gave a little smile at the memory. "This one night at the bar, he stood behind a petite blonde whose hair was almost as big as her torso. I knew he liked someone else, but I didn't know it was her. Tammie. I'd already disliked her from working with her at the bar, but this was electric loathing. She'd used so much Aqua Net, I worried the nearby cigarettes would spark into her shellacked hair, especially since my path to an exit was lined with drunk undergrads. There's no question she was adorable by any standard: toned legs, one of those double-V sweaters without a tank top underneath, so everyone knew she wasn't wearing a bra. She was that kind of girl, and it explained the swarm of boys surrounding her.

"While she flirted with all of them, she ignored Chris, who was keeping her tumbler full of vodka and cranberry juice. I almost lost it when I saw her wiggle her empty glass over her shoulder when he hadn't grabbed it fast enough. Who treats people like that? When he took the glass from her, she turned and gave him a brilliant, plastic smile and his face brightened. It was so hard to watch my friend fall for her tricks. Once he took the glass, she went right back to ignoring him. His shoulders slumped as he looked at the empty glass in his hand. He knew what was going on. I wanted him to set it down and walk away. Or even better, to dump the melting ice cubes over Ms. Big Hair. That can be very satisfying. Instead, he looked at me to make her a new drink."

MJ remembered how he smiled at her as she stomped down to his end of the bar.

"Tammie was a fool for not seeing how special he was, and he was a fool for thinking she was good enough for him. Of course, I wasn't so kind with the words back then. I may have said something like, 'Why are you buying that cuntch drinks?' "

"Cuntch?" Jerry asked.

"Chris and I like to mash up words. It's our thing."

Jerry laughed. "I see."

MJ continued.

"Much to my regret, I didn't actually call her that. But she did notice I wasn't making her drink. Or more importantly, Chris was not successfully procuring it for her. And she and I, well, oil and water. Without mincing words, I accused her of stringing along Chris. Her defense was that he had just as much of a chance of taking her home as the rest of her herd. Then I refused to serve her at her father's own bar. Good thing there was another bartender working that night or I might have finally lost my job there."

"What did Chris do?"

"He stopped getting her drinks." MJ smiled. "A few months later I finally asked him out."

Jerry raised his eyebrow.

"He was taking too long."

They entered the front door of Bonn Oir, all gold and green. It was a relief to get off the crowded sidewalks and into the calmer lobby.

"And now?" Jerry prompted.

"I think he's getting used by her again, and I can't stop it this time."

"You don't know that. Men are funny creatures. We like to have a purpose, to know we're needed. I haven't known you very long, but you don't come across as someone who needs help often."

MJ paused to let that sink in. She did need him. She needed him to keep her safe from pineapple, to cook when everyone got sick of eggs and takeout, to make life real. And she needed him to need her, too.

"I do need him."

"But does he know it?"

First her best friend and now this brief acquaintance? Maybe Lisa and Jerry had a point — maybe it was time to ask for help before she lost everything.

CHAPTER SEVENTEEN

MJ left Jerry at the elevators with the promise to buy him a drink for being such a great listener.

In her room she flopped on the bed, letting his advice sink in. It was the polar opposite of everything Barbara Olson hammered into her brain since birth. She was raised to not need others, to solve her own problems, and up until now, that had seemed to work — until it hadn't.

Her phone buzzed. Chris. Her breath caught with relief and surprise that he was actually calling her. He wanted to talk. She answered, heart in her throat, like a teenager whose crush was on the line.

"Hey. Glad you answered. How's it going?" Chris asked. He sounded so normal, like this was any other phone call. Not like they had barely spoken over the last few months.

"Good. It's been a busy day, one of those

days that seems to last forever because I've done so much. Lisa and I saw the Bellagio fountains and I made a new friend at the table." It was so easy to slip into normal conversation with him, to want to tell him every detail.

MJ got off the bed to look out the large window overlooking the glittering lights below her. It all seemed so far away. She knew how noisy it was on the street level, but from up here, it all looked like silent, moving lights. The distance played with the perception of reality.

"Cool." MJ waited for him to say more, until the silence stretched to match the distance between them.

"Is there a reason you called?" MJ asked, scrounging for something to keep the conversation going.

"Yeah. I need the password to the brokerage accounts. I want to update our finances and I can't remember where they are written down."

MJ leaned her head against the window, staring down the side of the hotel. She closed her eyes when the height started to make her dizzy. He was calling to get a password, not because he missed her. How could she broach everything she was feeling in the face of such a mundane request?

"It's on the Post-it under the phone on your desk."

"Great, thanks." And he hung up. MJ held the phone to her ear for a few more minutes, until she had to accept he wasn't calling back.

These roller-coaster emotions were too much. It was like her heart was being drawn and quartered, stretched to its limits. Each new tear stung as she realized how far she and Chris had drifted. Eventually, her heart would completely break apart. How much more could it take? Too many thoughts raced in different directions. She needed to calm her mind.

She looked in the bathroom at the palatial bathtub. If she stood in the middle of it, it almost hit her hips. Maybe a long bath and a movie would give her time to think. But she knew that wouldn't be enough. She needed her fix.

MJ pulled out her clothes for the night, one of the new outfits Lisa had convinced her to buy — a fitted cobalt-blue dress that hit her curves in the right spots, with ruching that hid the ones in the wrong spots. With the right bra and Spanx, it rocked her curves so well — Mae West would have been jealous.

With her heart still back in Wisconsin, she

couldn't really focus on the opportunities around her. She slipped into her evening finery and superhigh heels with rhinestones twirling around the stiletto. In her battle gear, confidence surged and purpose filled her. Time to go to work. She left the suffocating, silent room, eager to disappear into the game.

As she walked to the elevator, her phone rang again. It was her mom.

"Hey, Ma."

"Margaret June, I hear you're in Vegas! What are you doing there?"

During the elevator ride and the long walk to the poker room, MJ filled her in on everything, from Chris and Tammie to Doyle and his life-threatening cocktail.

"When are you going to learn to not accept drinks made by anyone but yourself? You should know better." That was her sage advice? Don't take drinks from strangers? MJ rolled her eyes and sat down on a bench near the poker room. The heels may have been a mistake.

"Is there a reason you're calling, Ma?"

"I almost forgot." Her mom paused. "I don't know how to tell you this, especially with so much going on right now with you and Chris. The timing isn't the greatest, but I hope you're happy for me."

"Ma, get to it."

"Well, me and Gordon are getting married! And we want to do it soon. Oh, maybe we can go to Vegas?" MJ could tell that Barbara held the phone away from her mouth as she shouted, "Hey, Gordo, what about Vegas?"

There was a muffled response.

"He likes the idea. I'll have to use the Google and look for information."

"Ma, it's just Google, not the Google. And that sounds like a lovely idea. I can get some info while I'm here. I'm really happy for you." Her words clanged as she said them.

"Could you? Find out where the best Elvis weddings are. Send me an e-mail when you can. Gotta go."

"Love you, too."

MJ held the silent phone in her hands, watching people come and go from the poker room. Slot machines jangled with their promise of easy riches, and tourists strolled by in comfortable shoes on their way to a buffet dinner or a show. Her mom could be one of those people in a few days, walking hand in hand with Dr. Vander-House, "Gordo," apparently.

MJ was so confused. She was hurt by Chris for talking to Tammie. She was angry at herself because it bothered her. She was happy for her mom, but felt betrayed after all the years of having "depend only on yourself" hammered into her head. Now Gordo would be her stepdad, making Mike her stepbrother. Holidays would be more interesting, at least.

With a wince, she stood and strode to the poker room, putting her name in and sliding into an empty place to get what she needed right now. Her once clear and organized life had been dumped on the floor like a game of 52 Pickup. She knew she needed to take the time to sort it all out, but all she really wanted to do was escape to the serenity of the felt.

MJ pulled up the corner of her cards. A pocket pair — tens. Not bad. She bet — finally.

The tables were full and raucous tonight and the players here were more aggressive than back home. Two opponents came with her — Larry and Moe, she called them. Curly had folded. The flop gave her a third ten, but there was a flush possibility. Fourth street — the fourth shared card, as she had figured out when Doyle kept using it during the lesson — made the flush more likely. She looked over the men, keeping her hands calmly folded in front of her. Larry and

Moe looked the same — relaxed and cool — while her heart raced and sweat dripped down her back. She had almost a third of her chips in the pot. She should fold. Larry or Moe probably had the flush; then she'd be out. Fifth street came and it made a pair on the board. She had a full house — tens over fours. There were other hands that could beat it, but not many. Larry bet and Moe folded. It was to her. She looked at Larry and there it was — little flick of his tongue. He hadn't done that when he had a straight a few hands ago. He was trying to see what she had.

She swallowed hard and shoved all-in, then returned to her pose. Larry smiled.

"I like you." He had a Russian accent. "I know you have me beat. You have the nuts, don't you? How's this? I fold if you promise to show your hand."

Against her better judgment, MJ humored him with an answer. "Now, dear, I don't show anything for free. If you want to see, you need to pay."

Larry laughed and folded his cards. "Smart girl."

MJ's chest eased and her muscles relaxed. All the misery of earlier was in the distance, too. She could think clearly and found that emotional detachment let her approach her

250

problems more rationally. Tomorrow was the tournament; she'd play her best and then she could go home and finally have the conversations she and Chris needed to have. No storming off. No quitting until they both had their say. They both needed to be reminded why they fell in love to begin with. Simple as that.

Larry seemed unfazed that she'd more than doubled her chips. Instead, he looked over her shoulder and his eyes widened.

"Bit of nice playing there," an Irish voice said behind her.

MJ turned in her seat and looked up into Doyle's grinning face.

"Nicer dress." He was looking straight down.

"Enjoy the view while you can." She turned back to the game.

He pulled an empty chair to sit behind her and chat while the next hand started. MJ looked at her cards and folded.

"What are you messing about out here for?" he asked.

MJ looked over her shoulder at him.

"Where else would I play?"

"The Fourth Leaf." He pointed to the VIP room.

"Are you going to front me the cash to get in there? Because I can't afford that."

Doyle looked at her chip stack pointedly. "Aye, I will. You played well this morning, and I want to play with you again — see how you do with real stakes."

MJ rolled her eyes. "I can't let you do that. I'm not good enough to play in there. I could lose your money."

Doyle smiled.

"Playing in there isn't about being good enough; it's about having the cash to not get wiped out. The players aren't any better than these guys. They just have more disposable income for you to take." He paused. "How about this: I'll front you the chips and if you end the evening up, you get to keep half the winnings."

"And if I lose?"

"Then I lose the money. That's why it's called gambling, right?"

MJ turned back to the game. She shouldn't really leave so soon after winning such a large pot — bad poker etiquette.

"Go," Larry said when she caught his eye. "You'd be a fool to turn down that offer."

MJ smiled at him and started racking her chips. Doyle stood and waved over an attendant.

"Can you rack MJ's chips and cash them out, please, then bring it to TFL? She'll be playing at my table."

The host nodded and Doyle took MJ's arm and led her back to the VIP room. Eyes touched her back, watching Doyle and trying to guess who she might be. She'd come looking for a distraction, yes, but Doyle might be a bit more than she could handle.

"And there we were, racing remote control boats through Treasure Island's pirate show. I thought we were finally going to get arrested," said Lloyd between laughs. An hour into play and MJ's — actually Doyle's — stack had dwindled, but she was laughing too much at the banter among these funny, familiar players. All of them, besides her and Jerry, were regulars in TFL. Their stories drove home how different — and exciting — their lives were compared to hers. The most excitement she found back home was coming up with believable excuses to get out of attending the never-ending circuit of at-home business parties — a woman only needed so many organic cleaners or expensive candles.

"MJ, has anyone challenged you to a prop bet yet?" Jerry asked. She had been surprised and happy to see his familiar face at Doyle's table.

She scrunched her face, thinking. "A prop bet? Never heard of it."

Doyle clapped his hands together, then rubbed them. "Well, lads, I think there's some fun to be had here. Let's pop her prop cherry."

"The first time is always the most exciting. I'm in," she said.

"So eager and she has no idea what we're talking about. My kind of girl," Doyle said.

"Be careful what you agree to. Prop bets are serious business to this crowd," Jerry said.

"So what are they?"

"Proposition bets. And they can be anything. We like to bet on everything, and half the fun is devising ridiculous wagers. For example, I once challenged Lloyd" — he pointed across the table — "to a paddleboat race across Lake Mead. I won ten grand off that one."

"I still contend you cheated," Lloyd said.

"How do you cheat during a paddleboat race?" Jerry rolled his eyes.

"Sounds like fun. I want in." MJ nodded her head.

Doyle leaned to whisper in her ear. "I'm sure I can think of a few interesting wagers. Money need not be involved."

MJ shivered as his breath moved her hair, but she gathered her wits and gently pushed him away.

"We'll have to see when the opportunity presents itself." MJ winked.

"Doyle, where are those lovely blondes? They added to the decor in here, even if they sucked the brain power out of the place," Jerry said.

"I'm looking to trade up. Perhaps a brunette this time." Doyle nudged his leg against MJ under the table. She stomped on his foot.

"You can't just trade up because you want to. What do you bring to the table?" MJ said.

Doyle smiled at MJ, his eyes twinkling.

"I make fantastic eggs in the morning."

MJ looked at him down her nose.

"I can make my own eggs." Truth. It was her one kitchen skill.

"Not as good as mine." Doyle smirked.

"And that, kids, is how a prop bet is made," said Jerry.

MJ laughed.

"Is that all it is? I challenge you to an egg cook-off?"

"Let's take it out to the floor," said Jerry. "We'll have a table out there to taste and vote. They won't know who made them, so no cheating possible." That last with a knowing look at Lloyd.

"Agreed. But we need to make the same

kind of eggs," Doyle said.

"I suggest scrambled. Basic ingredients. No bacon or cheese. This is a technique challenge," MJ said.

"Are you suggesting your technique is better than mine?" Doyle flipped a chip over his knuckles.

"I'm not suggesting it. I know it."

"Excellent. Now, the wager." Doyle leaned closer and whispered into her ear. "I win — you spend the night and I'll make you breakfast in the morning." MJ couldn't stop the blush from spreading. She would never be ready for that level of gambling. She pushed him back a few inches.

"That's not going to help my bankroll. I'd prefer cash. Five hundred says my eggs are better than yours."

"Done." He flipped his chip using his thumb and caught it on the back of his hand. "I'll have everything arranged and we can do this now. Hey, Ginger." He got up to speak with the attendant, explaining the items they'd need. Before she disappeared, he took the chip he had been playing with — a hundred-dollar chip — and slipped it into her hand.

MJ looked at Jerry. "This is the easiest money I've ever made." She could barely boil water, but she could make fantastic scrambled eggs. She'd been making them at least twice a week since the kids were born. Easy as pie.

A half hour later, Ginger wheeled in two carts with all the ingredients and equipment they'd need.

She kicked off her heels and wrapped an apron around her waist. No need to ruin her new outfit. Side by side, they whisked and seasoned while the other players cat-called and made side bets. MJ was pleased to learn she was the two-to-one favorite. Even Zoe and Ginger, the room attendants, were getting in on the action. Doyle leaned over and turned off her burner when she had her back turned, hoping to swing the odds in his favor. Rookie. She could make scrambled eggs with two toddlers hanging on her arms. Her heart pinged that they weren't here to see their mom kicking ass with her egg-making skills. She couldn't wait to tell them, but for now, she needed to keep her mind on the task at hand.

As soon as the eggs were done and plated, Zoe and Ginger whisked them out to the floor still hot. All the players in TFL lined the frosted windows to peek out at the non-frosted section, a reverse from the norm. The eggs were served, and the girls collected paper votes.

"I should have wagered more," MJ said.

"Confident, are you?" Doyle said. "You should have taken the first offer. I would have agreed to any sum if a night with you were on the table." His voice was husky in her ear, his Irish lilt dancing over the words and down her spine. He wasn't touching her, but she could feel every inch of him; the air between them could singe. She held his blue eyes with her own.

"I'm married," she whispered, then took a deep breath and spoke with a firmer voice. "And a night with me is not a prize to be won like a stuffed panda at the state fair."

His lips twitched into a smile, then turned as Zoe and Ginger returned. "The results are in."

Zoe waved the ballots. "We've counted and, based on our ten tasters, it's a landslide. MJ won."

The room echoed with hoots and demands for payment. Doyle bowed his head, took five one-hundred-dollar chips off his stack, and set them in MJ's open palm one at a time, careful to graze her skin with each addition, never taking his eyes off her face. Her knees softened with each touch. Ridiculous. Chris could once make her knees wobble with a wink and a smile — especially one of his special smiles. But that early excitement waned decades ago.

She knew there was a line she couldn't cross, but Doyle made her reckless. Whatever his reasons, he seemed to want her and made his desires clear. He made her feel beautiful and sexy and wild, made the line look too easy to skip right over.

MJ pulled in her rampaging emotions, using all the discipline she could find, and returned to the game, slipping the extra chips into her purse.

"All right, gents, let's have some fun with Doyle's money."

CHAPTER EIGHTEEN

The hustle and bustle of Vegas never stopped, especially at the Starbucks. There were two times a day when the city seemed to switch over. Around ten at night, the cargo shorts–wearing tourists were gradually replaced by beautiful women in designer dresses and impossibly high heels with well-groomed men in sport coats and pressed button-down shirts. They sat down to late-night dinners and went dancing at one of the many clubs just opening their doors. Around seven in the morning, the reverse happened. Stragglers, still robed in short, sparkly dresses and carrying their impossibly high heels or now wrinkled sport coats, arrived for a morning fix before crawling away to sleep off last night's fun, while fresh-faced folks, ready for a day at Hoover Dam or exploring the Neon Boneyard, clamored for their morning caffeine kick.

MJ had no intention of being up this early

after her late night at the tables, but back home it would be nine o'clock, and Lisa had been bumping around their room for a few hours — even getting in a little shopping on her way to meet MJ for breakfast. MJ was saving a table so they could decide how to spend their day.

"Here you go, love."

Startled, MJ looked up as Doyle set a coffee cup and croissant in front of her. She was surprised to see him in the Starbucks of all places.

"How did you know I was here?"

He pointed to the cameras in the corner. "I know people."

"Are you stalking me?"

"Is it stalking if I only did it once so I could surprise you?"

"Yes, it is. And it's a little creepy."

"Then yes, I was stalking." He sat down. "I didn't mean it to be creepy. Sorry." His voice slowed down, like it had when he was apologizing for the pineapple, so she could tell he meant it.

"No worries." MJ smiled, then waved as Lisa walked in, gesturing at the table, but Lisa pointed that she was getting a drink first. MJ popped the top off her coffee and stood to go add the requisite flood of cream she required, but stopped in her tracks. It had already been added. Doyle had already mixed it in. She took a sip. Perfect. She sat back down, dumbfounded at the simple gesture and how much it meant. It reminded her of Chris's habit of always having her old-fashioned ready and waiting when they met for a fish fry. He always did it even though she rarely acknowledged it. That needed to change. She couldn't take those kindnesses for granted. And she'd start with Doyle.

"Thank you. It's exactly right."

"My pleasure," Doyle said with a shrug, but a small smile belied his nonchalance.

Lisa joined them with her cup of tea. On a murky but highly rigid principle, she never ordered coffee at a Starbucks. She would have had her caffeine jolt from the hotel room's coffee machine already. She nodded to Doyle as she blew across the top of her cup.

"Well, isn't this lovely?" Doyle said. "We three, sitting and enjoying a nice cup of coffee and sunshine." He looked around at the handful of customers. From where they sat, they could hear them ordering. "Feck, this is dull."

"What do you propose?" MJ asked. "A prop bet?"

Lisa looked confused. "Huh?"

MJ explained while Doyle leaned back in his chair, seeing how long he could balance on two legs. Lisa grinned once she understood.

"Ten bucks that guy in the baseball hat and cargo shorts will order a frilly drink."

Doyle sat up, intrigued.

"You need to be more specific."

"Fine, he'll order a vanilla Frappuccino."

Doyle pulled out his money clip and peeled a ten off. Lisa added her ten on top.

"I'm in." He turned to MJ. "You want some of this action?"

She paused with a chunk of croissant halfway to her mouth. "I think I'll finish enjoying breakfast."

Over the next twenty minutes, Lisa earned a hundred dollars off Doyle as she rattled off ridiculous drink orders. Doyle started demanding she specify size, but even then she still got two right for every one she missed. MJ almost confessed that Lisa made a living guessing people's orders, but Doyle didn't seem to mind losing — it was the action he craved. MJ finished her breakfast and savored their friendly banter . . . well, at least it had been friendly.

"Bull pucky. I'm not going to believe it until I see it," Lisa said.

"I don't have one in my pocket."

"What does he not have in his pocket?" MJ asked.

"A mythical million-dollar chip he claims the casino has and uses."

"A single chip worth one million dollars?" MJ asked.

"Bonn Oir had a few chips made for the whales to use. Only a few people ever see them, and certainly not us lowly poker players. It wouldn't be practical. But there are a few players who like the cache of gambling with a single chip worth such a lofty sum."

"And he's full of green shit," Lisa said.

"It's the American Express black card of poker chips. You are chosen to get one. Until then, no one knows if it's real or not," Doyle said.

"He just wants to whip out his black card to impress you," Lisa said.

"I do not just whip anything out. I have some finesse, right."

MJ watched them volley back and forth, rolling an idea around her head. Lisa got up to get some more hot water. She was still a little buzzed from last night's intro to prop bets, and an idea started to grow. She wanted another heady hit.

"Prop bet," she whispered to Doyle. "One thousand dollars. You procure the chip within twenty-four hours."

"I don't want your money." He shook his head and squinted his shining blue eyes. "How about this? If I can't get it, I'll give you twenty grand. But if I do, you spend the night with me."

MJ raised an eyebrow.

"Do you not learn? We've been over this. Absolutely not. Try again."

Doyle ran his tongue along his teeth, his eyes skating over her skin.

"Fair enough. I win, I get to roll the chip over you." He picked up a coin between his fingers and demonstrated rolling it up his arm.

MJ's stomach fluttered. Being around Doyle was exciting; she never quite knew what he would do next. The unpredictability, so opposite from every other aspect of her life at home, needled her with prickles of anticipation. And everyone knows anticipation is the best part.

"Only already exposed skin, and you can't touch me with anything but the chip." That should limit the potential danger. Even at the cabana, she was well covered. But Doyle's grin had her second-guessing the bet before they even shook on it.

"Done." He put out his hand to shake; she took it. That kind of money would go a long way toward Kate's first year of college, but MJ had to admit the reckless part of her didn't mind losing, just to see what Doyle had in mind.

Lisa counted her tens onto the prematurely aged stone wall, her grin getting bigger with each crisp bill.

"I'm starting to understand the allure of gambling. I think Mama needs a new pair of shoes," Lisa said.

MJ tilted her head back to admire the ceiling painted to look like a sunny Italian sky. A gondolier sang while poling guests around the indoor man-made canals, and garlic wafted from the nearby restaurant, making MJ's stomach growl. They had dodged the salespeople offering free meals and show tickets in exchange for sitting through their condominium hard sell, and had made it to the safety of the pigeon-free Venetian sidewalks and squares.

"It's usually not that easy. You did have him at a bit of a disadvantage."

"He could have asked what I did for a living. It's on him for not doing his research." She laid the bills in neat rows, then gathered them up to do it again.

MJ pulled her phone out of her purse and checked her texts.

Tommy: I miss you.

Tommy: How do you do laundry?

Tommy: Dad's locked in his office.

Tommy: Never mind. Dad just came out. I'll ask him.

Kate: Why is Tommy doing laundry? He put my bras in the dryer!!!!!!

Tommy: I didn't know they weren't supposed to go in there.

Kate: Who is that hottie on your FB page? Go Mom!

MJ: Tommy, I'll take care of it when I get home. You shouldn't have to wash your sister's bras.

MJ: Kate, your bras will be fine. At least he's trying to help. What hottie?

MJ: Chris, what is going on there? Tommy is doing laundry?

MJ: I won $500 in a scrambled egg cook-off! I'll tell you about it when I get home. Tourney tonight — wish me luck?

MJ flipped to her Facebook page, and there at the top of her profile was the picture Doyle had taken of them. He had posted it and tagged her, with the comment "My new favorite."

"Did you know about this?" MJ held up the phone for Lisa to see. She looked up from her money stacking.

267

"Oh yeah — Ariana and I have been defending your honor in the comments. Don't read them." She gave MJ a stern look.

MJ flushed and untagged the picture.

Lisa and MJ made themselves at home in Doyle's cabana even though their host was absent, happy to take him up on his offer that they make use of it. He had surprised MJ at the coffee shop, letting down his guard for a moment, showing her a more genuine side. Maybe there was more to him than she thought.

Lisa had picked up where she left off yesterday before the pineapple incident, spread out on a lounge chair with her floppy hat covering her face. MJ pulled off her cover-up to reveal her new swimsuit, another acquisition from her shopping trip the previous day. It was a retro-cut black bikini, high-waisted to a few inches below her bust, then a full-coverage top that showed just enough cleavage — sexy, not slutty. MJ settled onto a chair, letting the vitamin D work its magic. The sun soaked into her early-spring, pale, Wisconsin bones, warming her from within. After a matter of minutes, she was drenched in sweat. The black suit drew the sun like a laser beam.

"It's fot out here," MJ said.

"What are you talking about?" Lisa said from under her hat. "No one but Chris understands the ridiculous words you make up."

"Fot — fucking hot."

"Language, my dear. We're old — we don't use the f-word."

MJ smiled at her friend, grateful she had come on this adventure.

"I'm going in the pool — I don't care how unhip that makes me."

Grabbing a huge towel and setting it at the pool steps, she descended into the delicious water. The sizzling heat dissolved as she walked deeper into the blue, cooling her body instantly. She settled onto the steps and scooped water onto her shoulders, chest, and arms.

"Can I help with that?"

MJ jumped and opened her eyes, squinting into the bright sunlight. Doyle stood above her on the pool deck, grinning down at her. He wore a white button-down Cuban shirt over green-and-white swim trunks. She couldn't see his eyes behind his mirrored aviators, but his saucy grin said it all. Something gold glinted in his hand — a poker chip dancing across his knuckles.

"Bringing me gold already? I prefer diamonds."

He picked up her towel and held it out to her.

"You'll be wanting to get out, right. I have something to show you."

She stood, the blissful water sloughing off her. The hot air sucked up the remaining drops, making the towel superfluous, but she wrapped it around herself anyway, tucking it securely under her arm. She followed Doyle into the shaded cabana, where a ceiling fan helped to keep the area cooler, and Doyle turned to her.

"I thought you might like to know what a million dollars feels like."

He held out his palm, where the gold chip rested with a black "$1,000,000" written around the edge, the shiny Bonn Oir insignia in the center. The gold wasn't just painted on, it was solid — molded into chip form. He'd actually gotten it.

MJ gaped. Crap, she'd have to fund Kate's college tuition the old-fashioned way.

"I thought it was a myth. Where did you get it?" She reached out to touch it. Doyle pulled his hand back.

"No, no, no. I promised I wouldn't let it out of my hands."

"Then how am I supposed to know it's real? It could be a fake." MJ raised her eyebrow.

Doyle's mouth twitched upward as he took a step closer to MJ, putting her within arm's reach of him. She could see the chips of silver in his blue eyes and the luscious pout of his bottom lip. God, so tempting. Not even so much the forbidden thrill as it was the attention. Doyle's flirtation in the last two days was more attention than she'd gotten from Chris in the last five years. Sometimes, it was just nice to be asked to dance, even if you had no intention of saying yes — and Doyle was definitely asking.

"You'll know." His voice whispered the words. He pulled on one edge of her towel, sending it to the floor. Curious, MJ held perfectly still.

Doyle's voice sounded gravelly as he studied her soft, visible curves. "I won't touch you, but you have lost a bet." He looked into her eyes to confirm his promise. MJ glanced down at the chip tucked into the palm of his hand. With a jerky movement, he popped the chip out of his palm, almost as if it sprang up on its own, then caught it back in the same hand. If her gut was right, and he was planning to push her limits, Doyle had just given her his tell. He always did tricks with the chips, and that was one of the most difficult — only a few players could do it and no one would think of it as a tell because they would be so impressed at the feat. Now was the time to test her theory.

"You're lying." Would he know she guessed?

"Fine. My skin will not touch your skin." If she was right that he had been bluffing, then he would do something different with the chip. He adjusted his hold on the chip and it danced familiarly across his knuckles, flashing as the lamplight glinted off the metallic surface.

MJ nodded. He was telling the truth now. He stepped closer so his feet touched the fallen towel that pooled at her feet. The soft breeze from the ceiling fan chilled her wet bathing suit, causing her to shiver. Standing before this almost stranger, in her bikini, MJ should have been embarrassed or reluctant. Instead, she savored the attention.

Doyle held the gold chip between his thumb and index finger, light enough that it could spin as if on an axis.

"Close your eyes."

MJ opened her mouth to protest.

"Trust me," he said.

She closed her eyes slowly as he set the cool, gold edge on the back of her right hand and rolled it up her bare arm. With her eyes closed, the sensation intensified.

Exposed, yet in the dark, her imagination slipped away like the towel at her feet. She imagined Chris doing something this seductive, this playful. Her heart thumped painfully at the thought, wishing her husband were here now.

The chip rounded her shoulder. Doyle angled it so he could slowly graze her collarbone. MJ could feel the air move as he molded his body around her, careful not to touch her except through the chip. He reached the other shoulder and the path sent flares through her, scattering her thoughts, making her breathe fast as she envisioned her handsome husband. As he reached the tip of her left hand, she took a deep breath.

"Well, that was illuminating," she said.

She opened her eyes. Doyle's face was inches from her own, so close she could taste his breath — mint and good whiskey. His look no longer teased but burned. MJ should stop this — she opened her mouth to speak.

"Keep your eyes closed, please," he said.

MJ obeyed. Doyle's clothes rustled as he moved. His movements swirled the air, making her skin hypersensitive, waiting for any accidental contact. He set the chip on her forehead, slowly rolling it down her nose.

She tilted her head back, anticipating the chip's kiss across her lips. Doyle slid the chip over her chin onto her exposed neck so she could feel its weight when she swallowed. He rolled it into her generous décolletage. A hitched breath from Doyle sent tension throbbing through her.

But it wasn't Doyle's face in her mind; it was Chris's. She pictured his lopsided grin and pink lips, his brown hair not quite long enough to curl around his ears. Her heart picked up the pace as the chip slowed, then crested her bikini top to continue on to the few inches of bare skin below. MJ inhaled, flattening her stomach as much as possible. Doyle chuckled, the sound lower than before, almost like Chris's laugh, the chip's path leaving scorch marks on her. She could tell he had shifted down to continue his game, but when she felt his hot breath flutter across her thighs, her composure broke. She squeaked and stepped backward, her feet tangled in the towel still on the floor.

As she fell, she watched Doyle's face transform from teasing to concerned to smiling. By the time her well-padded backside made contact with the cabana's teak floor, he was already laughing. Gone was the flirtation. Gone were the flashes of Chris. Back were her inhibitions — and how. MJ blushed and grabbed the towel to cover herself up, holding it under her chin like a bedsheet. The heat flooding her body was fueled with horror at what she just let happen.

"Oh, God." MJ pulled the towel over her face.

"It wasn't that bad," Doyle said. MJ could hear the chuckle in his voice.

"You didn't know what was going on in my head."

"I'd like to."

MJ flopped onto one of the nearby wicker chairs, covering herself in the towel. She looked at Doyle. He obviously wasn't going anywhere until she elaborated. She pointed to the chair next to her and waited for him to sit.

"I was imagining my husband."

Doyle's mouth gaped, but he recovered quickly. "Well, that's not where I thought this would go, but I'm okay with it if you are."

MJ smiled and leaned over so she could rub her backside. There would be a bruise there in the morning.

"I'm not discussing that with you," she said.

Doyle nodded toward her.

"Are you okay?" Doyle slid the gold chip

into his pocket. "Can I get you some ice? You hit the ground quite hard, right."

MJ waved him off.

"Thank you for showing me the chip. It feels a bit like I've joined a secret club."

Doyle settled back into his chair, crossing one leg over the other. MJ looked at him — really looked at him. There was no denying he was heart-stoppingly handsome and he could charm a boat from under a pirate if he put his mind to it. His ruffled short, dark hair implied someone else's fingers had recently roamed freely in it. A champion flirter, renowned ladies' man, and confirmed bachelor all rolled into one. Yet MJ got the feeling his intentions were more innocent than all of his actions implied.

"Why are you doing this?"

Doyle raised an eyebrow and spread his hands apart.

"Doing what?"

MJ took a controlled breath and tucked the towel around her.

"Pursuing me. It doesn't make sense. Nothing will come of it. I know you know that."

One side of his mouth slid up as he stood.

"It makes perfect sense to me, love."

Doyle winked and left the cabana.

CHAPTER NINETEEN

MJ sipped her blessedly pineapple-free cocktail and cuddled close to Lisa on a lounge chair with her phone between them. Doyle hadn't returned yet, so they were getting in an important phone call with Ariana.

"He did what to you?" Lisa asked.

"Rolled a gold chip up and down my body," MJ said.

"And you were only in your swimsuit?" Ariana said.

"Uh-huh." MJ sipped her drink.

"Not just any suit, a bikini — and she's rocking it," Lisa said.

"But he never touched you himself. Only with the chip?" Ariana asked.

"Yep," MJ said.

"That's hot," Lisa said.

MJ flushed at the memory.

"Sort of. It would have been hotter if it were Chris. I should feel guiltier than I do, right?"

"Maybe not. It was part of the bet. There's a certain honor to upholding your end of the bargain, even if it's pretty clear he timed it so you'd have privacy and minimal clothing," Ariana said.

"Are you giving me a pass?" MJ asked.

"You're having a midlife crisis right now . . ." Ariana said.

"Ouch," MJ said.

"I'm calling it like I see it. And you are. Admit it and it will go a lot smoother," Ariana said.

"You sound like you're speaking from experience," Lisa said.

Through the phone, Ariana took a few moments to collect her thoughts.

"I've seen what denial can do to a marriage. Over and over. A couple shows up in my office, one of them clearly trying to turn back the clock with fancy cars, tight jeans, or a flirty new boyfriend. You're going through a phase."

"I'm not a toddler."

"This would be a lot easier if we could put you in a time-out until you and Chris were ready to apologize to each other." Ariana chuckled. "Toddlers aren't the only ones who go through phases. You're moving on to the next stage of your life. Kate's about ready to go to school; Tommy doesn't need you as much. It's scary. If you can accept that that is what you're going through, it'll help you patch things up with Chris. Now, back to your Irish rogue."

MJ put her head in her hands.

"That is exactly what he is — a rogue. Hell, add an eye patch and he'd be a sexy pirate." MJ snorted.

"I almost forgot to tell you something," Lisa said. "This morning at Starbucks when you went to the restroom, I may have told him he was wasting his time and you'd never leave your husband for him." Lisa gave her a toothy grin.

MJ's jaw dropped. "You didn't."

"Uh-huh. But that's not the good part. He said he knew. I got the distinct impression that he has no intention of truly seducing you. He's up to something. Attractive women keep hitting on him, and he ignores them to focus on you."

"Are you implying I'm not better than all those other women?" MJ said.

"Of course not. I just thought it was an interesting tidbit," Lisa said.

"Agreed. And I get that vibe, too. He's also not Chris, who is apparently gadding around town with Tammie." MJ let out a little growl.

"We don't really *know* that. We've only

seen them get coffee," Ariana said.

"But he's deliberately not telling me about their friendship."

"Have you told him about your new friendship? Don't you think he'd like to know?" Lisa said.

"Ugh. Yes, he'd like to know, and no, I haven't told him. I need to get my head straight first."

"What's to straighten out? You love Chris," Lisa said.

"I do, but how can I explain all this? How do I explain the poker? How do I explain coming here without him? How do I explain how much I like the attention I'm getting from Doyle? Every time we talk, he freezes up more."

"Unthaw him with honesty. If it's going to fail, it needs to fail because of the facts, not because you aren't communicating. How many times do I have to tell you this before you listen to me?" Ariana said.

"When did you get all voice-of-reasony?" MJ asked.

"Look. You haven't done anything ir-redeemable. We've all flirted with a hand-some man. It's all fine. But hurry up and figure this out so everything can go back to normal," Lisa said.

"We'll be home soon. Thanks, you two.

My head's clearer about the Doyle situation. Love you!"

MJ ended the call and set her head on Lisa's shoulder. Lisa's body tensed.

"I'm a situation now?" Doyle had entered the cabana.

Oh, shit.

"It's not polite to listen to other people's conversations. They might be talking about you," MJ said.

"This is my cue to return to the sun." Lisa scampered from the room.

Doyle dragged a chaise closer to hers so they were side by side, like on a large bed. He pulled off his shirt and lay down. He was close enough they could touch. She scooted over to add some distance. He grinned, letting her know he noticed, and pulled out a box of crackers, the plain white ones that came in fancy cheese baskets.

"I want to hear more about my situation. I like being a situation." He rolled onto his side, propping his head in his lower hand and chomping crackers with the other.

"First — you're getting cracker crumbs on my lounge chair. Please desist or I'll need to ask you to leave."

"It's my cabana — I'll eat crackers on all the lounge chairs if I want." He chomped another one with gusto.

"Second — there is no Doyle situation you need to hear about."

"That's just a bald-faced lie. I distinctly heard 'Doyle situation.' " He set his snack down. "Really. Am I causing you problems?"

MJ shook her head, ignoring his toned torso. Sort of. She wasn't dead.

"No. I'm causing my own problems." MJ rolled onto her back. "It's time for me to get home. If I'm lucky, they can get us on a flight tonight."

Doyle frowned. "You can't leave."

"I don't belong here. I'm avoiding the inevitable — my life is moving on, and ignoring that fact isn't going to make it stop. I belong at home, where I can find out what's going on with my daughter's college applications, do the laundry so my son doesn't need to wash his sister's underwear, and thank my husband for keeping me pineapple-free for twenty years after I tell him how much I love him."

"Ah, I called it. There are problems." Doyle's mouth turned up at one corner.

"Don't look so happy about it. But, yes."

"I know I'm a little biased in this matter, but it seems a husband who lets his stunning bride go to Vegas without him maybe doesn't deserve her."

"It isn't that simple." MJ stared at the

tent's ceiling, where the fan spun in a quiet circle.

Doyle grabbed her hand. MJ pulled it back.

"Don't leave. Not yet. You've only been here a few days. There is so much more to experience." His face softened and he inched his hand toward hers again. "You really are a natural poker player. Most people play a lifetime and would still fail at our tables. You will only get better, but you need to keep playing with players who are more skilled than you. You can't do that back home. At least stay through the tournament like you planned."

She was torn. She wanted to fix her marriage, but it was only one more day. She had already become a stronger player; she wanted to find out how she'd do in the tournament. She and Chris had puttered along in a holding pattern for a few months now — their marriage could wait one more day. But maybe they could get started before she returned home. With a few quick taps, she sent him a siren-emoji text, their shorthand for "Call me ASAP."

After glaring down two clearly drunk college guys who staggered toward her, then sidestepping out of their way, MJ was glad she opted for the more conservative shoes. Plus, the endless walk through the casino's corridors tormented her feet. She had learned to skirt the edges of the floor rather than dodge the old ladies and hardened gamblers in the pits to reach the poker room, visible through the slot machines and across the table games that blocked a clear path.

MJ had left a message for Chris to call her back, then waited in her room for him to respond, yet still nothing. Even though she decided to finish the trip, she wanted to apologize to Chris for taking him for granted all these years. She hoped it would be the start of some real progress, but she couldn't wait in the room any longer, so she had applied her armor and war paint and readied herself for a night of cards. She straightened her shoulders, smoothed her hair, and tightened the backs on her large rhinestone earrings.

Her phone buzzed.

Chris.

She hadn't been this nervous since she'd asked him out for the first time. Going first in anything was always the most difficult, before you knew how receptive the audience would be.

"Finally," she said. "I was starting to worry."

"Sorry. I had the ringer off all day because of meetings, so I just saw your message. What's on your mind?"

MJ's body tensed.

She stepped into an alcove to get out of traffic and get a little privacy. She leaned one shoulder against the wall and tilted her head, leaving her hair to fall away from her neck.

"I've been thinking a lot."

"Between poker hands?"

"Yes, between poker hands and by the pool with Lisa." MJ swallowed. "We're growing apart." She spoke in a rush and her words slurred together.

"You are several states away."

"That's not what I meant. I miss you. I miss us."

MJ waited for him to say it back. Say that he missed her, too. She ran a finger down the patterned wallpaper, tracing the curves. He wasn't speaking. Her courage was fading. Perhaps if she had a better idea of how he felt.

"I want to be home," she added.

"Then come home."

"Before I do, I need to know something. Are you . . ."

From behind MJ, fingers traced a line from her earlobe down her neck and around to her collarbone. Startled, she squeaked "Doyle!" as she whipped around.

"Pretty sure I'm not Doyle," Chris said.

Doyle stood in front of MJ, grinning, close enough for her to smell his smoky cologne and mints. He wore fitted jeans and a blue T-shirt with a twenty-sided die that said "Nerd Poker" under a fitted black blazer. It worked. His eyes raked over her body like they could peel away her clothes. She rolled her eyes.

"Nice dress," Doyle said.

"MJ?" Chris said on the phone.

MJ cleared her throat, keeping her eyes on Doyle.

"Sorry, someone surprised me."

"I gathered. Someone named Doyle." Chris paused as it clicked. "Not Doyle Kane?"

Yes, Doyle Kane. And now he was standing close enough to hear Chris's response. His eyes flashed with voyeuristic enjoyment. MJ pushed him away.

"Yes, that one."

"You've been playing with him? Do you have any money left?"

"Actually, I've been playing with his money because I can't afford to play at his table. And I lost quite a bit of it last night." She smirked at Doyle, who stepped back toward her, until he was just a little too close.

"Really? You're hanging with the big boys, then?"

"I guess."

"That sounds amazing. Friends with Doyle Kane." His voiced sounded awed. MJ's mouth dried with disappointment. This was not the direction she wanted this conversation to go in.

"I wouldn't consider him a friend."

Doyle opened his mouth to say something and MJ put her finger over his lips to keep him quiet. She wanted to talk about their marriage, not Doyle.

". . . ask him about the tournament?"

"What?" MJ refocused, blocking out the feel of Doyle's lips under her finger.

"I said, can you ask him about the last GPF? I'm dying to know what went through his head during those last few hands."

"He was probably deciding which blonde to bring back to his room."

"Lucky guy."

MJ curled her fingers and pulled them back from Doyle's oddly soft lips.

"He's been unabashedly flirting with me. He knows I'm married, but he's relentless."

Doyle raised his eyebrow, clearly impressed she decided to play that card.

"Really." Chris clicked his tongue. "Doyle Kane thinks my wife is hot. Outstanding."

"Outstanding?" MJ could feel her anger rising and Doyle's amusement growing. She looked around as people walked past. A few pointed and slowed down, recognizing Doyle. She turned away from them.

"You have to be enjoying that a little bit."

"It doesn't bother you?"

"Should it?

"It would bother me if a woman was pursuing you." There, now they were getting to where she wanted to go. Honesty.

"Are you saying you wouldn't trust me?"

MJ swallowed. Yes, she supposed that's what she was saying.

"Of course not," she lied, hating herself for it. Every time she did, it was another brick in the wall keeping them apart.

"Exactly. You wouldn't do anything that I'm worried about."

MJ's heart broke a little. He didn't care, wasn't worried at all. Add in the guilt about the chip stunt and she felt incapacitated. The crease on her forehead found new depths as she traced it with a finger. She turned to the wall to avoid Doyle and ignore the people who had stopped on the other side of the hall. They were probably working up the courage to approach Doyle for an autograph. He decided to put them out of their misery and approached them, giving her some blessed privacy.

"I understand now." She shuddered a silent breath, struggling to keep control in her voice. She was just going to ask, get it over with. "So, Chris, you and Tammie hanging out at Starbucks. What's up with that?"

"What? Why would you say that?" He spat out the words after a weighty pause. "Are you accusing me of something?"

"I'm just wondering, since you haven't mentioned seeing her again. Ariana saw you."

"I don't know what Ariana saw, but it wasn't what you're suggesting."

"So you weren't at Starbucks with Tammie?"

"Really, MJ?" His voice rose in pitch. He never did that unless he was hiding something. "You think I'm hanging out with other women, especially Tammie?"

She would not cry. Her face strained to keep the gathered tears at bay, a headache blossoming behind her eyes. She knew the truth, and he wasn't telling her.

"Sorry I brought it up. I should have

known better," MJ whispered.

"Yeah."

"Of course. I better go."

The distance between them widened into more than states.

"Have fun."

She clicked the phone off and slumped against the wall. At least she hadn't cried, though her head was screaming from the effort of holding it back. She hadn't really thought this would all be solved with a call, but she didn't expect the juxtaposition between Doyle's playful attention and Chris's disinterest to be so stark. There'd been a time when Chris spoke to her with warmth, honesty, fun. Had she lost that forever? Could she go on without it?

Doyle still spoke to the fans, but MJ knew he had seen everything. With his back still turned to her, she slipped away to find some pain pills, hoping to take the edge off her blossoming headache but knowing they would do nothing to dull her disappointment.

CHAPTER TWENTY

MJ popped three overpriced-gift-shop ibuprofen into her mouth — swallowing them without water made her throat feel even tighter. She slipped her octopus ring onto her right hand, then twirled her wedding band. It spun with little resistance, almost ready to pop off on its own. Almost.

Even if she hadn't cried, humiliation wormed into her brain, like a corkscrew, embedding itself deeper and deeper. She shouldn't have taken the phone call in a public place; it twisted the corkscrew tighter to know Doyle had heard — she didn't want him privy to her personal life.

MJ made her way to the poker room, looking through the crowd for the tournament check-in. Instead, she spotted Doyle surrounded by fans. He looked up and detached himself from the small circle and greeted her with a lined forehead, leading her into the area where the other players waited.

"You okay?" His eyes searched her face for the answer. Before she could respond, he took her hand and slipped a small black velvet bag into it.

"What's this?" MJ asked.

"Something I thought might cheer you up," Doyle said, his eyes watching her every movement. MJ smiled at him.

"You shouldn't be getting me things." But her smile said otherwise. MJ loved unexpected presents. Not the obligatory gift for a holiday or birthday, but a little something just because. She felt a hard, heavy object inside the soft bag, about the size of a golf ball. She opened the drawstrings and let the object fall into her palm.

It was a pineapple — a beautiful, golden pineapple studded with topaz and yellow and light green stones. The leaves were a vibrant enameled green. She fought to hide how much his thoughtfulness meant to her — how badly she needed it right now. She couldn't keep the grin off her face.

"My mentee needs a proper card protector. And look." He pushed a button hidden among the sparkles, and the pineapple split in two. "It's a trinket box, too. You can put in money or mints or whatever." He shrugged his shoulders and looked up at her through his eyelashes like a child asking for permission, his face inches from hers. He looked vulnerable. MJ was confused.

"Your mentee?"

"You didn't think I'd let you play without a coach, did you?"

MJ was surprised at this change in Doyle's approach to her. Gone were the over-the-top flirtations and borderline inappropriate comments. Instead, a soft-spoken respect blossomed in his eyes.

"Thank you. It's beautiful. And very thoughtful." With him so close, she wanted to give him a quick hug or kiss on the cheek, but there were witnesses. People stood only a few feet away, snapping pictures of Doyle and her. Instead, she clutched the beautiful card protector to her chest.

"Doesn't that get annoying?" MJ used her eyes to gesture toward the nearby fans.

"You get used to it. I don't even notice it much anymore. Though sometimes it makes it difficult to get anywhere on time."

MJ looked around the poker room. The back four tables had been cordoned off. Currently people lined the velvet rope separating the participants from the audience. Though Doyle wasn't playing, no one was about to tell the reigning champion he couldn't stand on the player side. This was the event her trip to Vegas was molded around. If she won this small, forty-person tournament, she would get entered in the Global Poker Finals. The entry alone was worth twenty thousand dollars! The GPF was *the* big poker event — the World Cup of the poker world. MJ tried not to focus on this, that tonight was like baseball's wild-card play-off game. Each seat had chips stacked and ready for the tournament to begin, ten spots at four tables. The other tournament players hovered around the edges, sending quick glances in her direction, waiting, like she was, to be told where to sit. She took a deep breath and ran her fingers over the pineapple's leaves, the hard enamel smooth and flawless. Doyle bumped her shoulder.

"I'm glad you like it."

"It's the perfect surprise — especially since this won't kill me." She bumped his shoulder back.

"Perhaps you'd like to reward me properly later." He tapped his thumb against his lips.

So maybe the flirtation wasn't retired completely.

"If my thanks isn't enough, then I'll have to return it." MJ sighed dramatically. "Which is too bad, because I really do love it, and every time I use it, it will make me think of you."

She turned her attention back to the fidgeting players, starting to compile a list of their quirks. For the best players, the game had already begun. Sweat trickled down the back of her knees, a sure sign her nerves had entered Code Red. The crowd noise quieted as the announcer started pulling names and seat assignments from a bag, interrupting her assessments. When MJ's name was called, she gave Doyle's arm a quick squeeze.

"Any last words, Coach?"

"Patience. You're an unknown and they're going to wonder about your connection to me. Use that," he said. "And don't hesitate to come talk to me between hands, even if it's just for a stretch. That's what I'm here for. Good luck, MJ."

She nodded and took her seat. Within minutes, it was shuffle up and deal. The dealer sent the cards around and MJ set her new trinket on her hand with pleasure, enjoying the weight of it and the ridiculous memory. The nerves she fought to control a few minutes ago faded away. After months of using the poker table as an escape, the snapping of cards and clinking of chips relaxed her. She assumed her position of stillness, clasping her hands in front of her even when she wasn't in the hand, using the pineapple as a focal point.

She folded her first hand and gave Doyle a quick look over her shoulder. He smiled, but looked more nervous than she felt. In his right hand, he flipped and popped a poker chip, never bothering to look at it but catching it each time. A stunning brunette wearing a body-skimming black sequined dress and five-inch heels approached him from the other side of the rope. MJ couldn't hear, but Doyle said a few words, then moved to stand along the wall between the poker room and TFL, where a few of the VIPs were peeking out the glass. She gave Jerry's laughing eyes a little wave.

She studied the players at her table, making assessments she knew she'd adjust as the game went on. She'd learned a few things about poker in the last few months that the Gents couldn't have known in their friendly game. Poker was lonely. Sure, players often chattered, but in games at casinos or especially at a tournament, any conversation was just as calculated as the calls and raises. Every twitch, every bet, every fold was a clue into a player's mind. A few of her tablemates started out aggressive, going in big and scaring off the others. MJ kept folding, playing the part of "insecure woman." In these early rounds, she only forfeited a small amount of money when she was in the big- or small-blind position. She could see Doyle pacing, annoyed with her play. Lisa had appeared next to him and flashed her a small wave when she noticed MJ looking in their direction. One player curled his lip as he watched her fold the latest hand — she dubbed him Sneer. Let them make their assumptions.

A few hands later, the small blind was to MJ. She had a nine and a ten of hearts. Not an awful hand, but not great for what she was planning: to go in big and catch the table off guard. Only two other players had called the blinds: Sneer and another man she named Nose, for obvious reasons, were hoping for a cheap look at the flop. That wasn't going to work this time.

"I raise." MJ quadrupled the big blind. The player to her left folded, leaving it up to Sneer and Nose to call, fold, or raise. Sneer folded. He obviously didn't have a good hand. Nose stared at her. MJ sat with her hands folded around her pineapple, her thumb grazing over her tattoo. She saw Doyle freeze and his head turn quickly to the last remaining player. What had he noticed? She stopped moving altogether, focusing on her breath. In. Out. In. Out. All her play for the rest of the night would be based on how she behaved right now. In. Out. In. Out.

The lights above the table reflected in the green enamel leaves of the pineapple. She could count the lightbulbs. There were four. Nose's stare burned the side of her face; the blood in her neck throbbed. She counted to ten in between blinks. She recited the lyrics to "Walk Like an Egyptian." At last, the player tossed his cards onto the table faceup. He had folded two queens.

"Could you beat that?" he said.

MJ ignored him. She didn't have to show him. He had folded to her, so she won regardless. She slid her cards to the dealer and scooped in her chips. It wasn't a huge win chip-wise, but the players at the table thought they knew something about her. Now the fun could begin.

She rolled her new trinket between her hands, the cold stones pressing against her palms. Such a sweet gesture — Doyle had gone out of his way simply to make her day a little better.

The last time Chris gave her a surprise was on their anniversary, and it was to apologize for ditching her. If he'd been concerned about making her day better, he would have been on time. She knew her husband didn't care she had left, or that Doyle behaved as if he had an intimate agenda. She knew her husband was keeping secrets from her.

She knew Doyle made her feel special the way her husband used to.

She knew she missed that feeling.

The day after tomorrow, she'd leave to go back home. Doyle stood opposite her, his arms crossed over his chest, his right thumb resting on his lips. Their eyes met and he winked. MJ recalled seeing him for the first time on TV after he won the GPF. That night, she had been full of hope that her marriage was on the mend, and now she questioned whether she wanted to fight for a man who so clearly didn't appreciate or even want her.

People call New York the city that never sleeps, but that title should really belong to Las Vegas. Where else could you buy Chanel at three in the morning? MJ and Lisa stopped in front of the Chanel jewelry store in Bonn Oir's mall. She hadn't won the tournament, but she wasn't upset — the allure of poker was waning for her. Plus, she'd won a few grand, and she wanted to do something frivolous with it. Drawn by the sparkling displays, MJ pulled Lisa across the threshold into a whole new world. She wanted a memento of her victory here — something just for her, something sparkly.

A young woman, way too perky for the time of night, walked up to MJ and Lisa. Her black suit looked tailored to her trim figure, with simple, elegant jewelry adding a subtle touch. A more-than-ample hint of cleavage spilled out from the fitted shirt under her jacket, so clearly she wasn't stupid.

"Can I help you find something?"

"We're just looking for fun," Lisa said. "Celebrating."

"Would you like to try on some things?"

"Really, we're just looking," MJ said. "We don't want to waste your time."

"Speak for yourself," Lisa said under her breath.

The saleswoman smiled and motioned around the store. "There's no one else here. Please, let's play dress-up with extravagantly priced jewelry. I can only polish the cases so many times before the fumes start to mess with my brain."

MJ looked around her. They were the only ones in the store, aside from the security guard stationed at the entrance. She looked at Lisa, who looked more awake than she had during the hours-long tournament.

"I'm not going to say no to that. Where do we start?"

"Well, if you were going to buy something, what would it be?"

MJ twirled the teal octopus ring she wore for good luck. It covered three fingers and had cost twenty dollars at a street fair.

"Rings. Big ones. And sparkly."

The saleswoman grinned and held out her hand.

"I like your style. My name is Clare."

She pointed to herself and Lisa, who had already wandered to the earrings. "MJ and Lisa."

"I'll be over here falling in love," Lisa called.

"The best rings are over here." Clare stepped behind the counter and pointed to where MJ should meet her. She unlocked the case and pulled out a black velvet tray full of gorgeous.

"Wow," said MJ. "I'm getting shivers just looking. You're really going to let me try them on?"

"That's what I do. Here, put this one on — it's our most expensive one in this case."

The ring dwarfed her octopus. A lion's head made entirely of diamonds threatened to blind her. She slid it onto her finger, weighing it down.

"How much?"

"This one is about two hundred thousand dollars, but we do have a safe in the back where there are a few rings in the seven figures."

Her eyes nearly doubled in size and she pulled the ring off.

"It makes me nervous just to wear it. Can I try that one next?"

MJ pointed to a flower-shaped ring, Chanel's latest incarnation of the classic camellia. White gold and tiny diamonds formed three tiers of petals, with a gigantic diamond at the center. Off to one side, a leaf added asymmetry to the otherwise balanced flower. If MJ could have any ring in the entire store, this would be it. She slid the bauble onto her right ring finger, tilting it to catch the light from above. Little rainbows jumped off the facets.

"So pretty," MJ mumbled. "How much?"

"Fifteen grand."

MJ winced.

"But you get the cute Chanel shopping bag to go with it," Clare added.

With a smile, MJ wiggled her fingers, making the sparkles dance.

"You've given me something to dream about, Clare."

"Don't tell me you're planning to buy your own diamonds," a deep, kind voice said from behind her.

"Jerry!" MJ said, delighted to see him one more time. Lisa's and her flight left in twenty-six hours, so she had no plans to return to the poker room. "It's good to see you."

Clare took this as a cue to pull out the earrings before Lisa decided to climb into the case and get them herself.

"You played really well tonight. I see Mr. Kane's quite taken with you."

MJ rolled her eyes.

"He's quite taken with anything in a skirt." MJ waved to the store. "Are you shopping?"

Jerry's smile dimmed a bit.

"Not today. I like to come in and look. It reminds me of my wife."

MJ wanted to know more but didn't want to prod into anything too personal. Her patience paid off.

His voice more gritty than before, Jerry continued, "Sylvia passed a little over a year ago. I used to buy her baubles, usually when I did something stupid. Sometimes just to see her dimples when I handed her the box."

Jerry's eyes shone as he picked up MJ's

303

right hand and tapped the camellia ring.

"These were her favorite."

MJ squeezed his hand.

"She obviously had excellent taste, in jewelry and men." He clearly still loved her deeply. "How long were you married?"

Jerry's eyes grew distant. "Forty-seven beautiful, challenging, and perfect years."

"Challenging and perfect?"

He smiled the smile of someone who knew, who had been there, who had seen it and planned to share.

"There were times we couldn't stand each other. Once we spent six months not speaking — no baubles could help that time. A day didn't go by that I didn't think of cutting my losses and moving on. I found out later she felt the same way."

"What happened?"

Jerry tapped his chin with a thick, well-groomed finger.

"It was never just one thing. I didn't replace the toilet paper, she didn't cook my steak right, I snored, she talked during football games. A million stupid things that added up to silence."

"How did you stay together? It sounds like you were both miserable."

"That's the secret, isn't it? When the love is real, even when you can't find it under mountains of hurt feelings and shuttered emotions, it's not really gone. All it takes is finding one new reason to fall in love. Just one, and all the other reasons become clear again."

"What was the reason that time?" MJ asked.

"I came home early from work." Jerry told the tale without a pause, as if it were a memory he visited often. The story unfolded evenly and slowly in his deep, rumbling voice, giving MJ time to absorb every word. "I remember pulling into the garage, irritated I would need to mow the lawn. I sat in my car with the windows open and could smell the tuna noodle casserole she had made for dinner. And I hated tuna noodle casserole. I put the car in reverse, to hit the club for scotch and cigars with the boys, when I heard the most beautiful voice coming from the backyard. I got out of the car, not even shutting the door, and snuck around the house.

"Sylvia had her back to me, hanging sheets on the clothesline. The sheets snapped in the breeze. I could smell the bleach she used to keep them white. Her hair was piled on top of her head with an apron tied around the faded blue dress she always wore to clean. I hated that ratty old dress, but on that day it was the most beautiful thing she owned. Everything about her was more beautiful than ever before. I had never heard her sing, which was why I hadn't recognized that it was her right away.

"At the time, we'd been married for ten years, we had two energetic boys, and I didn't even know she could sing. In that instant, I fell in love with her all over again."

"What did you do next?" MJ had to know how it ended.

"I helped her finish hanging the laundry, of course. She sang to me every day after that."

MJ swiped at the corners of her eyes.

"Thank you for sharing that with me."

"Thank you for giving me a reason to." Jerry yawned. "I guess it's time for the old man to get to bed. It was lovely seeing you again, Miss MJ. Good luck to you." He nodded and left the store, grazing his hand over the Chanel logo near the entrance, clearly wanting to be alone with his memories.

MJ wanted to find hope for her and Chris in Jerry's story — that she'd return home and they would both swoon all over again. In another thirty years, she wanted to share her story about that time her marriage almost ended with some forlorn fool, but she couldn't envision finding some new talent or personality quirk to fall in love with. What could possibly be left to discover after twenty years together?

CHAPTER TWENTY-ONE

MJ walked. The sun was still low in the early-morning sky, but she couldn't sleep, so she had left Lisa to have the king bed to herself while she burned off her demons. At barely seven o'clock, the sidewalks were mostly empty. The handful of people out were either employees going to and from work or reluctant vacationers who had to get a run in before a day of gluttony. The eight lanes of road were mostly empty, too. She stopped in front of the Mirage, where a man-made lagoon featured lush palms and a large stone outcropping. During the day, water tumbled over the rocks in playful waterfalls as birds cawed in the background, but at night it would transform into a showy volcano. The rising sun had still not moved high enough to be seen above the rock waterfall. Watching those early rays, she tried to divine what her husband was doing over the many miles. Back home it would be shortly after nine. It was Saturday, so Tommy would be tossing a ball against the roof and catching it when it rolled off, and Kate would be curled up with a book or texting with her friends. MJ would normally be at home folding laundry or loading up on groceries. She missed their faces, their awkward teen bodies, all elbows and knees. Had Kate gotten any acceptance letters while she was in Vegas? Had Tommy eaten all the pizza rolls and Pop-Tarts?

She pulled out her phone and fired off some texts to Tommy and Kate, eager for their responses.

Now what about Chris? Everything was so familiar. She pictured his ruffled brown hair and clear blue eyes. The way he used to kiss her like she was the only thing in the world and he would die if she didn't kiss him back. He hadn't kissed her like that in months, maybe even years. Did he kiss Tammie like that? Did it matter? More than anything, she wanted to feel that yearning for him again. Doyle's attentions reminded her of the first thrills of young love, the anticipation when you didn't know your lover's every move before they did it. He surprised her constantly. It was exciting. So why did her mind keep returning to a face that hadn't surprised her in years?

■ ■ ■ ■

MJ sipped a gin and tonic at the bar. Ten in the morning was a bit early, but it was technically noon back home. Lisa decided to sneak in one more spa treatment and MJ declined, knowing she'd be unable to truly relax. They planned to have a long, expensive dinner tonight, before turning in for their ridiculously early flight — with an eternally long layover in Denver — but a free trip was a free trip. Waiting for the day to pass made her feel adrift, untethered, and a bit wild. She watched her ice melt. A hand slipped into her field of vision and set down a small box. A small Chanel box. An open, small Chanel box containing the Ring.

She looked up at Doyle, who was leaning on the bar next to her, admiring her with his dancing blue eyes as if there was nothing else he wanted to look at more than her.

"How did you know?"

"You forget, I know people. You'd be surprised what a few extra tips here and there can get you."

"That's still creepy — you know that, right?"

He shrugged and she resisted rolling her eyes. "Please tell me you didn't harass poor

Clare — she was delightful."

"I assure you, Clare was well compensated for assisting me."

He nudged the box toward her.

"I can't accept that," MJ said as she pointed at the box. She was looking at his face, so she noticed the tiniest of flinches. He didn't expect that answer, or had hoped for a different one. If she hadn't been playing so much poker, she never would have noticed it, but watching people this way was becoming second nature.

"It's not a gift. It's a wager, right," Doyle said, his lips wrapping around the words, drawing her eyes to them.

MJ's eyebrow rose.

"Heads-up," Doyle continued. "You win, you get the ring."

MJ smiled. The thrill of the game kicked in — and how could it not with such a perfectly sparkly pot?

"And what do you win? I can't afford to match that bet."

Doyle's mouth twitched upward; his eyes crinkled.

"A kiss." He lifted one finger. MJ shook her head.

"So, I could win an extravagant fifteen-thousand-dollar ring and all you could get is a kiss? From me?"

He nodded.

Her pulse rushed, thrilled at the idea of owning the beautiful ring. The possible kiss had nothing to do with it, right? She looked at his lips, soft and easy to smile. Everything about Doyle was new to her, and exciting. If they kissed, she didn't know what would happen next. No preset choreography.

She turned to him, uncrossed her legs, and stood in front of him, inches from his face.

"Challenge accepted. But we'll have to play now — Lisa and I have dinner plans."

Doyle nodded and grinned his approval. MJ looked around the bar. At this time of the day it was quiet. Each table had a bowl of pretzels. "I have a deck of cards. Let's play here. Pretzels for chips."

She cut her teeth on poker playing with bar snacks. She could win this. "A little unorthodox, but I like it. Let's go, then."

They settled into a corner booth, and MJ split up the pretzels evenly between the two of them. Doyle ate the odd one, salt lingering on his lips. Would his lips taste salty? She shouldn't want to know.

MJ dealt the cards, but more than one game was afoot. With each hand, Doyle brushed his lips, or licked them, or bit them.

His stupid ploy was working; he was

slowly taking all her pretzels. MJ gave her head a little shake and switched her focus to his hands. She thought she knew his tell. He'd pop a chip from the center of his palm when he was bluffing. That's where her advantage lay. His hands arranged his pretzels into neat lines, then into stacks, then back into lines. As he would with a chip, he tried to roll one across his knuckles, which was when she realized her mistake. He couldn't do his tell with pretzels, couldn't pop one out from the palm of his hand. She'd have to outplay him the old-fashioned way.

But she had lost this hand as well, her pile getting progressively smaller. Plus Doyle kept eating them, making the available pots tinier and tinier.

MJ picked up a pretzel to flip between her fingers as Doyle dealt the next hand. She missed having real chips to flip and clink, never mind the advantage it gave her over Doyle. His hands shuffled the cards, barely touching them as they arched and shushed. Tiny movements, yet creating so much chaos.

She'd need to change up her play if she wanted to beat him, but how? MJ crushed her pretzel.

"Pressure getting to you?" he said. "You

can always concede." He arched an eyebrow at her. MJ swallowed.

"No, I've just decided it's time to end it."

She peeked at her cards, a seven and a two, off suit — the worst possible poker hand. She pushed all her pretzels into the middle.

"All in," she said, folding her hands in front of her, using her thumb to rub against her tattoo.

Doyle's eyes caught her thumb movement and he grinned. Without looking at his cards, he said, "Call." He flipped over a jack and a ten.

Damn.

"Are you going to show me? I showed you mine," he said.

She didn't want to. He'd think she was an idiot card player for going all in with a seven-two off suited, or worse, that she wanted to lose so she had to kiss him.

"You may as well flip them, love. I know you have shite." MJ gave him a baffled look — how could he know? "You tap your tattoo when you bluff. I noticed it during the tournament."

Double damn.

She thought she knew his tell, when he knew hers as well. Nothing to do but play it out. Poker was a game of luck, too. MJ

314

flipped her top card, the seven. Doyle raised an eyebrow. She flipped over the second card, the two. He laughed out loud, then clasped his hands together.

"Brilliant!"

Her stomach leapt in anticipation and her mouth went dry. She expected him to make some ridiculous comment about foreplay, but then his brow furrowed and his shoulders stood at attention. Could he be as conflicted as she was?

Doyle dealt the flop. Two kings and a ten. The ice in his glass clinked as he took a sip of whiskey.

He set the turn down — a seven. They both had two pairs. Doyle had tens and kings, and MJ had kings and sevens. They looked at each other, neither exactly sure how they wanted it to resolve.

They both watched as he slowly laid the final card on the table. MJ's heart clunked to a stop. A three. She had lost. Somehow, she didn't think she'd really lose. Both pairs of eyes blinked at the outcome.

"And that is that, right," Doyle said.

It's just a bet. Besides, she had to uphold her end of the bargain — honor among gamblers and all.

Their eyes met as his hand trembled and reached to cover hers on the bench between them. MJ looked down to where they touched. His hand covered her wedding ring so she couldn't see it. Her eyes lifted back to his heartbreakingly blue ones. He was just as caught between the past and the future, and he wasn't finding any answers at the poker tables, either.

MJ started to pull her hand away, but he tightened his hold. Doyle rubbed his thumb across her wrist, circling her tattoo. But the intimacy of the gesture only reminded her of Chris, so she pulled her hand away completely, touching her wedding ring with her right hand. Doyle's shoulders slumped and his eyes closed. They were both so alone . . . but maybe they didn't have to be.

She slid closer to him so their hips were touching and reached out with one hand to curl around the back of his neck, pulling his lips to hers. She could smell his skin — freshwater and smoky peat. Her eyes fluttered shut as her lips made contact, soft and warm, like a sun-drenched peach and good whiskey.

It was new and different and . . .

Horribly dull.

She leaned in closer, pressing against him while he slipped a hand into her hair. Each noise in the restaurant amplified, clamoring for her to stop the kiss and look when she heard whispers and what sounded like Doyle's name. Unable to stop herself, she started to laugh.

Doyle squished his eyebrows together and opened his mouth to speak but nothing came out. He was handsome. He was charming. But kissing him was like the never-ending pasta bowl from the Olive Garden — perfectly adequate, but not what she really wanted and ultimately regretful.

"I'm sorry," MJ said. "That was . . ." She searched for the right word. "Bland."

He leaned back against the cushions and held the hand that had just been in her hair against his chest.

"I'm so glad you said it. I may as well have been kissing my sister."

MJ snorted.

"It wasn't that awful." She looked at him and started laughing again. "Okay, it was. I'm a one-man woman and you aren't him."

"Thank God for that."

She put her head on his shoulder. "What are we going to do now?"

"Well, it appears I have a ring to return."

MJ sighed as she looked at the pretty sparkles dancing against black velvet.

"It is lovely. Good-bye, beautiful." MJ sighed and sat up straight so she could look him in the face. "I've just realized, I don't even know where in Ireland you come from."

His lips curved up in a small, tight smile.

"Lisdoonvarna. It's in County Clare on the west side. Close to the Cliffs of Moher." Doyle's eyes grew distant, looking through time to his memories. "I'm the eldest of eight and my mum and da' own the village pub. It's been in our family for generations. I grew up pouring pints of Guinness and listening to the village gossip."

MJ leaned toward him. She didn't expect to actually have something in common with him: they were both born and raised at the tap.

"What happened?"

"Fiona happened."

"It's always a woman, isn't it?" MJ said.

"Always." Doyle tapped his thumb on his lips, taking in MJ's reactions, deciding whether he should share the rest of the tale. MJ waited patiently, holding his gaze.

"Fiona was my childhood love. I was certain I would marry her and we'd be together forever, running the pub like my parents do, having a barrel of little ones."

Doyle closed his eyes at the memory, pausing to take a sip of water, and continued.

"And we did. Almost. We married young

— I was twenty-two, she was twenty-one. I thought she was happy. Then the day before our first anniversary, she left, leaving just a note with some nonsense about wanting more." Doyle had lowered his eyes and scooped up a handful of pretzels.

"Wait . . . are you still married?"

Doyle's mouth twisted into a wry smile.

"Technically."

"Why?"

"Divorce is still a last resort in Ireland. Most couples go their own ways until someone wants to get remarried."

"How did you get here?" MJ enjoyed this deep dive into Doyle — he was so much more than she expected. And a much better friend than lover.

His voice quavered. "I started drinking a bit more than I should have and playing poker with the local crew in the back of the pub. I buried my heartbreak with gambling, whiskey, and women — bit of a cliché, really. But I discovered my years of listening and observing in a pub paid off."

MJ's heart went out to him — she knew how that felt.

But the moment was interrupted when her phone started buzzing. She flipped it over to see the name, glanced back at Doyle, and said, "It's my son — he never calls. I need to take this."

Doyle nodded his head. "Of course."

"Honey, what's up?" she asked.

"Mom?" His voiced sounded scratchy — more little boy than young man.

"I'm here. What's going on?"

"You need to come home, Mom. Now."

Panic raced through all the possible options: car accidents, drugs, fire.

"What happened?"

"I was in Dad's office on his computer and I found something."

"What did you find, Tommy?" Her tone had taken on an edge.

"He has divorce papers in there. Are you getting a divorce? Is that why you're in Vegas? Because you don't want to be married anymore?"

The D-word echoed in her head. Divorce. MJ wrapped her free hand around her stomach and folded over as much as the booth would allow.

"Mom?"

"I'm here." She shook her head, then slid off the bench, gesturing to Doyle to follow. A frown on his face had replaced the introspection of a few moments ago. "I'll be on the next flight home."

She picked up the pace as they left the restaurant. Doyle jogged ahead to get the elevator. She signaled with her hands what floor she needed.

"I'm scared, Mom."

"It's just a misunderstanding, baby. I'll be home soon and I'll talk it out with your dad. I love you."

"Hurry home."

MJ's heart broke for herself and her son. But she had to keep it together until she could get home and talk to Chris. MJ texted Lisa.

MJ: Come back to the room. We've got to go to the airport now. Tommy found divorce papers.

Her phone pinged back immediately.

Lisa: On my way. I'll call the airlines, you start packing.

She flung open the door to their hotel room and tossed the phone on the bed, not registering that Doyle still followed her. She crammed clothes from the closet into the half-full suitcase.

"What happened?" Doyle said, walking around to the bed.

MJ went into the bathroom. She returned a minute later with her arms full of toiletries, no time to waste repacking her toothbrush kit.

Doyle moved in front of her and put his hands gently on her cheeks so they made eye contact. "Hey, what happened?"

MJ blinked, as if he were a speck of dust on her eyeball that would go away if she blinked enough. He didn't.

"It appears my husband has divorce papers on his computer. I need to go home. Now."

Doyle frowned as he watched her collect stray items and toss them into her overflowing suitcase. She could tell the hotel to ship anything she forgot. Closing the suitcase and jumping on top of it, she stuffed anything sticking out back inside. She tried to zip it shut but couldn't keep it closed and zip it at the same time.

"Can you help me?"

MJ hopped onto the luggage, wobbling to keep her balance while Doyle zipped it shut.

"What can I do?" he asked.

"Nothing," MJ sighed, and yanked the suitcase off the bed and started pacing while she waited for Lisa to return.

Doyle pulled out his phone. "Give me a moment."

MJ walked to the large window, willing herself to cross time and space to get back home. To hug her frantic boy and kiss her husband. She had to make this right. It couldn't be over. She couldn't lose him. It didn't seem real. Or maybe now it was too real. Lisa burst into the room and rushed to MJ, hugging her tight.

"I called, but there isn't anything else that leaves earlier than our current flight. We'll just have to tough it out. I'm sorry."

MJ couldn't wait that long — with the layover, they wouldn't be home until late tomorrow afternoon; her skin itched for action, to get home now.

Doyle closed the phone and walked to them.

"The hotel will take you home on their plane. They can be wheels-up by six."

MJ whimpered in relief.

"But how?"

"I'm a very good customer."

That good luck had to be an omen. If she got home fast enough, she could fix this. She would finally explain everything to Chris. Her body trembled with energy to keep moving forward, keep moving toward home, keep moving toward Chris. One thing had gone right. More had to follow, right? All she needed were a few more lucky breaks.

CHAPTER TWENTY-TWO

As the jet pulled into the private hangar, MJ shook Lisa awake. Once one eye was confirmed open, MJ said, "We're here. They're going to drop us off at your car in the parking structure."

Lisa nodded — still not ready to talk — then folded the soft cashmere blanket, and set it on one of the few squishy leather chairs that populated the cabin.

"I could get used to traveling like this," Lisa finally said, sipping the cold bottle of water the attendant had delivered right before descent.

MJ could only nod. As soon as the plane stopped moving, she unbuckled and paced in the small area. Like a well-oiled machine, the crew opened the doors and got their luggage ready to go. A car waited in the hangar to whisk them to Lisa's SUV. She would need to send Doyle a cheese basket, at least, even though she would never be able to repay him properly for all he had done for her. If it weren't for him, she wouldn't be getting off this plane ready to fight for her marriage. The flirtation made her realize it was Chris or nothing.

They had landed right before midnight. Through the open hangar doors, she could see a light, warm April rain, the kind that promised lush grass and blooming flowers in the morning and made the air smell like earth and growing things.

Once settled in the driver's seat, Lisa zoomed through the empty highways to get MJ home as quickly as possible — while still obeying all posted speed limits, of course. After the non-stop noise and lights of Vegas, midnight Milwaukee seemed sleepy and very dark in comparison. The farther west they drove, the darker and sleepier the city became. And the closer to home, the faster she wanted to speed through the streets.

At last, Lisa pulled into MJ's driveway. The house was dark, no one inside expecting her until tomorrow. She ached to run into the house and wake everyone up. With a quick wave to Lisa, she grabbed her suitcase and walked through the door.

Daisy woofed once when MJ entered the dark house, then trotted to give her a proper tail-wagging greeting. She had the dog, at least. Daisy walked halfway through her open legs and stopped, waiting for MJ to bend over and hug her around the middle. She buried her face in Daisy's fur, wanting to hear the reassuring thump-thump of her doggy heart.

Easing the door shut, she snicked the lock. Other than the refrigerator hum and the ice clunking in the ice maker, the house was quiet. What did she expect at one in the morning? She set her suitcase in the laundry room and pulled out her pajamas. Might as well change clothes down here so she didn't wake up Chris.

She'd only been gone a few days and she felt like a stranger in her home, an intruder so meaningless the dog couldn't even muster a real bark. The kitchen was cleaner than when she was in charge, there were no baskets bursting with clean laundry awaiting folding, and the floor even looked swept. The faint hint of bleach wafted from the nearby bathroom. The only sign of untidiness was Kate's and Tommy's homework stacked on the kitchen table. She rifled through the papers. Kate was reading *Eleanor & Park* for English class — yellow stickies cluttered the book's edge like a bird's wing. Tommy's precalc homework was riddled with eraser marks. Next to the homework lay another sheet of paper, with many of the same problems, but in Chris's handwriting. He had helped Tommy with his homework — he'd never done that before. She envisioned her boys side by side, speaking more numbers than words. She could practically hear it all in her mind.

Beside the homework lay Kate's iPad. MJ flipped it on and scrolled through her texts, e-mails, and photos. In the album were several pictures of Chris and Tommy cooking dinner — it looked like spaghetti. They were laughing and having faux sword fights with the uncooked noodles. While she wished she could have been a part of the fun, knowing that this memory existed was almost as good. No matter what Chris thought of her, he obviously loved their children as much as she did.

What had Jerry said? You just need to find one new thing to love, and then you'll remember all the rest.

A tsunami of images flooded her, sucking the air out of her lungs. Her first taste of lemon custard pie, Chris's laugh, holding hands during Kate's and Tommy's births, his preference for boxer briefs, Sunday-morning pancakes and bacon, his special smile just for her. The memories were so much and not enough. How could she ever doubt that she loved this man? That she needed him every day?

She tiptoed up the steps, avoiding the creaky ones like a teenager sneaking in after curfew. After standing in the doorway to her bedroom, listening to Chris's breath, slow and rumbly, she slid in between the sheets, lying still, not even breathing. Chris moved, but MJ stayed as far on her side of the bed as possible. He sprawled on his side, face crushed into his pillow, his sandy hair messier than normal. She lay a foot from him but felt as far away as if she were still in Vegas. She had to be closer.

How did this chasm form? It was just a small crack a few months ago. But that's how it happens. Ice can split the strongest boulder; add a little water to the tiniest crack and give it time. MJ turned to face him, to watch him sleep in the moonlight. A tiny snore wheezed from his nose. He was really and truly asleep. She laid her hand over his still one, twining her fingers between his, listening for any sign he was waking. Another rumble, louder than the last. She relaxed into the sensation, easing her tense muscles and warming her worried heart.

She had spent the flight thinking about

Doyle's and her failed kiss. It was so telling. Chris was her one and only. The only one who could send shivers through her body and make a room disappear around her.

She breathed into the heat flooding her body from where their hands connected. Were the papers a bluff to make her confront their problems? Would Chris really leave her? He wouldn't, would he? Not when they still had this connection. But he could. A connection when one party was asleep didn't count. She struggled to keep her eyes open, not wanting to miss one moment of lying in bed with him, knowing it could be the last time. Her eyelids drooped as she let all the distance between them dissolve. She wanted to take in as much as she could, store it up to get her through whatever was going to happen, like a squirrel saving nuts for winter. If she saved up enough, she could make it through the icy time to come. She needed his warmth and love. And she would take everything she could now.

She fell asleep blissed out, holding his hand, remembering his long-ago proposal.

MJ had tossed her keys onto the counter, scattering the bills and pizza flyers. Dishes piled in the sink and the tiny kitchen floor needed sweeping. How could two people who were never home make such a mess? She pulled off her work clothes as she walked down the short hall to their bedroom, carefully hanging the suit coat and skirt, and tossing her heels into the corner. It seemed illogical for her feet to hurt so much when she sat at a desk all day, trying to find people jobs for the staffing agency. She peeled off the control-top panty hose, cursing as she snagged the material, sending a run from thigh to toe. Chris wasn't home yet from his job at a nearby bank branch.

Their tiny apartment consisted of one bedroom, one bathroom, a tiny galley kitchen, and a postage-stamp living room. It wasn't much, but it had a small patio and a view of a farm field out the window over the sink. They'd moved in together after college, figuring they could afford one decent apartment rather than two separate hovels in bad parts of Milwaukee.

She'd worried if they lived together he'd smother her, but so far, no smothering. He respected her need for quiet, for space. He let her read alone on the porch while he made a pizza from scratch for dinner or played Nintendo. And he respected that she liked to take charge of their life — paying the bills, buying the toilet paper — yet he stepped in to pick up tasks she hated, like taking out the garbage and, of course, cooking.

In her comfy sweatpants and baggy T-shirt, MJ flicked on the radio station to keep her company while she cleaned the kitchen, then made dinner. It was Taco Tuesday night — one of the few meals she could usually handle. As she turned the browned meat and seasonings down to simmer, she heard the door open.

"Mmm, gotta love Taco Tuesday. Never gets old." Chris appeared in the kitchen, his tie hanging loose and his suit a bit too baggy. He kissed her neck where it met her shoulder, sending a whirlwind of butterflies aloft. She turned into his arms to further the matter — the tacos would keep. Chris's hands trembled as they dove into her hair, pulling it from the loose ponytail. His kiss seemed urgent and needy and she matched it, letting the passion lift her away from thought and dissolve in a swirl of heat.

With a quick inhale, Chris pulled away, jarring her senses back with the harsh fluorescent light humming above them. His eyes burned into her as they both worked to control their breathing. She stepped toward him, wanting to continue, but he held up his hand and shook his head.

"One second. I need to say something first."

He slipped his hand into his baggy pants pocket, then took a knee on their freshly swept kitchen floor. What was he doing? They hadn't talked about this yet. She lost her breath and tried to take a step back, but she was already pressed into the sharp edge of the counter.

"Moon." Chris started to speak. His voice quivered with nerves. "You've made my last few years complete. I can't imagine living another day without seeing you every day and I don't want to. I know this isn't a proper ring, but believe me that the sentiment is. MJ, will you be my wife?"

He looked up at her with long lashes offsetting his eager eyes, so certain of her response. Her chest hurt from lack of oxygen. She felt him slide something onto her ring finger. It wasn't cold and hard like she expected, but as it settled into place, MJ's knees buckled and the kitchen went black.

She woke to a cold cloth on her forehead and Chris's concerned face above hers, eclipsing the ceiling light in the kitchen. He smiled into her eyes.

"Too soon?" Chris asked.

It all came rushing back at once — the

proposal, the bent knee, the ring. MJ put her hand in front of her face. Instead of a sparkling diamond, she saw a cheap tin ring with a clear plastic gemstone. That explained the unusual sensation. She searched for words to explain how she did love him, how unexpected this was. She'd never thought about marriage before. Her mom had never married; she had always assumed she'd be the same.

"I'm . . . sorry."

Chris shook his head.

"Don't be. I knew it was a risk. Hell, it's not even a proper ring. Can we forget this ever happened? Maybe pick up where we left off before I lost my mind."

MJ shook her head.

"No, don't take it back." She reached for his face. "I just never thought I'd find someone like you, someone I could trust with my heart forever. Yes, yes, Chris Boudreaux, I will happily be your wife."

When she woke, she was alone. On Chris's pillow lay the divorce papers and a photo.

As MJ rubbed the sleep from her eyes and stretched, remembering the events that brought her home, her hand hit the papers lying on Chris's pillow. Attached to the front was a photo printed off the computer. Even through the pixelation, there was no question it was her and Doyle kissing in the booth. She remembered the whispers, the constant photos being taken by fans. Someone must have posted this online, and Chris had found it. Her stomach plummeted. She knew exactly how he must have felt, as she experienced the same thing after Ariana's phone call. But she wasn't demanding a divorce. Anger replaced the shock, and she hopped out of bed determined to put an end to this nonsense. He would understand once she could explain. He had to understand.

She sniffed burned toast from the kitchen and padded downstairs to see Tommy fishing a charred bagel from the toaster with a knife.

"Honey, use the bamboo tongs, not a knife." MJ grabbed the tongs and extracted the bagel as Tommy stared at her. She tossed the bagel in the garbage and put a fresh one in the toaster. As she slid down the button to restart the process, Tommy snapped out of his daze, wrapping his arms around MJ and crushing the air out of her lungs.

"Mom! You're home. You came home." He had tears in his eyes.

"Of course I did. I told you I was going to

on the phone yesterday." She brushed his hair out of his face and kissed him on the nose. She had to reach up to get there. He'd grown more during her short absence. A piece of her healed.

"I missed you so much," he said.

MJ held him close and soaked up the familiar boy smell of grass and fresh air. Even at his age, he still had it, with a whiff of aftershave on certain days. She let him go after a few moments.

"So, who applied for the job of housekeeper? The house has never looked so good."

Tommy blushed and looked down at his shoes.

MJ's mouth dropped.

"You did this? By yourself?"

Tommy nodded. The floors were swept, the dishes were in the dishwasher, and even the cupboard fronts lacked their normal layer of food splatter.

"I don't know, I think I might keep you."

"Please, no. A brother shouldn't have to wash his sister's underwear."

MJ laughed.

"You are absolutely right. Kate should have been doing her own laundry." MJ checked the clock; it was past eight. "Speaking of, where are she and your dad?

Shouldn't he be pancaking it up?"

Tommy buttered his bagel and started shoving it in his mouth. Between bites, he managed to explain.

"Dad was gone when I got up, and I don't think Kate came home last night."

MJ went from proud of her son's responsibility to disappointment at Kate's lack of it.

"She didn't come home? Is your father aware of this?"

He shrugged his shoulders.

She took a few deep breaths. It didn't take long to get back in mom mode. "I'll track down Kate."

Tommy kissed his mom and headed downstairs, a spring in his step as he bit into an apple.

At least things seemed better with him; now to find her daughter.

MJ called Kate's cell and she picked up after a few moments.

"Hey, Ma, what's up?"

"Where are you?"

MJ could hear rustling in the background and Kate cleared her throat.

"In my bedroom. Why?"

MJ squinted her eyes. Kate didn't know she was home. Two could play at this game. She walked up the stairs and entered Kate's room. The bed was made and everything was neat and tidy.

"Can I talk to Tommy?"

"Um, no. I think he's outside."

That little shit.

"Okay, so do you want to tell me where you really are?"

"What do you mean?"

"I'm standing in your bedroom, and Tommy just went to the basement. I know you aren't home."

Kate went silent. MJ couldn't even hear her breathing.

"Kate?"

"You're home?" Her voice squeaked it out.

"Yes. I'm wondering why my straight-A daughter is lying to me. I know you're about to graduate, but we still have things to do around here. We need to sort out why you aren't getting any acceptance letters. Tell me where you are and I'll come get you."

MJ heard more rustling.

"I'll be there in a few minutes," she mumbled, and clicked off the phone.

MJ checked the time; she'd give her ten minutes before she called again. She returned to the kitchen and shuffled through the unopened mail on her desk. Still no letters. She searched for the Marquette admissions department's phone number and hoped someone would be in the office on a Saturday morning. After a few rings, a young voice answered.

"Hi, my daughter applied a few months ago and I'm just following up on her application."

"I can't tell you the status, but I can let you know we've received it. What's the name?"

She knew they had received it, but thought she could wiggle a little more info out of this student who was stuck answering phones on a Saturday.

"Boudreaux, Kate."

She could hear some clicking in the background.

"I'm not seeing anything. Let me look her up by social."

MJ gave it to him.

"I'm sorry, but I'm not finding a record for her. We don't have the application."

"That's not possible. She filled it out months ago. Maybe it was entered incorrectly."

"If that's the case, then it was your daughter who made the mistake. It all feeds from the application."

MJ mumbled her thanks and hung up.

MJ couldn't fit together the pieces of this

puzzle. Kate was meticulous about getting her work in on time; it didn't make sense that her applications would be any different. Yet she recalled when school counselor Kyle had mentioned he wasn't getting any transcript requests. She called Northwestern and UW-Madison and got the same responses — no application on file. She knew if she called the other dozen schools, she would get the same response. It was the middle of April and her daughter hadn't applied for college.

Kate walked in the door with forty-nine seconds to spare. Her face paled when she saw MJ standing behind the island, tapping her fingers; then MJ saw her straighten her spine, preparing for a confrontation. Her little girl had too much of MJ in her. She slid a cup of hot cocoa across the counter, but Kate only looked at it.

"I'd rather have a cup of coffee," she said.

"I'd rather wake up knowing what roof my teenage daughter is sleeping under. Looks like we both lost."

MJ wanted to pull her daughter into her arms, but she needed to know what was going on here. She folded her hands on the counter in front of her and waited.

"Why do you even need to know? You weren't even here," Kate said.

Guilt smacked MJ in the face. Smart girl — she'd gone right for MJ's weak spot.

"We'll discuss my deficiencies as a parent later. You first."

Kate poked at the marshmallow floating in her cocoa, her mouth a thin line.

"Tommy told me what he found on Dad's desk." She turned her brown eyes up to MJ. "How could you do this to us? Why did you have to play poker? How come Dad is never home?"

"Nothing has been signed." MJ tapped the counter, thinking about how to handle this.

Kate looked up.

"Mom. Are you and Dad going to get a divorce?"

MJ looked into her daughter's large brown eyes, the eyes of the little girl she used to kiss after a tragic tricycle accident. Now they looked at home in a young woman's face, a woman old enough to ask the question she'd been avoiding herself.

"I don't want to, but we have some work ahead of us. Even grown-ups make mistakes that need fixing, and your parents have really made a mess of things. No matter what happens, we're both here for you and Tommy. Always." MJ's throat tightened up at the thought of putting her kids through a divorce. She sipped her coffee to loosen it up. "That still doesn't explain where you were last night."

"I was at Bree's. Her ex-boyfriend won't leave her alone and it's freaking her out. She needed a friend so I went over there after dinner."

MJ studied her daughter for any lip biting or finger picking. There was nothing. She was telling the truth.

"Keep me posted on your whereabouts from now on. Don't lie." Kate nodded and turned to leave. "One more thing — can you tell me why Marquette has no record of your application?"

Kate's eyes widened; then she bit her lip.

"It must have gotten lost. Computers aren't perfect."

MJ narrowed her eyes. "Then why did I get the same information from Northwestern and UW?"

MJ almost felt bad for Kate as she slumped in defeat and tears welled in her eyes. MJ wanted to pull her into her arms, but they needed to sort this out first.

"Why, Katie?" MJ asked.

"I freaked out. You kept on me to get the applications out, get the applications out. It's such a big thing." She spoke between ragged breaths. "College changes everything. I couldn't do it!"

That wasn't how she'd raised her kids.

"That's not true, you can always B-DIO."

Kate's face turned red as the tears fell faster.

"You aren't listening to me. I couldn't B-DIO, Mom. It was too much. I couldn't do it alone. I'm not like you. I needed help."

MJ winced — she had done this. She was too focused on her own issues; she completely missed her daughter's dilemma. No matter what MJ had screwed up in Vegas, Kate was not going to be collateral damage. MJ could make this right, at least. She walked around the island and wrapped her arms around her daughter. Kate opened her mouth to protest, then shut it, leaning into her mom's embrace.

"I've screwed everything up," Kate moaned.

"Sweetie, that's what we do. We muck it up and we fix it. Everybody makes mistakes, but it's how we fix them that matters, that shows our true character. We're Boudreauxes — we're tough and feisty and smart. You haven't done anything that can't be fixed." MJ looked at her daughter.

"I can't B-DIO."

"And you shouldn't. There's no more B-DIO. From now on, it's B-DIT — Boudreauxes Do It Together."

Kate took a deep breath and used her sleeve to sop up the tears, her body trembling as her emotions worked their way out, but MJ already knew it'd be okay — for Kate, at least.

CHAPTER TWENTY-THREE

It was Pavlovian — if MJ was with Lisa and Ariana, she wanted the familiar smell of coffee and fresh-baked scones. Ariana's office smelled lovely enough, like lilac. Comfortable with squashy chairs and pleasant impressionistic art, her office was safe and nonthreatening. It reminded her a bit of a funeral home, except this was where a marriage came to die. Being here instead of the coffee shop was one more sign that everything was different. She'd kissed another man, played poker with the highest of rollers in Vegas, and Chris wanted a divorce. Not to be outdone, polished and professional Ariana had been having a fling with a twentysomething counselor. Yes, everything was different.

"So, these are what they look like." Lisa had the divorce agreement in her hands.

"What were you expecting? Stone tablets?" Ariana said. She held out her hand for the papers and Lisa relinquished them. She flipped through them with the ease of someone who knew exactly what to look for. "This seems fairly standard and the terms are more than fair. Do you want me to negotiate?"

MJ snatched them back.

"No. I'm not going to sign them. These are just a scare tactic. He'd been pushed to the edge and didn't know what else to do. But we can still fix this."

Lisa squeezed MJ's hand while Ariana tapped a pen on the desktop.

"People don't serve divorce papers as a scare tactic. He's serious. How did you find out?"

"Tommy called when he found them. Then Chris left them on the bed while I was still sleeping."

"And what about this?" Ariana held up the photo. "It doesn't look good for your case when anyone can find proof of infidelity online."

MJ shifted in her armchair.

"It was a bet." Her friends leaned back in their chairs, crossed their arms, and waited for MJ to keep talking. "I know. I know. I was lonely and vulnerable. Chris had cut me off. Yes, it was actually a bet, but he wouldn't have held me to it. It was a low moment, and so I kissed him." MJ looked down at her hands in her lap as if this were another poker game, but this was no game.

"And? Tell her what you told me." Lisa said.

A pathetic chuckle escaped MJ's throat.

"It was so incredibly boring. I would have been more titillated kissing Lisa."

"That's a given," Lisa said.

"The truth is I only want Chris and even though I'm terrified it's too late, I'm not giving up until I make this right."

"Have you talked to him about Doyle?" Lisa asked.

"No. And I'm not sure how."

"No more delays, no more secrets," Ariana said. "That's your only recourse if you don't want to end up signing these." She poked at the papers, bright white against the dark wood of the desk. MJ hated the sight of them. If only she could toss them in the shredder behind Ariana's chair. But the problem wasn't with the paper; the problem was something she caused, and she would fix this.

"We'll talk today."

The Boudreaux family rode in silence to tae kwon do. When MJ had tried to speak, Chris had turned up the radio. She watched him without turning her head. His jaw twitched and he gripped the steering wheel until his knuckles turned white. As soon as he pulled into the parking space in front of the dojang, the kids hopped out, probably grateful to escape the tension.

"We'll meet you inside," MJ said out the open window. She turned to Chris. "We need to talk about this."

He didn't turn to her. His hands still strangled the steering wheel. "What's there to talk about? The document is straightforward."

"I'm not signing those papers, especially without talking first."

"We grew apart. You've never needed me. Now you've replaced me."

"What are you talking about? I haven't replaced you for anything."

He finally turned to look at her, his blue eyes a blaze of tortured memories.

"Doyle." Her mild-mannered husband practically growled out the word.

Now was her chance to explain that stupid kiss. Explain all the different ways she loved Chris, how she loved him more than ever now. This was her chance to fix everything. She had to find the right words, the perfect words to make it clear how much she needed him in her life. Without him, she'd been bobbing along like a forgotten plastic bucket left at the beach. Chris huffed his impatience and MJ squeaked out the first of her confessions.

"It was a bet and I lost, but it —"

"That's your explanation? A bet!" Chris's voice filled the car. Panic spread from MJ's core to her fingertips. She rubbed her hands on her knees. Why on earth did she start there?

"He doesn't matter. And you were with Tammie . . ."

"If this is your attempt to salvage our marriage, I know I don't want to be in it anymore."

"So it's okay for you to be with Tammie, and I can't have an awful kiss with Doyle after you were so cold to me?" She was doing this all wrong.

Her face hurt from holding back her tears, which had turned from guilty to angry, but a few escaped, searing down her cheeks. He was avoiding her question. Chris closed his eyes for a few moments. When he opened them, he spoke in a whisper.

"I bumped into Tammie at the casino." MJ raised an eyebrow. "We reminisced about college. She shared that life wasn't going great — she had gotten a divorce and moved here last year to be farther from her ex. Then it got worse. She was diagnosed with cancer and didn't have anyone to talk to, so we started meeting up. She needed someone to turn to during her treatment, and I was able to share all my worries about us."

"Wait. She has cancer?" MJ struggled with her sympathy for Tammie. She needed to focus on her marriage first. "You could have told me."

"That's the thing. I couldn't. I tried a few times, but it was like talking to a wall." MJ flinched. "And then you were gone all the time and I didn't understand what had happened. My best friend was gone and this other person seemed to understand and was willing to listen. We were there for each other. It was just talk."

MJ studied her husband. He was telling the truth. It was so plain on his face, as was the hurt she'd caused him. But why Tammie?

"And not for one second did you think she was playing you? Tammie does not like me."

Chris looked confused, then certain.

"Of course she wasn't playing me. She was sick and alone. You're the one who still doesn't like her. She got over that ages ago."

MJ rolled her eyes and opened her mouth

to speak, when her phone buzzed. Chris's eyes narrowed.

"Are you going to get that?"

"No."

"It's him, isn't it? You wouldn't want to miss that." Chris opened the car door and started to get out.

MJ's heart broke. She threw her phone at the dashboard, where it bounced off and fell to the floor, still buzzing — the picture of her and Doyle filling the screen.

"This isn't what I want!"

Tears stung her eyes as she struggled to find the words to convey her hurt and guilt and anger. Chris paused and got back in the car, then pinched the bridge of his nose, waiting for her to continue. All the rational and calm parts of her brain had melted. Her breath came in short gasps as she rubbed her knees even faster.

"You left me for a card game, MJ."

"You left me first! You missed our fucking anniversary for cards. And that wasn't the first time. You get a free pass, but I don't?"

"I didn't kiss anyone!" Chris banged on the steering wheel.

"It was a bet! And it sucked." MJ's throat hurt from yelling and crying.

"So it only counts if it's a good kiss?"

Words choked on their way out, unable to

get past the pent-up anger and hurt gushing out of her. Chris grabbed the door handle again.

"You've been keeping me at arm's length for twenty-five years, waiting for me to leave you like your dad left your mom. Well, congratulations, it's finally fucking happening."

He got out and slammed the door.

MJ folded over, her chest heaving for air between sobs. How did this all get so out of control? She'd just wanted to have an honest talk and save their marriage, and its demise seemed certain.

She needed to pull it together long enough to watch her children. They deserved that.

She'd taken a few deep breaths, when her phone buzzed again. A text from Doyle. She picked the phone off the car floor.

I want to sponsor you in the GPF. You in?

MJ scrunched her face and chewed her lip. But truthfully she knew the answer before she even finished reading the question. Poker was no longer on her radar. It had caused her too many problems, and the excitement was too convenient of a distraction.

MJ: No, but thank you for the offer. I'm done with poker. I have more important

things to focus on. Good luck, Doyle.
Doyle: Thanks. I'll need it. Off to the
homeland. Family. Luck to you, too.

She looked through the window as her
children moved to the floor for their group's
turn.

With one last wipe to dry her face, MJ
slid on her glasses, hoping they would block
the worst of her tear-ravaged skin, and
walked into the studio alone.

CHAPTER TWENTY-FOUR

After an awkward car ride home, MJ followed Chris into their bedroom and shut the door. She watched as he stood in the closet, staring at his rack of clothes.

"The kids were amazing. I took some great pictures."

He picked nonexistent lint off a shirt while the muscles in his jaw shifted under his skin and his eyes glistened.

"Chris?"

"I think I should leave." The words shot out like missiles aimed at her heart. MJ looked at him, praying she had misunderstood.

"What?"

"I need to not be around you for a while."

MJ leaned on the wall, blinking back the shock of his words and swallowing her tears. "If that's what will make you happy."

"Jesus Christ, MJ." He waved his hands in the air. "None of this makes me happy."

Without another word, Chris packed a bag, hugged the kids, and left. MJ stood in the kitchen and watched it all happen. After the door banged shut, Tommy and Kate turned to their mom, broken hearts stamped on their faces. She held her arms open and they both came in for a hug. Pulling back after a moment, she looked at her downtrodden children. Seeing the pain on their faces made her more determined.

"This isn't over. I'm not giving up so easily. Remember, B-DIT." She kissed their cheeks. "Now, I need to make a few phone calls. Will you be okay for a bit?"

"What are you going to do?" Kate asked.

"First, I'm going to call Grandma. We'll take it from there."

She squished them to her one more time, then went upstairs to her bedroom, clutching her phone in her hand. She gently shut the bedroom door and let all her strength drain out of her. MJ flopped onto the bed, their bed. She held Chris's pillow to her face and inhaled. She couldn't give the scent a label — it wasn't soap or deodorant; it was just Chris. It was comfort and love and happiness. She didn't want to live her life without smelling him again.

Barbara would know what to do. She curled onto her side and held the phone to her ear with her top hand. She didn't know how she was going to explain what happened, how she screwed up her marriage, and then her mom answered.

"Hi, honey," Barbara said, her voice bordering on giddy. "I'm so glad you called. I have official information."

"Ma," MJ whispered. "It's over."

Without giving her a moment to respond, MJ told her about kissing Doyle, Chris giving her divorce papers, and the horrible argument.

"MJ, you and I are such different people. I never had the option of a real partner. Your father was all problem, no perk. I had to do everything myself, and I shored myself up by teaching you to do the same."

"I make my own choices, Ma. You didn't make me ignore Chris or kiss Doyle."

"You're right there, but I've watched a lot of marriages over the years from behind the bar, and if you're going to save this one, you need to show him you've changed. You need to put your heart completely in his hands. I'm not sure how you're going to do that, but no simple apology will do. Get vulnerable, open yourself completely — no holding back."

MJ chewed her lip, absorbing her mom's words. How could she show Chris she was a different person? She used her sleeve to dry her face, leaving smudges of makeup.

"Thanks, Mom." Some of the anxiety had left her body already. Time to do as her mom said. "How's Dr. VanderHouse?"

The contentment rushed back into Barbara's voice.

"He's exactly what I need him to be. I know the timing is awful, but Gordo and I are eloping to Vegas. Elvis will be marrying us!"

"Wow, congratulations." MJ tried to muster the requisite excitement, but her emotions couldn't switch gears that quickly. She wrapped up the phone call and hugged Chris's pillow to her, taking deep breaths. As she processed what a Vegas wedding meant, an idea formed. She had said she was done with Vegas, but perhaps just one more trip, one more huge gamble.

She texted her mother.

Would you mind if the kids and I tagged along?

MJ zipped up her suitcase and pulled papers out of her back jeans pocket. She laid them on the bed, then set her gum-ball machine engagement ring on top of them. She'd deal with those later.

Tommy came out of his room carrying his

overstuffed duffel bag.

"Ready to go, Mom," he said. "Dad's coming with us, right?"

MJ opened her arms to her son, and he flew into them just like he used to when he only came up to her waist. A few weeks ago, she would have distracted herself from her uncertainty and heartache with a game of poker and let the pain trickle to the floor ignored, but no more. It was time to clean up this mess. "Let's stick with that optimism, but prepare yourself for the worst."

"Mom?" Kate walked into the hallway, and MJ folded her into a group hug.

"What if he doesn't. What if —"

MJ put a finger to Kate's lips.

"No what-ifs. If he doesn't, he doesn't. Then we'll work it out. But dwelling on the what-ifs will blind you to the wonderfulness of what is. We've gotta live life with our eyes open."

MJ kissed her daughter's cheek.

She pulled her kids close, savoring the feel and smell of them in her own home, storing it up. Chris would forgive her. He had to. These people were her life.

She gave one last squeeze.

"Now get your things in the car. I've got a few things left to do. Wheels up in five."

Kate and Tommy thundered down the

stairs, shoving each other to get down first. Some things never changed.

MJ turned back to the items on her bed, unfolding the documents. How could a few pieces of paper end years of commitment and family? Ariana had explained all the legal terms, but reading each word in the agreement was another paper cut to her heart. They had both held back in their marriage, but if this was going to work, they both needed to be one hundred percent committed, no partial credit. Seeing Chris's controlled signature on the last page was a huge lemon squeezed into all the bleeding nooks, stinging like hell.

How did they get here? They'd fallen in love so long ago — an actual millennium had passed. MJ remembered the days of catching fireflies with Kate and Tommy and spooning mashed sweet potatoes into their squirming-baby mouths. Amid that chaos, everything had made sense.

She thought back on all the mistakes she had made in the last few months, starting with their anniversary. She'd known something wasn't right in their marriage, but she was a fool to think a game based on bluffing could help. Poker had given her a false sense of relief, but it wasn't an escape. It merely multiplied their problems. Marriage didn't work that way. It was all in or folding. She had tried to slow-play it.

MJ picked up the ring. Some dust still clung to the edges of the plastic gem, but she'd gotten most of it off. On the papers she traced Chris's signature with her forefinger. What did he feel when he signed this? Relief? Terror? Sadness? Self-righteousness?

No, Chris hadn't been perfect either. He had shut her out when she needed him most. He'd been perfectly content to allow the distance to grow between them. And he should have known that rekindling any type of relationship with Tammie, even a very platonic friendship, would hurt her. No, there was enough blame for both of them.

She slid the old ring onto her finger, all in. She laid the papers out on her dresser and pulled a pen from her back pocket. As she put the pen to paper, all the what-ifs she told Kate to ignore charged through her head, nearly trampling any hope she had that the gamble would work. Tears fell as she signed, smearing the ink.

She was blowing on it, hoping to dry it quickly, when her phone buzzed.

Lisa: He's here.

She had texted earlier, asking Ariana and

Lisa to help her find Chris. She needed to see him one more time before leaving for Vegas. As usual, her friends didn't let her down. She gave the ink one more puff of air and slid the papers into an envelope before rushing to the car.

The door to This Great Coffee Place jangled as she pulled it open, yanking it harder than intended. She'd told Kate and Tommy to stay in the car, but like the headstrong children they were, they didn't listen and had followed her inside. It was packed for late morning. A handful of local writers hammered away at laptops in the corner. The PTO had set up shop at one of the larger tables, chatting more than planning the next elementary school dance. MJ cringed to realize she was about to give them some new fodder. Her eyes found Lisa, standing behind the counter and pointing to a table near the window. Her stomach turned in on itself when she saw Chris sharing a table with Tammie.

She had to do this now. The plane was leaving in two hours.

Lisa had stopped taking orders to better watch what MJ would do. The room went silent, collectively recognizing something out of the norm was afoot.

MJ strode to stand right in front of Chris, clutching two envelopes in her right hand, the tinny engagement ring proudly displayed on her left.

Chris opened his mouth to speak to her, but she held her hands up.

"No, please don't say anything. Let me say what I need to say; then I'll go."

He nodded and crossed his arms in front of himself. MJ looked around at all the expectant faces. Tammie leaned forward with voyeuristic anticipation, her face gaunt from her recent treatments. For once, MJ ignored her and everyone else, letting the room dissolve until it was just she and Chris, like when they kissed.

"From the moment you boosted me onto that counter and charmed me with that lemon custard pie, I knew you were extraordinary. You had a direct line to my soul, and over the years, I did everything I could to block it up. I didn't like needing you so much. Every time I didn't share my thoughts because I didn't want to fight. Every time I didn't ask for help when I was overwhelmed. Every time I wished you were with me instead of playing poker but didn't tell you — each a little brick I stacked between my heart and you. I made a wall so high and thick that I couldn't remember all the reasons I loved you — and there are so, so many."

MJ knelt on the floor in front of him, grabbing his hand with her left. He didn't pull away, so she kept going.

"You got stuck with a broken person who refused to admit how much she needed you. But I do.

"I need the special smile you only give to me. I need your pie every year on our anniversary because I still can't make it. I need you to order my old-fashioneds on Friday night and make up ridiculous words that only we understand. Marriage isn't supposed to be perfect. It's messy and frustrating and full of compromises. It's toilet seats left up, it's rained-out vacations, and arguments over how best to do the taxes. But it's also finding new reasons to love the person you're with."

MJ paused to catch her breath.

"I screwed up and I am so sorry. I thought kissing another man would give me answers, but it only proved I was asking the wrong question. You are the answer. You're the only person I can trust with my heart. I need you in my life — there is no substitute, no one else for me, and there never will be."

MJ squeezed his hand and stood up. She set the two envelopes on the table.

"The kids and I are going to my mom's wedding. One envelope is the signed divorce papers. The other is a ticket to Vegas to join us. My heart and soul are yours completely. If you can forgive me — even if you only *think* you can — I want you to join us."

She bent over and put her hands on the sides of his face, soaking up his blue eyes, afraid this might be the last time, and set her lips on his. She let them linger, memorizing the taste and feel and smell of him. She pulled back and with her face a few inches from his, she whispered, "I need you, Chris. Please, please come to me."

Chris's eyes shone a bit more than before, but he didn't say anything — she'd told him not to. When she stepped back, the rest of the café came back with a rush. MJ was painfully aware everyone had witnessed her confessions. Everyone would know whether they stayed married or not. But the only one who mattered was staring at the two envelopes.

She turned and left, the bells echoing in the silence behind her.

CHAPTER TWENTY-FIVE

The tiny outdoor chapel was a riot of greens. Lush moss traced a curved path to a backdrop of ancient-looking stones under a gentle waterfall, which formed a tiny clear pool. The walls were thick green hedges decorated with thousands of white lights. A border of Irish moss dotted with tiny white flowers edged the base and irregularly shaped paving stones framed by neatly trimmed grass formed an unconventional floor. Sheer white fabric tented above them, decorated with more white lights and small hanging lanterns. The whole area breathed with life and magic.

MJ, Kate, Tommy, and MJ's mom had arrived before the VanderHouse contingent. Her mom wore a swishy A-line cream dress with elegant lace sleeves. Her graying hair was pulled back in a soft chignon at the base of her neck. She glowed with so much happiness, MJ couldn't help but feel the same, even while a piece of her was still back home. She daubed at her eye with one of the many tissues she'd tucked into her bra.

"Shouldn't you be in hiding somewhere, Ma? Dr. VanderHouse is going to notice you when he walks in."

Barbara waved her hand at MJ's words.

"We're too old for that nonsense. We're going with what makes us happy. And he's going to be family — you don't need to call him Dr. VanderHouse. Gordon will do."

As if summoned by magic at the mention of his name, Dr. VanderHouse — in a crisp gray suit and lavender tie — entered the chapel, his eyes ignoring everything but her mother. Any doubts MJ might have had about this marriage evaporated. His adoration for her mother couldn't have been clearer. He went straight to her, pulling her in for a kiss.

The kiss stretched into awkward territory. MJ hadn't noticed who entered with him until a male voice cleared his throat and brought the couple back to the present. Mike and his husband stood close by the door.

MJ went up to Mike and gave him a huge hug — he was going to be her stepbrother, after all.

"Hey," MJ said. "It's nice to see you."

"You, too," Mike said. "MJ, this is Brian." Brian leaned in closer to shake MJ's hand, keeping an eye on the door.

"When do you think Elvis is going to get here?" he asked. "I'm dying to know if he'll be a young, sexy Elvis or a drug-addled, fat Elvis." His face reflected the giddy delight in his voice.

MJ snorted. She liked him immediately. "I'm rooting for a young Elvis."

Brian shook his head. "No way — five bucks he's full-on white jumpsuit and muttonchop sideburns."

"No gambling. It's a wedding," Mike said.

"It's a wedding in Vegas — I'm pretty sure an oddsmaker is part of the package," Brian said, winking at MJ.

From beyond the greenery, they heard someone singing "Can't Help Falling in Love."

Barbara squeaked in excitement.

A businesslike assistant preceded the singer into the chapel, silently directing everyone into position for Elvis's entrance. At last, in all his spangled, white-jumpsuited glory, the Elvis impersonator entered. His black wig formed a towering pompadour, a deep V dove almost to his navel, and a guitar hung over his shoulder. He shimmied his way to the front, facing the giddy couple.

MJ couldn't keep a smile off her face, especially when she noticed Kate and Tommy giggling to each other. MJ owed Brian five dollars.

With practiced ease, he slipped the guitar off his neck and handed it to the assistant. In a spot-on imitation of Elvis's drawl, he began.

"We are gathered today, to celebrate the miracle of love between this beautiful woman and this handsome man."

Elvis paused, giving the wedding party time to soak up his presence. The sequins on his outfit sparkled, adding a disco-ball effect to him. Everyone had a sparkle or two dancing on them, making them a part of the special ceremony. He was a one-man portable party of love.

"Love, it's a beautiful thing," he continued. "Barbara and Gordon, love has brought you to this moment so you can proclaim it for all to hear.

"But this proclamation isn't just for today. Today is about committing to loving eternally, every day, with all your heart. Love doesn't take a vacation to Hawaii; it doesn't recognize time or age. It needs to be tended to every day."

Barbara and Gordon held hands, absorbed in each other's eyes.

As MJ listened to Elvis, a warm, strong hand slid into hers and the familiar scent that lived in all her happiest memories caused her breath to hitch. She couldn't look because she knew she'd ruin her mom's beautiful wedding by making a scene. Instead, she clutched Chris's hand, worried he'd disappear if she let go. She poured all her heart into that grip, sending him all her love, hoping he'd feel it. Fat tears of relief tumbled down her cheeks. She looked down at her feet as she wiped them away with one of her stashed tissues, noticing a white box next to Chris's black dress shoes.

On her other side, Tommy elbowed Kate and the two stood grinning. Elvis pulled two rings from somewhere in his jumpsuit and set one in Barbara's hand and one in Gordon's.

"Barbara and Gordon have prepared their own special vows for each other." Elvis nodded to Gordon.

Gordon cleared his throat and gently took Barbara's hand, partially sliding on the ring.

"My dearest Barbara, I'll never fall in love again if you love me tender. I'll buy you blue suede shoes and never take you to Heartbreak Hotel. Please wear my ring around your neck to soothe my burning love." His voice cracked. "I want you, I need you, I love you." He slid the ring onto her finger.

MJ leaned into Chris, wanting to be as close to him as possible. Now it was Barbara's turn.

"My surprise, my Gordon." Her voice was strong and clear. "I'll be loving you too much, baby, if you'll give me all your love. I'll take you to Blueberry Hill and I'll never have a suspicious mind. Don't be cruel, and take care of any fever. I want you, I need you, I love you."

Elvis pulled out a spangled handkerchief and dabbed his eyes.

"I'm all shook up," he said. Everyone chuckled. "Barbara and Gordon have declared their love and commitment in front of their family, friends, and the King of Rock 'n' Roll. With the power vested in me by the state of Nevada, I now pronounce you husband and wife. You may kiss the bride."

While the newlyweds sealed their vows, Elvis sang "Love Me Tender" and encouraged all the guests to dance. Kate and Tommy quickly got out of the way while the adults began swaying to the music.

Chris pulled her in so close that she had to wrap both arms around his neck and rest her head in the space between his shoulder and ear. She never wanted the music to stop, for the moment to end, but all too soon, the last notes drifted into the sparkling lights surrounding them.

As the other guests moved forward to congratulate Barbara and Gordon, MJ pulled Chris to the back corner of the room.

"MJ." His voice cracked with relief.

"You came." She searched his face for a clue.

"I . . . I wasn't going to. I couldn't get that picture out of my head. But then I went home to our quiet, empty house, and it didn't matter anymore. I love you so much it makes me stupid." He laced his fingers with hers. "I thought about what you said at the coffee shop, how open and honest you were. I knew I couldn't live without you."

A sob of pure relief escaped her mouth.

"I don't want us to be over." His voice broke. "I said so many things I didn't mean. I have always wanted you, MJ. Always. I just needed to be reminded why. And I'm sorry I took so long. I should have followed you out of Lisa's."

Tears shimmered in both their eyes.

"I let you push me away. When I thought I had lost you — I didn't fight for you. That's my biggest regret." He took a step closer to her, the air between them electric. "But never again. You are the first and only woman I've ever loved, but I stopped showing you that. You deserve to know every second of every day that you are adored, and I promise to show you a million different ways. I never want you to doubt me again. I would do anything for you."

MJ grabbed his shirt and pulled him in the last few inches.

"Then kiss me."

He did, and everything disappeared around them.

"Congrats, Ma." MJ hugged her mom close, both women wiping tears.

Barbara took her daughter's face in her hands. MJ saw the wise woman who raised her, but also a new side — a carefree side, an in-love side. The pressure of living life and raising a daughter — even a full-grown daughter alone — had lifted. She pulled Chris into their small circle. "Elvis was right, you two. You need to tend to your marriage." She gave them both a squeeze. "Now get out of here," she whispered. "I'll make sure the kids don't get into too much trouble."

MJ didn't need to be told twice. She snagged Chris's hand and pulled him out of the chapel, leaving behind two kids whose future therapy bills had just gotten a lot cheaper. He paused long enough to pick up the white box that was at his feet. Her heart thudded as everything slowed around her. More than their hands connected them — strings made from a thousand memories intertwined to bond them closer and tighter than a welding torch binding steel to steel.

She yanked him into an empty elevator, holding his head between her hands, their bodies inches apart. He settled his free hand on her hip, letting it skim her curves, revisiting their dips and rises.

"You came," MJ said again, scouring his face with her eyes.

His mouth twitched into a half smile. "How could I not? You told me to."

She ran her fingers through his hair, which had never looked better.

"So, you do what I tell you now?" she teased.

"Always and forever." Chris's hand slid up her side as he nipped at her bottom lip, sending shivers across her body.

The elevator dinged on their floor. MJ backed out of it, keeping Chris close, inches from connecting. Holding his gaze as she backed down the hallway, she stopped when she got to her door.

"Will you get the key?" MJ asked.

Chris looked at her dress for pockets.

"Where is it? You don't have a purse."

MJ smiled and flashed her eyes down. Chris's face turned wicked. He pushed her against the door as she threw her head back, giving him more room to search. He slid a hand into her bra, inhaling as his fingers grazed the soft skin. MJ bit her lip as his hand made contact, finding the key card immediately, but ignoring it as he chose to explore more. He dipped his head down to kiss her through the satin.

"Open. The. Door," she said.

With a grin, Chris pulled out the card, then leaned into her harder so she could feel the torment was not one-sided. Chris fumbled and opened the door, causing them to stumble in. He yanked her in tight, kissing her while backing her toward the chair, dropping the box on one of the end tables. When her legs hit the back, he spun them around and sat down, leaving her standing. His hands followed her legs under her dress until they reached the satiny edge of her underwear. Leaning his head against her stomach so she could feel his hot breath through the thin fabric, he clenched the top of her underwear with his hands and pulled them down, nearly tearing the fabric in his haste.

This was no step one, two, three — she had no idea what would happen next. He took his hands off her to unbutton his own pants, his trembling hands struggling with the basic coordination.

Without waiting for him to kick them off his ankles and with her dress hiked to her hips, she crawled into his lap and exhaled as their lips found each other.

Her husband had come to her. She was home.

"After that, I'd consider letting you kiss other men on a regular basis," Chris said.

MJ threw a cloud of bubbles at him, but they broke apart midair like a mini-blizzard, so she kicked him under the water, sloshing it against the sides. They'd ordered up some champagne and food and took their party to the giant tub. Chris had moved the mysterious white box in there with them.

"Too bad — you're stuck with all my kisses from now on."

Chris's face relaxed. She slid across the tub to sit next to him and slipped her hand into his, leaning her head on his shoulder. Her curiosity had finally lost patience.

"What's in the box?"

Chris smiled his special smile and pulled the box toward him.

"I was wondering when you were going to ask."

Careful to not get it wet, he opened the top and tilted it so MJ could see inside.

"Is that what I think it is?" But she knew what it was before he confirmed it with a nod. She could smell the tart lemon. "You brought this all the way from home?"

"We didn't have one for our twentieth, so I thought we should celebrate now."

MJ scrunched her face.

"Not exactly . . . you didn't have any. I, on the other hand . . ."

She watched him put the mystery together, ending with the room-filling laugh she loved once he figured it out.

"You ate an entire pie that day? You really were tipsy." He set the box down and pulled her tighter.

"Where did we go so wrong?" she asked.

He kissed the top of her head. "We stopped talking about important things."

"Let's not do that again. And what about Tammie?"

"She really is in a tough spot. She's not an easy person to like, but she's trying to change that."

MJ pursed her lips. "I'm on it."

Chris tilted her chin up so they could look at each other.

"You're an amazing woman." He kissed her nose. "What about poker?" Chris asked.

"Over it. Someone once told me that most regular poker players were searching for something on the felt. I don't need to search anymore. I had what I needed all along."

CHAPTER TWENTY-SIX

MJ stared at the license plate that used to frazzle her. HOT MAMA. Tammie opened her door and eased herself down from the high perch, her head wrapped in a colorful scarf.

MJ opened her door and slid out, too. She didn't have to move too fast to catch up.

"Hey, Tammie," MJ said.

Tammie looked up and cringed. Next to her bright pink lipstick, her skin was drab, and her too-loose yoga pants hung off her like elephant skin. Hair poked out from under her fabulous silk scarf, but not much.

"I need to speak to you," MJ continued.

Tammie's shoulders slumped lower.

"I'm sure you do, but I really don't have the energy for it today. Can we get into it another time?"

"No, that's not it."

Tammie looked confused.

"Chris mentioned you're going through

some tough stuff, so . . . if you need help picking up your daughter or anything, let me know."

"You're offering to help me. Really?"

"I've realized we all need some help from time to time." MJ smiled and meant it. "Chris and I have been through some shit, but you were the least of it."

Tammie stood a little taller.

"I appreciate the offer. Some days it's tough to get here."

"Then send me a text, and I'll pick her up. You need to keep up your strength. I'll have Chris make you some meals, too. You need to eat more." Tammie raised her scrawny eyebrows. MJ smiled. "Trust me — you don't want my cooking."

"You're the first person in this whole town to offer any help."

"Well, you haven't made it easy to like you, but let's see if we can change that. My friends Lisa and Ariana agreed to help, too, and they are also much better cooks than I am."

Kids started streaming out of the school, like ants fleeing from a flooded anthill. They swarmed around the two women and escaped into waiting vehicles. Tammie's eyes followed the passing students; she was trying to hide the welling tears. She nodded, lips tight in a line. MJ pulled her into a hug and felt the tears free themselves and dampen her shirt.

"It's not too late. We're both different than we were in college."

Some horns started honking in the pickup lane, angry moms venting their own frustration at the world. MJ smiled and waved. Last fall she was there, fighting against the drop-off lane, fighting for something more, not realizing it was all right here. Tammie's daughter joined them, looking confused at her mom embracing someone.

"Mom?"

"Hey, baby, let's go." She turned toward her vehicle.

"Tammie, plan on me bringing her home until I hear otherwise from you, okay?"

Tammie smiled with gratitude and nodded, tears still hanging in her lashes. Tommy and Kate joined MJ as she returned to her car; the horns started honking again as she climbed behind the wheel with a big smile on her face, no longer annoyed with the routine in her tiny corner of the world. She loved every bit of it.

The crowd bustled around MJ and Chris as they stood in front of a stall, her first time at this farmers market. A quartet of teenagers sawed away at the *Brandenburg Concertos,* an empty violin case collecting spare change and wrinkled dollar bills. There was a stall for anything — fruits and veggies, syrup, meat and cheese — but not so many that a trip here would eat up the whole morning. They'd left the kids at home. Tommy was in the middle of his baseball season and Kate was helping Ariana at her office for the summer, payment for the strings she and Kyle yanked to get her into UW-Madison. In front of them was a stand owned by the restaurant where they might have reconciled if MJ hadn't lost track of time, A Simple Twist. They sold locally grown produce and amazing desserts, especially a coconut cake to die for. Just looking at it made her mouth water.

"So, what's for dinner?" MJ asked. Chris grinned at her joke.

This was their solution, the plan they came up with. Each weekend they'd hit the farmers market and make dinner together. He would teach MJ how to cook a new dish, then they'd head out for a night at the theater, or the latest superhero movie, or even the casino for an evening of casual poker — only if they could play at the same table. MJ loved the sight of Chris standing alongside her at the cutting board, dicing vegetables and sautéing something delicious. Sometimes the kids would eat dinner with them; sometimes it was just the two of them. But they were together.

"What do you want?" He slipped his arm around her back and pulled her in close, so they were standing hip to hip, admiring the cacophony of color before them. He nuzzled her ear, sending shivers down her spine despite the warm summer air. She could feel his weekend scruff brushing her cheek.

"I don't really care, as long as we have that cake for dessert."

She pointed at the huge, frosted delicacy, sprinkled liberally with toasted coconut. A giant man, complete with tattoos, beard, and a bandana, stopped in front of her. He wore a sleeveless chef's jacket with the name Harley stitched onto it, and despite his imposing appearance, his eyes crinkled with kindness.

"Do you want me to wrap one up for you?" he asked.

"Yes, please," MJ said. As Harley boxed up a cake for her, Chris picked up a bunch of asparagus and looked at her. "How about grilled lamb chops and asparagus? Maybe you can make baked potatoes to go with it."

MJ rolled her eyes. She could manage a decent baked potato now, most of the time.

He kissed her softly on the lips, trying to keep it brief, but MJ wrapped her arms around his neck, the produce selections still cradled in his arms, and pulled him in for more.

"Ahem." Harley cleared his throat, holding out the cake box to them. "It's nice to see a couple so in love, but you're holding up the line."

MJ tried to blush but couldn't muster it. She was too happy and too in love. She handed over the money for the cake and vegetables and stepped away from the table, admiring Chris as he maneuvered their purchases into the tote bags they brought with them. Rediscovering Chris's passion for food gave her another reason to adore him, a whole new side of him to love.

How many people were lucky enough to keep falling in love with the same person over and over? So much luck in her life, MJ thought . . . not to mention love and lemon pie.

ANNIVERSARY PIE

BY CHRIS BOUDREAUX

Back in college, I made a simpler version of this pie — a plain crust, filling, and canned whipped cream. Over the years I've amped up the lemon flavors. A good recipe, like a good marriage, is always improving — and I can honestly say it's better than ever before. Pie up!

Crust

The crust is the hardest part of this recipe — not because crust is hard to make but because the rest of the recipe is so simple. If you prefer, feel free to use your favorite piecrust recipe for a single crust — or even a store-bought one. This is my favorite because I've added in a little extra lemon flavor. I like to use a food processor, but you can use a mixer or do it by hand with a pastry blender.

1 1/4 c unbleached all-purpose flour
1/4 tsp table salt
2 tbsp sugar
2 tbsp lemon zest
6 tbsp unsalted butter, chilled and cut into
1/2-inch slices
4 tbsp lard, chilled and cut into 2 pieces
2 tbsp lemon vodka, chilled
2 tbsp water, chilled

In a food processor, mix the flour, salt, sugar, and lemon zest together, about 3 to 4 pulses. Add in the butter and lard. Pulse until the butter and lard are broken down into pea-size pieces or smaller, 10 to 15 pulses.

Dump the flour mixture into a separate bowl and sprinkle with the vodka and water. Using a fork, mix until it comes together. Using your hands, form it into a 4-inch disk, wrap in plastic wrap, and chill for at least 30 minutes.

Flour the counter and roll out the dough into a 12-inch circle. Loosely roll the dough around the rolling pin, then unroll it into the pie plate, forming the dough to the pie plate. Trim overhang to a 1/2 inch and tuck under, pinching or using the tines of a fork to form an edge. Chill for another 20 minutes.

Preheat oven to 425 degrees. Line the crust with foil and fill with pie weights (I use a pound of dried beans). Bake for 15 minutes. Remove the foil and weights, then bake another 5 to 10 minutes, until crust is golden and crispy.

Filling

1 14-ounce can sweetened condensed milk
4 egg yolks
1/3 c heavy cream
2 tbsp lemon zest
1/2 c fresh lemon juice
pinch of salt

Preheat oven to 350 degrees. In a medium bowl, whisk all the ingredients together until fully combined.

Set pie plate on a baking sheet (this makes it easy to take in and out of the oven) and pour the filling into the baked piecrust. The piecrust doesn't need to be cooled.

Bake pie until the filling edges are set but it still wobbles in the middle, about 15 to 17 minutes.

Cool completely on a wire rack, then refrigerate for at least four hours before topping with the whipped cream.

Lemon Syrup

This is the kick in your pants that makes this pie extra delicious. Trust me.

1/4 c fresh lemon juice
1/4 c sugar

Combine juice and sugar in a small saucepan and bring to a boil for 2 minutes. Cool.

Brush 1/2 of the syrup on the cooled crust of the lemon pie. Reserve at least 2 tbsp for the whipped cream.

Whipped Cream

1 c heavy cream
2 tbsp lemon syrup

Using a mixer, whip the cream and syrup together on medium until combined, then raise the speed to high until stiff peaks form.

Spread onto to the chilled pie filling and serve.

ACKNOWLEDGMENTS

Rachel Ekstrom, you are my agent extraordinaire, always ready to answer my random questions and provide much needed wisdom. Most importantly, thank you for introducing me to the mouth-watering strawberry hotcakes at Pamela's Diner!

Kate Dresser, my other half! This book wouldn't be here without your spot-on feedback and much-needed enthusiasm — especially in those moments when I stared into the inky depths in the Pit of Despair. You knew what I wanted this book to be before I did, and you're almost always right, except about my geeky shout-outs — then you're wrong.

Kristin Dwyer, not only are you a brilliant publicist who works her ass off for my books, but you are my DVR soul mate.

Thank you to the fantastic team at Gallery, including but not limited to: Louise Burke, Jennifer Bergstrom, Ciara Robinson (who catches all the embarrassing mistakes I make), Becky Prager, Susan Rella, Liz Psaltis, Melanie Mitzman, Diana Velasquez, Mackenzie Hickey, Davina Mock — I'm so honored to be a part of the Gallery family!

Merci to Baror International, Inc., who does such an exceptional job with foreign rights.

To all my writing friends whom I can count on to beta read, talk me off a ledge, and share a celebratory cider — Sarah Henning, Sarah Cannon, Carla Cullen (especially for our long car rides to hash out story ideas), all my Debs (Karma Brown, Colleen Oakley, Sona Charaipotra, and Shelly King) for sharing our exciting debut year together, all my wise Tall Poppies (there are too many to list), and lastly, Mark Benson and Melissa Marino — you see the good, bad, and ugly, and still respond to my texts.

Thank you to Stephen Amell — for inventing and sharing the word "sinceriously," and inspiring my characters to invent their own words.

Thank you, Joan Folvag, for your unending support of *Cake* and letting me borrow the name of your wonderful coffee shop. You really do make the best scones!

Courtney and Jim Marschalek for letting me shamelessly steal your adorable meet-cute and Anniversary Pie tradition for MJ and Chris. I owe you some baked goods.

My family and friends for being so supportive and not too judgmental that my house is a mess all the time because I'm "working," even when working looks a lot like playing on the Internet.

A special shout-out to my mom, Mary Guertin, who inspired Barbara's independent, will-do attitude. There is nothing you can't do!

My kiddos, Ainsley and Sam — thank you for being just as excited as I am that I make up stories for a living, and understanding that when my office door is shut, you need to figure out who has control of the TV on your own.

John, my one and only, you are my first reader, and for *L3,* you were also my poker expert, letting me know when I got it all wrong. I can count on you to call my bullshit, make me laugh when I'm too stressed, and give me time when I need to work. You're always willing to read my latest revision on a moment's notice, and your feedback always makes my stories stronger. Without you, none of this would be possible.

■ ■ ■ ■

READER'S GROUP GUIDE: LUCK, LOVE & LEMON PIE

AMY E. REICHERT

This reading group guide for Luck, Love & Lemon Pie *includes an introduction, discussion questions, and ideas for enhancing your book club. The suggested questions are intended to help your reading group find new and interesting angles and topics for your discussion. We hope that these ideas will enrich your conversation and increase your enjoyment of the book.*

INTRODUCTION

Sometimes, you have to risk it all to reap
the ultimate reward.

Milwaukee-area wife and mother MJ
Boudreaux is becoming increasingly frustrated with the state of her marriage. But,
rather than feel angry with her husband,
Chris, she is more concerned about how
she isn't that upset by his lack of attention.

In an attempt to make more of an effort
in her marriage and reignite their love, MJ
picks up Chris's favorite hobby, poker, so
that they can spend more time together. But
when MJ discovers that she is quite a
talented poker player, her show of good
faith only causes more strife. Tumult arises
in her marriage when MJ chooses to spend
more time on the felt top of the poker table
than at home with her family.

After picking up a tournament win, MJ
finds herself in Las Vegas, where she attracts
the attention of poker's most notorious, and

handsome, bad boy. MJ must make the riskiest bet of all — follow her new exciting lifestyle or go home to her family — and her decision just might cost her everything.

TOPICS & QUESTIONS
FOR DISCUSSION

1. At the start of the novel, MJ acknowledges that she and Chris have not been on the same page. Rather than expressing her concerns to her husband, MJ proposes, "It's easier if I just fix it myself. I just need a plan of attack (39)." Is MJ's idea irresponsible? Immature? What do you think of her strategy to "fix it"? If you were her, how would you approach the situation?

2. While contemplating her marital issues, MJ asserts, "Perhaps love was like any other habit, practice it enough and it becomes a part of you (50)." Do you agree? Does love need to be practiced, or should it just come naturally? Is a relationship doomed if it requires so much work?

3. Lemon custard pie is a symbol of the love and commitment MJ and Chris share. Do you have a favorite culinary dish that is

associated with wonderful memories? How has this dish become so special to you or your family? Why do you think people oftentimes commemorate special moments or celebrations with food?

4. MJ's family has their own motto — Boudreauxes Do It Ourselves (B-DIO) — that they recite in times of encouragement and decision-making. Do you and your family have your own family motto? What does it mean? Does it continue to influence you today?

5. Communication, or lack thereof, is a major source of contention amongst the characters in the novel. Discuss the paranoia and distrust that percolates within MJ and Chris's marriage because they avoid their issues. How could some of their problems been resolved if they had talked about their feelings? How has lack of communication also affected MJ's relationship with her daughter, Kate? Is there someone in your life that you fail to communicate properly with? Why do you think that is? How do you overcome it?

6. Since MJ had an absent father, her mother taught her from a young age about

the value of independence. How do you think her mother's values influenced MJ's mentality on love? Is her self-reliant approach clouding her ability to reconnect with Chris?

7. *Luck, Love & Lemon Pie* offers a wealth of knowledge and insight into the world of poker. Have you ever played poker? What have you learned about the game while reading the novel? Would you risk your odds at the poker table?

8. While playing poker, MJ feels engaged and attentive. She says, "Her body settled into a zone, muffling the ambient sounds to a low hum. She matched her play to the even and controlled breaths she took. If she were a yogi, she might wonder if she'd achieved nirvana. This was bliss (165)." Is MJ romanticizing poker, or do you think she really is that connected to the game? In what ways is poker an escape for her? Can you relate to MJ's sense of connection to an activity or sport?

9. Discuss Doyle's motivation in pursuing MJ. Why is he so intrigued by her? Can he be trusted? Does MJ ever cross the line when spending time with him? In what

ways is her new friendship with Doyle a coping mechanism for her circumstances at home?

10. Denial, silence, and jealousy plague MJ and Chris's marriage throughout the novel. Were you sympathetic to their struggles, or do you think the downfall of their marriage is their own fault? Is it normal for such hardships to exist in any long-standing relationship? How can a couple overcome these issues?

11. Jerry shared with MJ that he, too, had marital problems with his wife, but they persevered. He said, "When the love is real, even when you can't find it under mountains of hurt feelings and shuttered emotions, it's not really gone. All it takes is finding one new reason to fall in love. Just one, and all the other reasons become clear again (304–5)." Do you agree? Do MJ and Chris find one new reason to fall in love, or is it too late?

12. Who is Tammie Shezwyski? Given their complicated history, are MJ's malignant feelings toward her warranted? How does her attitude toward Tammie change by the end of the novel? Like MJ and Tammie,

have you ever repaired a relationship with someone you once considered an enemy?

13. The essence of this story is about self-discovery and strengthening romantic bonds. Is it possible to cultivate your own interests while also maintaining a healthy and loving relationship? Or do you risk losing one or the other? What have you learned from MJ and Chris's experiences? Are they able to find the balance they need for their marriage to survive?

ENHANCE YOUR BOOK CLUB

1. Test your baking skills and make a lemon custard pie. Find a recipe online, try Amy's recipe on page 383 or try *Taste of Home*'s recipe here: http://www.tasteof home.com/recipes/mom-s-lemon-custard -pie.

2. Read Amy Reichert's first novel *The Co-incidence of Coconut Cake* for your next book club meeting. The novel follows a talented chef and the food critic who brings down her restaurant, and how their chance meeting turns into a delectable romance of mistaken identities. You can even make coconut cake as a special treat for your group!

3. Are you ready to get lucky? Head to a lo-cal casino for a night out with your friends, and try your hand at the poker table. Or if

you're feeling a little more adventurous, plan a trip to Las Vegas!

4. Explore your own interests and sign up for a dance, art, or baking class. Or pick up a new hobby, like golfing or poker, just like MJ. Try something new — and have fun!